Title:	The French Honeymoon
Author:	Anne-Sophie Jouhanneau
Agent:	Grainne Fox
	UTA
Publication date:	April 15, 2025
Category:	Fiction
Format:	Hardcover
ISBN:	978-1-4642-2940-4
Price:	$27.99 U.S.
Pages:	288 pages

Please send all reviews or mentions of
this book to the Sourcebooks marketing
department: **marketing@sourcebooks.com**

For sales inquiries, please contact:
sales@sourcebooks.com

For librarian and educator resources,
visit: **sourcebooks.com/library**

Praise for *The French Honeymoon*

TK

TK

THE
FRENCH
HONEYMOON

a novel

ANNE-SOPHIE
JOUHANNEAU

 sourcebooks
landmark

Published by Sourcebooks Landmark, an imprint of Sourcebooks
P.O. Box 4410, Naperville, Illinois 60567-4410
(630) 961-3900
sourcebooks.com

Cataloging-in-Publication Data is on file with the Library of Congress.

Printed and bound in [Country of Origin—confirm when printer is selected].
XX 10 9 8 7 6 5 4 3 2 1

To Scott

B ubbles simmer quietly on the water's soapy surface. Underneath, her pale skin is creamy, her hair undulating like tentacles. Her body is letting go in peace.

A moment later, her bluish lips rise, regaining some of their original color as her face breaks through. She takes in a lazy breath, as if she hadn't just been deprived of air, until the weight of her head pulls her back down. She tries to focus on what should be an easy enough effort, but it proves too hard and she once again dips beneath the water. Her pruned hands grip the tub's sharp rim. She pushes hard, but there is no strength left in her arms.

Even through the foggy depths of her brain, she understands that time is running out. Nothing happens for a while. In and out. Up and down. Suddenly she is sliding backward and lifting up a little. The small progress lights something inside her. Hope, or maybe a flicker of clarity about what is going on. She must do something, tell someone.

I know what you did.

You'll never get away with it.

She reaches a hand over the side of the tub while she still can. The tips of her fingers crawl spiderlike along the floor, blindly searching for her phone. They wrap around it a few moments later but it feels too heavy, unattainable. *Almost* unattainable.

Eventually she loses her grip. The water's call becomes stronger. Irresistible.

The surface fizzes for a few angry seconds.

And then the bubbles vanish.

CHAPTER 1

Taylor

NOW

S ometimes Paris is a terrible idea.

The shiny gray taxi spits me out onto the narrow street, then continues on before disappearing around the corner. This is the Paris of postcards or, rather, of Instagram. The cobblestones are charmingly uneven, a centuries-old church peeks above leafy trees, and ornate lampposts line the sidewalk. The air smells sweet and damp, the asphalt still wet from rain, but the sky is bright and cloudless. It's early afternoon on an otherwise lovely summer day.

I've so often dreamed of this trip, but I never imagined it would happen like this, with my mind in disarray and adrenaline coursing through my veins.

The few passersby pay me no attention, or at least see nothing wrong with me. So I approach the hotel, take in the SONNEZ SVP sign, and ring the bell as instructed. I listen to the drum of my heartbeat until it's replaced by the buzz of the door clicking open.

The floor is tiled in a faded geometric pattern, drawing the eye from the lobby to the small café area behind it, which is lit up by a skylight. There are (probably fake) plants in corners, a bench with stained cushions lining the wall in front of round metal tables, and wiry lights dangling from the ceiling. It's plain but modern, and looks clean enough.

There weren't many places still available in Paris—it's late July, a perfect time to visit—so I booked the first hotel that seemed reasonably priced, expecting the worst, as I always do. As I always *have* to. But this is…fine. Almost nice, even.

There's a short line to check in and I go stand behind a bald man in a dark-blue blazer. He keeps rubbing his hand against his forehead with a handkerchief, which makes me realize I'm not exactly dressed for the occasion. I'm wearing skinny black jeans, a gray V-neck T-shirt with tiny holes at the seams from being washed too many times, my trusty lace-up boots, and the leather jacket I found in the trunk of my car after I parked at the airport. Not summer attire. Not Paris chic. A few minutes later, the bald man pockets his key card and rolls his flimsy suitcase toward the tiny elevator I'm only now noticing.

It's my turn.

I step forward, meeting the eyes of the attendant behind the counter.

"Madame," he says softly, warmly.

He's about my age, late twenties, with sharp features: a crooked nose, a thick mane of dark hair, pitch-black eyes, and tan skin that contrasts with the white of his perfectly ironed shirt. He's tall and lanky, his fingers so long and delicate that I fixate on them for a moment.

"Checking in?" he says, assuming that I don't speak French.

I think about correcting him, but I don't want to attract attention to myself. I can be your average American tourist. Unremarkable, clueless. That's what I've been most of my life. It's not hard.

"Oui." The word catches in my throat.

His face brightens with a soft glow as he smiles. I shouldn't be noticing this.

"May I have your name?"

He's asking but it's not really a question. It's a thing men do, making you feel like you have a choice, like you're in control, when in fact, they're the ones pulling the strings. By the time you realize you've been played, it's too late to stop the game.

"Taylor Quinn," I say, staring him in the eyes.

Amir—that's the name on the tag pinned to his shirt—raises an eyebrow as he checks his computer. "I don't see a reservation." His tone is apologetic. Kind. "May I ask when you booked with us?"

I take a deep breath. It's an innocent question. He doesn't know. He *couldn't.*

"Last night," I say. "Though I guess it was early morning Paris time. It was a little…spur-of-the-moment."

If he sees the tension on my face, he doesn't show it. "Ah, yes! The system can be…how do you say…*buggy* with last-minute reservations. Here you are. I see you now."

There's something about the way he says it—with his thick, singing accent, that makes my spine tingle. He sees me. I am being seen.

Then something changes in his face. His smile widens and his eyes fill with surprise. "Oh, um…congratulations!"

He looks behind me and scans the small lobby, his expression turning more into a question mark with every passing second.

"I'm sorry?" I say, following his gaze.

There's a couple behind me, loaded up with two small children and double the amount of suitcases. They looked pained, showing more than a hint of impatience at all the time this is taking. I don't disagree.

Amir shoots another glance at the front door, but whatever he's looking for, it's not there. "It says your booking"—he points at his screen, frowning—"that this is your honeymoon." He lowers his voice on the last word, as if sharing a dirty secret.

Oh, that.

It had sounded like such a wonderful idea: a Paris honeymoon. A lifelong dream of visiting the City of Lights, the real love I'd been waiting for finally coming along, fantasies shared in the dead of the night. And then…I see myself pounding the steering wheel of my car with a rage I often suspected was inside me but had never let out. Looking over my shoulder as I marched into JFK airport. Heading to the ticket counter and asking if there was space on the next flight to Paris. There was! *There was.* And how did I want to pay? *Cash. Cash?* The airline representative's curious tone when she asked; my eyes struggling to meet hers when I confirmed. *Yes, cash.* The words resonated between my temples, because they couldn't have come out of my mouth, could they? I wasn't *really* going to Paris right then and there, was I? The question circled in my head in an endless loop as I sat straight in 37E, while all around me screens lit up with the latest superhero movies or old episodes of *Friends.*

And then they closed the door. We were about to take off, and the voice on the speakerphone was asking all passengers to switch off their phones. My mind scrambled as I tried to think ahead to what I needed: somewhere to sleep. I typed in the keywords frantically, half hiding my phone under the leather jacket on my lap as a hostess, with a hair bun so tight I could see the shape of her skull, moved through the cabin. After I selected a hotel and room type, there was a question: What is the purpose of your trip? I wrote the truth.

Amir keeps staring past me, but if he's looking for the husband part of this honeymoon, he'll be waiting a long time.

I'm not prepared to share that information so, when the silence has gone on too long, he clears his throat. "If there's anything we can do to make this special trip even more memorable, please let us know."

"Well, um, thank you," I say, pretending not to notice the amused look on his face. "Merci beaucoup," I correct myself, as if it's going to make me look any less like a sad excuse for a newlywed.

He moves along gracefully. "I'll need your passport and a credit card."

I hang onto my bag tighter, my fingers gripping around the worn cross-body strap. "Excuse me?"

The young family shifts behind me, mumbling a little louder. Their children have started to roam around the lobby, and the boy is attempting to climb inside a cleaning cart parked by the wall.

"It's something we have to do," Amir says. "For safety. And it's the law. We have to record everyone who comes through here."

The law. It makes me shiver.

Of course hotels require identification. I knew that. But I hadn't thought about leaving a trace. No one can know I'm here. Now I have no choice. I carefully unzip my bag and slip my hand inside to retrieve my passport. It's crisp and clean. Never used before. I hand it over.

"Will you take cash?" I say.

Cash is the one thing I happen to have plenty of.

"Absolutely, madame," he says as he turns around to face the small copier on which he flattens my passport, cracking the spine open.

While he's not looking, I open my bag a little more. Wads of bills threaten to spill out, dollars mixed with the euros I changed at the airport, all fighting for space. I never actually counted the money. I saw it and took it, like it was mine. Ten- or maybe twenty-thousand dollars, that's my guess. More money than I'd ever held in my hands.

"Did you have a nice trip over?" Amir says, taking the bills I pushed his way.

"Yes, very nice, merci."

"And will you need help with your luggage?"

I don't know what comes over me. The exhaustion, maybe, or the dreadful realization that my life has been slipping away from me, the spiral going downward faster and faster, the end an inevitable crash.

"It was stolen. We… My… It's just me for now." The words come out in a whisper, and then it's too late to take them back.

Another attendant arrives then, a woman with long red hair, also wearing a crisp white shirt. The parents behind me let out an audible sigh of relief at finally getting help.

Amir smiles back at me, like I'm the only one here. "I'm sorry to hear that." Then, he leans over and lowers his voice. "I shouldn't be telling you this, but Paris is not always safe. I'm sure you'll have a wonderful time but it can be… Well, I would watch yourself." He glances at my bag. "And your belongings."

So he saw the money. *Great.* And there I thought I could go unnoticed.

He types on his keyboard for a few more seconds, before adding, "I upgraded you to our honeymoon room."

"Oh," I say, ready to protest. I'm not used to random acts of kindness.

"It's on a higher floor, overlooking the courtyard. Not much of a view, but it's quieter. And there's a bathtub, too."

"I won't need that." It comes out harsher than I intended, and the confused look on his face makes me think twice. "I mean, merci beaucoup. That all sounds lovely."

He smiles back. "This way you can relax after everything that happened to you."

He has no idea how right he is.

"Here you go, Madame Quinn," Amir says now, giving me the key card.

He doesn't take his hand back right away and our fingers touch for a brief moment. I hate how that makes me feel. I hate that it makes me feel anything at all.

"And if there's something we can do to make your stay with us more pleasant, please don't hesitate to ask. My name is Amir."

He watches me look at his badge again, an excuse to linger.

I thank him once more—always that need to please, good old Taylor that I am—then make my way to the elevator, clutching the key to my honeymoon room, still not quite believing that I'm doing this. As the metal doors close in front of me, trapping me inside this tiny box propelling me upward, a cold fact dawns on me. I'm alone in a foreign city. If anything happens to me, it could be days before I'm found.

But I couldn't stay home.

I had to get away.

And Paris was my only possible destination.

CHAPTER 2

Cassie

NOW

A squeal escapes my lips when we enter our suite, after I managed to hold myself back throughout the lobby. The *gilded* lobby, I should say. It has floor-to-ceiling mirrors, glistening chandeliers so imposing they'd kill whomever was underneath if they collapsed, and thick black carpet, the kind that makes you feel like you're stepping on clouds. It's all too much, too expensive, too fancy. Everything I thought I'd never have. Most people only go on their honeymoon once, right? It's supposed to be the trip of a lifetime. So of course I want to be here. I do. Yeah, I definitely do.

As I take in my home away from home for the next week, I'm glad I let Olivier book our accommodation. There's a king-sized bed made up in white linen with black trim, monogrammed with the B from the hotel's name. Fresh white flowers arranged in a tall vase give off a powdery scent that I wish I could capture on my phone. The black velvet armchairs look deep enough to curl up in, and the wooden dresser is so polished I can see myself in it.

Hi, Cassie. Looking good! Maybe a little tired, too, but nothing a filter can't fix.

On the right, I spot a walk-in closet that seems bigger than my bedroom at home. *Our bedroom*, I guess. Nope, actually. It's still *my* bedroom. My space. But this, here, is something else. On the left, the door to the bathroom is open enough for me to spot the claw-foot cast-iron tub and a whole lot of marble. Shiny, shiny, shiny.

And there's more. I walk to the other side of the room, leaving my dear husband behind. Olivier decided to carry both our bags up, even though a porter insisted he'd be happy to take them to our room. I read that in luxury hotels like this, you don't have to do anything. They can wake you up at a certain hour, recommend and book restaurants, and even organize your whole stay if you want them to. I might want them to, actually. Everything happened so fast and I haven't had a chance to think about, well, anything.

Even before opening the French doors—is that what they call them over here?—I can already see the Eiffel Tower standing tall in the distance. Frankly, I don't know why people fuss over a metal sculpture so much. What am I not getting? But I do know this: staying in a hotel suite overlooking Paris's most recognizable monument means something. Money, glamour, love in the air.

I'd drown in jealousy if I weren't me. I step out onto the balcony, my phone at the ready. There's a light breeze in the air, which wakes me up a little. I dozed off on the plane—thanks to the sleeping pills I got for the trip—but the taxi ride over put me back to sleep.

Sounds from the street travel up, mostly cars honking and the hum from the bus that just stopped. Not *so* glamorous—I'll mute the video. I record it all: the big phallic iron thing of course, but also the perfectly lined-up slate roofs with their cute little chimneys, the creaminess of the facades, and the balconies decorated with perfectly groomed potted plants. Then I turn around, catching my reflection in the spotless glass of the doors, and give a casual wave for the camera, like I feel so normal about being here. Like I'm in my element, when everyone knows that... Nope. They only know what I tell them. What I *show* them.

When I'm done filming, I immediately hit Play. Even though I'm here, experiencing it live, I can't help but marvel at how it all looks: the pastel-blue sky above the roofs, the soft glow of Parisian summer, my fresh blond highlights catching the sun, my hair *literally* glowing.

I don't overthink it on the caption. I think this two-thousand-dollar-a-night view will do all of the explaining.

Honeymoon Day One
Pinch me! 🌼 🌼 🌼

Back inside the room, Olivier is slouched in one of the armchairs, staring at the wall. Not at his phone. At the *wall*. The bare one.

"You were right," I say. "This place is perfect."

Olivier slowly turns to me, like he forgot I was here. "Glad you like it."

I'll admit the honeymoon wasn't exactly part of the plan, but things change. Sometimes you have to shake things up a little.

"Mind if I take a quick video?" I say, already pressing the red button.

"Why would I?"

I stop and frown at his sharp tone. Olivier straightens up. "I mean, of course," he adds. "Do whatever you'd like."

His tone is still a little cold and I almost want to say something. Instead, I swivel my phone around, making sure to catch every fine detail: the delicate fabric lampshade, the chilled bottle of Dom Perignon waiting in a silver engraved bucket, and the flat, wall-mounted TV. Little Cassie would have flipped her lid.

"Smile!" I say, as Olivier is about to enter the frame.

He does. It's not one of his warm, charming smiles, but I don't think you can tell through the screen.

I hit Share on this one as well, then decide it's time for a break. If I post too much, it will start to look suspicious, like I'm not having fun because all I do is snap pictures of the fun I'm supposedly having. Plus, a little mystery is always good. Let them wonder.

"I think I'm going to lie down for a moment," Olivier says, kicking off his shoes.

He goes to sit on the bed and rubs his eyes, then presses his palms against them. A nap would do me good, too. I feel dehydrated enough that it hasn't even occurred to me to pop that free champagne bottle open. Free champagne! And the good stuff, too... Dom Perignon is the good stuff, right? But I'm not sure I want to be next to Olivier right now. He's been acting weird since I sprang this surprise trip—nonrefundable flights and all—on him. But he must have gotten over it, because we're here now.

I leave him to it and head to the bathroom, where I start running the bath. The hotel provides free lavender-scented salts, which smell like summer in heaven when I open the glass jar. *This is the life*, I think, as I step into the steaming-hot water. This is *my* life.

I stay until my fingers are pruned, the bubbles are gone, and the water is cold. When I come out, I feel like a new person. Refreshed, reset. I may not have thought through this whole Paris affair, but now that I'm here, I might as well enjoy it. The thick robe I wrap myself in feels like a man's embrace. Cozy and soft. Though I don't think Olivier has ever hugged me like that. Shaking the thought away, I open the door wide to get rid of the fog so I can better read my phone screen, but I'm distracted by the fact that the bed is empty, the sheets still tucked in.

He's gone.

The comments have trickled in, fast and furious, during my bath. I got the latest iPhone a couple of weeks ago, and I didn't want to take the risk of it falling in the water. I'm still not used to being able to spend over a thousand dollars like it's a drop in the ocean.

Sooooo pretty
Oh em gee!
I'd kill to be you rn

It feels like everyone I know—well, *almost* everyone—is on their devices, ready to clock how wonderful my life is. How happy I am. How in love.

Where the fuck is my husband?

I head over to the door to peek out onto the hallway, half expecting him to be out there. The man likes his privacy. Or maybe he just likes being alone; I don't know which it is. I wonder if I should call or text him. But I'm not that kind of wife. We're not that kind of couple.

He'll be back soon enough. True fact: He can't live without me.

I take more pictures of the room, the view, the bathwater before I let it out, and of me in the new dress, a mini black lace thing I bought for this trip. I heard French girls wear a lot of black; it's supposed to be chic. Olivier told me I should wait to go shopping in the city, but waiting is not something I'm good at. Anyway, the dress does look quite stylish, especially against the red Chanel lipstick I grabbed from duty-free at the airport, along with a new pair of sunglasses. I've never been able to treat myself like this before. Look at me. Turns out I *am* marriage material after all.

Every now and then I listen for any sounds, but there is no sign of my husband. My French husband. My disappearing act of a husband. It's not the first time he has done this, but the fact that it bothers me is a new feeling. This is his city, his country, and I don't even speak the language.

Now I'm starving. I pick up the room phone to dial the restaurant, browsing over the leather-bound menu as the ringtone beeps in my ear. No answer. I'm about to try again when a buzzing sound comes from the door, the lock unlatching. I don't want Olivier to think I was looking for him, so I put the phone down.

"Hey," he says, taking me in: dressed, made up, and ready to go. He changed, too. He's wearing a pair of dark-blue jeans and a navy polo shirt. That's when I notice that his suitcase is open. He looks freshly shaven and his hair is wet—he's clearly showered. Where? How?

"Had a nice walk?" I ask casually.

He nods, giving me nothing. I'm not going to ask where he went. Olivier has that detached air about him—he exudes confidence. I was so impressed when I met him. This sophisticated French guy was interested in me. He asked all these questions. He *cared*. He was prim and proper, and yet he didn't look down on me. Quite the opposite, actually. I notice the shopping bag he's carrying, in a shade of mint green, with elaborate, all-caps lettering.

"Macarons," he says, with an amused grin at the greedy look on my face, "from Ladurée. Do you know it?"

Is there a hint of arrogance in his tone, or am I just imagining it? The first time I heard his accent, I thought it was so perfect. Exactly what I needed. But now…

Well, now we're here and I've never tried real French macarons. So.

"I thought you'd like them," Olivier says, sitting on the bed next to me.

I can't help but smile. The rectangular box inside the bag is mint green as well, and I open it to a festival of colors: round little pastries in shades of pink, blue, yellow, and brown. No wonder you see them all over Instagram. They're so photogenic.

Ignoring my rumbling stomach, I grab the bottle of champagne, the melted ice dripping on my dress. I lay it on the bed next to the macarons, then wipe my hands on the sheets. Olivier watches as I snap a few pictures.

First Paris treat! Thank you, hubby! Don't mind if I do.

My throat tightens as I hit Share. I'd never actually call Olivier "hubby."

Still silent, he props down on one elbow as I polish off two of the macarons—a strawberry one and then a salted caramel. They're sweet, crunchy, and flavorful. Delicious. I keep eyeing the box, debating about eating another one. But then something strange happens. I feel bad. I *have* put Olivier through the ringer lately. Pushing the guilt out of my mind, I lift the box in his direction, a silent, *Want some?*

He shakes his head. "No, you enjoy. This is for you. All of it."

I bring another macaron to my lips—pistachio this time—my eyes never leaving his.

Olivier sits up, facing me, and sighs. His features soften—his jaw goes slack and his shoulders relax. He *is* handsome; that has not changed. Not very tall but nicely proportioned, with broad shoulders. I wasn't sure about the goatee at first, but it does suit him, especially since he keeps it perfectly trimmed. The package is nice; I wasn't completely out of my mind when I decided to go to his place that night after we met three months ago.

I force a smile. "I was going to call the front desk and order room service, but maybe we could go down and eat at the restaurant?"

"Let's not," he says, so quickly it takes me aback.

"Well, um, I need to eat."

Why do I sound like I'm justifying myself? I can go there and order whatever I want. I can. And maybe I will. Still, I don't move.

"We'll go out," Olivier says. "Les Deux Magots is just around the corner."

Should I know what that is? Actually, should *he* know that I don't know?

He checks his watch. "If we leave now, we might beat the lunch rush and get a table."

I feel my shoulders soften. Right, of course. I may not know a lot about my husband, but I do have the bare bones facts. He lived in Paris before moving to New York last year, which means he knows this city better than I ever could. Besides, eating at the hotel restaurant is probably a tourist move.

"Right, sure. And then what?" Planning ahead isn't really my thing, but I wish I'd at least googled the top things to do in Paris. "What should we do this afternoon?"

Olivier gets up and looks down at me, his gaze unreadable. "It's a surprise."

A tiny voice tells me to beware.

"Come on, let's go," he says, holding out his hand.

"Will you at least give me a hint?" I try to sound lighthearted, but sometimes I feel like he can read through me, like he's always two steps ahead, no matter what I do.

"Nope."

He walks over to the door, ready to leave. I snap a pouty selfie before following him.

Hubby has a surprise planned for our first day in Paris. Am I
lucky or what?

But the truth is, none of this has to do with luck. You know when people say they met the right person at the right time? That the stars aligned and it was all meant to be? We were the wrong people coming together at the worst time, and the sky must have been pitch-black.

CHAPTER 3

Olivier

Let's be clear about one thing: Cassie came on to me first. At the hotel, women often did—I was manager of customer relations after all—which felt nice until I realized I never got to do the choosing. They chose *me*, flirted with me, cooed about my "cute" accent, as if I were a child showing off a trick and not a thirty-two-year-old man with a serious job in one of the world's most thrilling cities. Some also invited me back to their room, and I always politely declined. It was tempting, of course, but I'd never do anything so stupid as to compromise my job.

Cassie was different. She *literally* came to me, as in I met her in front of the apartment I rented in Brooklyn Heights—a small but functional one-bedroom on the basement level of a sprawling brownstone. It's a thing I discovered quickly about New York City: the rich lived on top of the poor, crushing them into the darkness. Here there was no pretense of equality. Though I wasn't poor, per se. Not yet anyway.

When I spotted my landlady in front of the house, my first impulse was to hide in the corner bodega. I'd procrastinated telling her I had to break my lease, and now that her husband had died so suddenly two days earlier, I was seriously considering packing up my few belongings and going without a word. By the time Ms. Crowes noticed the apartment was empty, I'd be back in France. But then, I saw that she was busy chatting to a young woman and figured I was safe.

"Oh, Olivier!" Ms. Crowes said as I approached, seeming overexcited to see me. "This is Cassie, Tim's daughter." Then, she turned to the young woman. "And this is Olivier, our tenant. Well, *my* tenant now, I guess. Olivier rents the downstairs unit." She talked so fast that her cheeks were flushed by the end of the sentence.

"I'm sorry for your loss," I said to Cassie.

Her face showed no emotion. I didn't know my landlord had a daughter but if I did, I would never have pictured her looking like this. Her blond hair was on the wrong side of yellow—a shade New York girls avoided with five-hundred-dollar coloring appointments, which we sometimes booked for our guests—her eye makeup was too heavy-handed for daytime, and her wrap dress gaped too much at the neckline, though I couldn't tell if that was intentional. Her slouchy black bag tried to be on-trend, but was clearly fake leather. These were the sort of things I'd started paying attention to since working at Bhotel. Now I could spot a Rolex a mile away, counting down the days until I could afford one of my own. Still, there was a mix of fierceness and fragility to Cassie, in her stark gaze and round baby face, her chin pointed upward in defiance. You could tell she was trying. She wanted to be *someone*.

"Cassie's staying with us for the funeral," Ms. Crowes said, her voice shaking. "With me, I mean."

I had been getting ready for bed when I'd been startled by the red flashing lights of an ambulance out the window. Intrigued, I'd gone outside just as the medics were loading my landlord—or rather, his body—onto the van. I'd consoled poor Ms. Crowes as I helped her book an Uber to follow him, which is how I'd learned about the fatal heart attack. My last days in New York were ending with a corpse, as if things weren't bad enough already.

"Really sorry for your loss," I said again, glancing at my front door. So close.

"Is your fiancé on his way?" Ms. Crowes asked Cassie. But before she could respond, the older woman's cell phone rang and she excused herself with a weak smile.

"Where are you from?" Cassie asked me, an eyebrow raised.

"I'm French." At that point, most people, most *women*, would start gushing about that one time they went to France, the best meal they ever had at a restaurant tucked at the end of a tiny street in Saint-Germain, the way the Eiffel Tower twinkled in the night, how magical the city felt, and wasn't I lucky to be from there! I usually said, *Yes, yes, so lucky*, not pointing out that I'd emigrated to another country across an ocean for a reason. Many reasons, in fact.

But Cassie didn't say anything.

I wasn't sure what to make of the amused smile that appeared on her lips, so I felt compelled to explain. "I work at a luxury hotel chain, Bhotel. My bosses in Paris sent me over to manage guest relations at our Madison Avenue location. We have the most amazing views over Central Park."

Best left unsaid: the fact that I'd had to practically beg for the opportunity to come here, or that I'd been let go nearly three weeks ago, due to some bullshit restructuring brought about by the American investors.

"Very cool," Cassie said, her eyes narrowing with intrigue. "Did you know my father well?" Her tone was clipped, far from devastated. More like provocative.

"Only a little. I helped him move stuff into their basement when he needed an extra pair of hands. That sort of thing. Tim was a nice man."

"Hmm…" Cassie said, casting a loaded glance at Ms. Crowes, who was now standing at the top of her stoop, absorbed in her phone conversation. "A nice liar then."

I didn't respond. It sounded like more drama than I wanted to involve myself in, which was none. I already had plenty of my own.

"Did you know he had a daughter?" Cassie said.

"No, sorry." I searched my mind for an excuse to get out of the conversation, but something about it made me feel a little better. It was good to be reminded that other people were fucked up, too. "Did *you* know him well?" I added without thinking.

"Nope. He took off when I was three, maybe four. I didn't know he lived in the city and definitely didn't know he had *this*." Cassie looked back toward the house. I couldn't tell if she meant the brownstone or the put-together wife. Probably both.

"I'm sorry—" I started mechanically.

"And then she—his "new" wife—calls me out of nowhere, tells me *all* my father's children should be there, and that it'd mean a lot if I came. To *her*, because of course it's all about her. The 'right' thing to do or whatever. She said she'd pay for my trip. I'm sure she just felt guilty for everything I didn't have growing up, but I never come to the city so…"

So…Cassie was using her estranged father's sudden death as an excuse for a vacation. My interest was piqued now. "Where do you live?"

"A small town two hours north, in the Hudson Valley. You wouldn't have heard of it."

Ms. Crowes had gone inside, and judging from the relieved look on her face when she answered the phone, she wasn't coming back out to hang out with her loving stepdaughter. I was starting to forget I had better things to do, such as leaving the country before being kicked out of it, since my visa, which was tied to my job at Bhotel and only valid for a month after my employment ended, was now expiring in mere days. I told myself I wasn't actually curious about Cassie. I only welcomed the opportunity to take my mind off my situation for a minute. "Your mother didn't tell you about him?"

"If I knew he had all this"—again she pointed at the house and the pretty tree-lined block—"I probably would have turned up here a long time ago."

"Families…" I said with a shrug. I hadn't spoken to mine in years, but the memory of our last interaction was carved in my brain forever.

Cassie's eyes lit up with a mischievous air. "So you're French…like, from France?"

It wasn't the first time I was asked the question. Americans—even the worldly New Yorkers—could have such a narrow-minded view of immigration, of what it meant to "be" from a different country.

I only had time to nod before Cassie continued. "And you're coming to the memorial tomorrow?"

I hadn't planned on wasting one of my last days here by attending my landlord's funeral. My time in the city had taught me that you never really knew New Yorkers, even the ones who lived right above you. Most of them were particular about what they revealed, and only did so when and if it served them. At first I found it thrilling—here I could be a totally new person, all my past mistakes forgotten—until it worked against me. I never saw it coming. My boss was kind and friendly, a blank face, up until the very moment she told me I was being let go, my visa and my future here be damned.

"Please!" Cassie said, pressing her hands together as if in a prayer with a smile. "I won't know anyone there."

She pouted, trying, and failing, to look cute.

"What about your fiancé?" I asked. I still fully intended to walk away and never see her again, but I thought she took my question as a sign that I was flirting back.

As I said that, we both glanced at her ring finger, which was bare.

"We're not… It's complicated. Come on. They have a cellar full of expensive wines. She's hosting a wake afterward and I'm sure she'll put some out. And if not, I'll get it myself. She owes me. She owes me *so* much."

I let out a small laugh, before I realized that Cassie was suggesting stealing her dead dad's wine from his grieving widow. Then I grinned openly. That sounded kind of fun.

We did just that. I had been so motivated by the work opportunity in New York that I'd perfected my English to the nth degree, always practicing my accent and looking up the meaning of new words I encountered. Still, the pastor's sermon and the religious verses flew right over my head. They also seemed to go over Cassie, who wore a dress too short to be appropriate. She paid little attention to the service and focused instead on casting judgmental looks at the mourners, especially Ms. Crowes, who was flanked by her and Tim's two sons, in their late teens.

We drank the wine, ate the food, again and again. Cassie asked me questions about France and Paris, but she was also curious about life in "the big city." I gave her the varnished version New Yorkers feed to out-of-towners: the bright lights, rubbing elbows with celebrities at the latest brunch hot spot, the endless options of amazing things to do at any time of day and night. Cassie lapped it up and it made my heart twitch.

At first, coming to New York had been an exit route, a solution to my desperate urge to get out of France. But now I genuinely loved it here. I was a brand-new me with a real career and a half-decent apartment. I'd even started to make friends with some of my colleagues. I was creating a life for myself here, and losing my job meant losing it, too. I hadn't even had a real chance to make it in the Big Apple. Hadn't saved anywhere near enough money. It's not just that I wasn't ready to leave. I *couldn't* leave. Or at least, I couldn't go home.

I didn't remember how Cassie and I ended up at my place. Correction: I didn't *want* to remember. Anytime I did something bad—like sleeping with a girl right after her estranged father's funeral—I found it easier not to connect the dots in my memory. Did it really matter how Cassie came to straddle me on my couch, her breath thick with booze as she unbuckled my belt?

She was still there the next morning when I woke up. An hour later, she got dressed and left. I figured it was the last I'd see of her.

But she knocked on my door that afternoon—once, twice, three times—until I answered.

"Hey, what's up?" I hung in the doorframe, blocking the way.

"I think I'll stay in the city for a while, check out some of these spots you told me about." Cassie pushed past me and slipped inside.

A few questions popped into my mind: Did she have a job? Even if she wasn't actually engaged, was anyone waiting for her back home in her country town? But I didn't care enough to ask—I *really* should have cared enough to ask—so I went to fish out my two remaining beers from the fridge. Cassie dragged a dining chair back and sat down, accepting the bottle I handed her like we did this all the time.

She took a swig. "Maybe you could show me around." Then another one. For a small woman she drank thirstily.

My mind started buzzing, and not only because of the hangover. Since being let go from Bhotel, I'd spent every waking moment trying to figure out how I could stay in the States, and by now I knew two things for sure: the only solution cost too much, and I was running out of time to make it happen.

Still, a sliver of hope gnawed at me. Cassie shouldn't have come back, but she did. If I could convince her, I'd get another shot at making it here. But how? I had nothing to offer.

"I'm kind of broke." It wasn't quite so simple: I'd saved every penny I could since moving here, but it didn't amount to all that much. A few thousand dollars paled in comparison to the debt I'd racked up back in France. Though it was much easier to ignore it while I was here.

I'd heard about immigrants paying American citizens for a fake marriage, which led to a very real green card. It was the golden ticket to staying in the country legally—to be able to work, and then maybe even start a business. Make real money again. *The American way.* Many actually got away with these marriages. It wasn't so hard, apparently, but you had to pony up big money to the person who agreed to be part of the scheme. I didn't have that. I didn't even have a fraction of that.

Cassie smirked. "Come on, it'll be fun."

My prospects for my last few days here amounted to wallowing in self-pity as I wandered the streets—making up stories for what I would tell people back in France. In reality, no one would care about what had happened to me. My parents didn't speak to me anymore. My brother couldn't even look me in the eye. And as for the friends I used to have, well…they'd have my head on a stick if they ever saw me again.

I took a long sip of my beer, not wanting to seem too eager. I had nothing else to lose, so I might as well try. "What's first on your list?"

CHAPTER 4

Taylor

NOW

Thump. Thump. Thump.

The muffled sound comes to me like in a fever-fueled dream. My eyelids feel glued together and I have to force them open to come back to the land of the living, where everything is dark.

Thump. Thump. Thump.

I feel around the bed, jogging my memory. Crumpled sheets are twisted around my half-naked body. I'm in a hotel room. I fell asleep. When I was a little girl, I often thought about my bed. How big it was, with plenty of space for me to spread out. How soft the linens were, washed with care on a regular basis. How comfortable. In truth, it wasn't really any of these things, but any bed is more comfortable than no bed at all. I felt lucky. No, grateful. There was a roof over my head and, for a long while, it was the best I could hope for.

"Ménage! Housekeeping!" a voice comes from behind the door, along with what I now recognize as a knock. The accent is neither French nor English.

Before I can respond, the door unlocks, letting in a sliver of artificial light. A cart rolls through it, pushed inside by a cleaning lady in a brown uniform. That's when she sees me, the body in the bed. I sit up, try to shake myself awake.

"Pardon, pardon!" she says, covering her eyes with one hand and stepping back.

I'm wearing my T-shirt and underwear. My bra, jeans, and leather jacket are folded on the back of the desk chair.

"Can you—" I start, then try again. "Pouvez-vous revenir plus tard?"

I'm not entirely sure if I said what I wanted to say, but she nods, then grabs the Do Not Disturb sign.

"Sur la porte!" she says, as she hooks it over the handle on the outside of the door. Her tone is half-scolding, half-panicked.

"Désolée," I shout, but she's already gone.

Huh. I didn't know I spoke that much French, even though I've been studying it for years. First at school, reading my study books cover to cover before the year had even started, and then later with an app. I kept wanting to take lessons, too, but I never had the money for that.

I reach for my phone, my lifeline. The screen is black. Jamming my index finger against the home button, I'm only greeted by the "recharge battery" flashing sign. Crap. I look around the room for a charger, forgetting that I didn't bring one. Because I didn't bring anything.

Putting aside my useless phone for a moment, I get up to open the shutters—the latch squeaks painfully before releasing them to the light—and take in my surroundings. If this is the special room they reserve to honeymooners, the other ones must be tiny. I hardly have enough space to walk around the bed. There's no wardrobe, only a rail attached to the wall and a handful of hangers dangling from it. Underneath, a wooden shelf covers the world's smallest fridge, with three kinds of water, a mini bottle of Coke and a can of orange juice packed tight in there. Next to the fridge is a safe-deposit box.

The hotel attendant's words ring into my ears. *Paris is not always safe.* I open my bag, grab most of the cash and shove it in the little black box.

Then, I add my phone. Before I can think about it too much, I close my eyes as I type a four-digit code at random—one I can't memorize. Slamming the door shut, I so desperately want to feel a sense of freedom at being cut off from the world—unreachable, unfindable—but instead, every cell in my body lights up with a mix of fear and guilt.

But there's also the thrill of what awaits. Paris is out there.

Fifteen minutes later, I'm showered, wearing yesterday's clothes, and on the street, where the air smells like baked bread rolled into cigarette smoke. The hotel is off Les Halles on the Right Bank, close to a lot of shops. I glance at the windows as I pass by. There's an optician with wooden heads on display—lips painted red for the female mannequins and twirling mustaches for the male ones. On the next corner is a pharmacy, with a blinking neon-green light in the shape of a cross above the door and, inside, a line several people deep. A flashing sign also indicates the time: 10:34. Running the math, I realize I must have slept for fourteen hours. I had a lot of catching up to do.

Further down, a strong waft of butter and dough hits me, making my stomach grumble. As soon as I walk inside the boulangerie, my mouth waters at the sight of the golden pastries and the glazed fruit—strawberries, apricots, apples—topping shiny little tartlets. Behind the register, the shelves are full of different types of baguettes: épi, ficelle, aux céréales, tradition, etc.

A memory comes to me. I'm three or four, running my finger against a glass partition, my mother watching as I make my pick. *Just one thing,* she says with a strained smile. *What are you getting, Mommy?* Her smile disappears as she glances inside her coin purse. *Just one thing for you.*

This memory doesn't really exist. I'm pretty sure I made it up in my head and nurtured it over the years I've spent without her, since we were ripped apart. Pretty sure, but not certain.

I buy a croissant, a pain au chocolat, and an espresso in a tiny paper cup, which I eat and drink standing on the sidewalk outside the bakery, ignoring the dismissive looks of a few older passersby. It's okay if they're shocked by my poor manners; I don't have to care what people think of me over here. Swallowing the last bite, I crush the paper wrapper in my fist before dropping it in a trash can.

I keep walking. It could be ten minutes or two hours later when I see a woman step out of what looks like an expensive hair salon. Moody portraits hang in the window, behind which I notice a row of leather seats. The woman's auburn hair is shiny and blow-dried to perfection in bouncy curls. She slips on her sunglasses and looks back at her reflection in the window with obvious satisfaction.

My heart does a little somersault. This is exactly what I need. Soon I'm sitting in one of these chairs, communicating with hand gestures and some Frenglish with the tattooed stylist behind me.

"You want what?" he says in the mirror as he runs his hands through my long, unkempt brown hair. His accent is the thickest I've heard so far and it takes me a moment to translate in my head.

"Quelque chose différent. *Très* différent." I try a smile, but my throat feels like I've swallowed a bag of cotton balls.

"Couleur? Coupe?"

I nod. He raises an eyebrow, then pulls a strand and studies it carefully. "You're sure?"

"S'il vous plait." I try to sound confident, like this is merely a style choice, and not like I have to change everything about me. I can't keep roaming the streets looking like this.

"So why you're in Paris?" He runs his hands through my hair, giving me a head massage in the process. It takes me a while to relax into it but then it feels kind of nice.

"I'm visiting family," I start. My eyes widen as they meet his in the mirror. I didn't intend to say that. I didn't intend to give anything away.

"You have French family?" He can't help but look down at my basic jeans, scuffed boots, and faded jacket. It's too warm for it, but I needed something to comfort me. A security blanket of sorts.

"Yes. I mean, no. Forget… Oubliez…" I try to switch to French but the language is not the problem.

"It's nice you visit," he says. Maybe he's choosing to ignore what I said, or maybe he didn't understand me. In any case, I need this to stop.

"I've always wanted to come to Paris."

My family history is not one for strangers. I've seen enough pitying looks for a lifetime, enough pats on the shoulder and claims of being so sorry for what happened when I was a child. How lucky I survived. Was it? Luck, I mean. I didn't die, but what came after felt like it wasn't much better.

For the next couple of hours, I bury myself deep inside gossip magazines telling stories I don't fully understand about famous people I don't know.

"Et voilà," the stylist says, running a soft brush across my neck. It sends shivers down my spine.

Looking up, I'm faced with glossy, dark-blond locks with a few lighter strands, chopped in a chin-length wavy bob that hangs around my face like perfectly draped curtains. I've never liked my nose—too pointy—or my jaw—too sharp. To be honest, I've never liked much about myself.

"What do you think?" The stylist seems genuinely curious.

"It's…good?" I reply.

He shoots me a questioning look through the mirror. "You're happy?"

I know what he means—am I happy with this new hair—but no sensible answer comes. It does look good, but I've never let myself think about my happiness before. I smile and nod. That's all I can do.

When it's time to pay, he protests at the amount I drop on the counter.

"Too much," he says, sliding a few bills back my way.

"It's a tip…pour vous," I explain, confused.

He points at the price list. "You pay what is written. Tips are not done here."

"Take it," I say, pushing the money back.

I walk away before he can say anything more. Where I'm from, it's not done to steal a whole wad of cash, either. Part of me wants to get rid of it as fast as possible, so I can forget I even took it. But the other part knows that when this money runs out, my time's up. And then what?

A few streets down, I enter a boutique with lots of florals and swingy skirts in the window display. Inside, I let the young sales assistant, with her braided hair and bright lipstick, guide me through racks of chic dresses and striped T-shirts. I've worked retail on and off for years, but I never buy new clothes for myself. I grew up on hand-me-downs that were too small for me, like my body was too big for the world I found myself in. Later on, the idea of spending money on myself felt as foreign as the possibility I might one day come to Paris. Back home, I go to thrift stores, stick to a palette of black and gray so everything matches, and wear every piece until it falls off me.

But now I have money. *For now* I have money. I tell the sales assistant that my luggage was stolen, again with that lie, when *I'm* the thief. I'm the one over here, getting away with a crime. I buy everything she suggests and then some, including a red dress with daisies that makes me feel like I'm in costume, and the kind of ballet flats you see on every other French girl. I change into a black polka-dot skirt and a white T-shirt, which I pair with my boots, before leaving the store.

Back on the street, I start to notice the intricate molding on the buildings' ivory facades, the imposing wooden doors painted in various colors, and the pigeons clambering down the pavement, alert for any crumbs. I'm not a city person but there's a lightness to Paris. People smile, laugh, even. They look around themselves, noticing, like I do, the little pieces of street art painted on the walls, the greenery in the tidy little parks every few blocks, and the ambient charm.

I stop at a few more stores along the way, stocking up on new lingerie and a few other accessories. Eventually I get to Le Marais—the hip neighborhood in the heart of the city—and come upon a lively corner café with a terrace spilling onto the street. In the building above, oversized teddy bears with sweet faces look down from the windows. Their smiles give me the creeps but my feet are aching from the hours of walking, and I haven't eaten anything since the pastries this morning. I stare at an empty table long enough that a passing waiter motions for me to take a seat.

I do, stacking all my shopping bags on the chair next to me. Then I allow myself a deep breath. The hardest part is over.

"Bonjour!"

Expecting the waiter has come back to take my order, I force a smile on before I look up. It's a trick I learned as a little girl—always start smiling before the other person can see you. This way it has time to reach your eyes, which is how you make it look genuine. But it's not the waiter speaking; the voice comes from the man next to me. He has thinning salt-and-pepper hair and is wearing thick-framed glasses with a plaid short-sleeved shirt, a newspaper folded next to a half-drunk beer.

"Belle journée, n'est-ce pas?"

There's something cringeworthy about the grin on his face, like he's trying too hard. I scan the space between us, trying to convey the fact that I don't think he's talking to me. It does little to deter him.

"You speak French?"

"No," I say, focusing on the menu in front of me.

But my throat tightens, my mind swinging back to the safe in my room. Has anyone noticed I'm gone or tried to reach me? I peek inside my bag, but of course my phone is not in it.

The waiter comes back, at last, and I order a glass of white wine. Whichever one he recommends is fine by me. He takes the order of another table behind me, and it's not until he's out of sight that the plaid-shirt man speaks again.

"I saw you before."

My heart pounds in my chest. I don't have to respond to him. I can be here, sitting at a terrace, drinking a glass of wine. But something in his tone—something slimy and pervasive—makes me look in his direction.

"You were standing right there." He points at the other side of the sidewalk. "You looked lost." I let out a sigh, almost relieved. He doesn't know anything. "Are you lost?"

I'm not. I'm exactly where I'm supposed to be. Where I have every right to be. The man is still waiting for my answer. I hate that I feel the need to give him one, to comply with what society—let's be honest, men—expect of me. Be spoken to and you shall reply. That's what Good Taylor does. *Did.*

"I'm fine," I say, but my voice is croaked, and I probably sound the exact opposite of fine.

The man takes a sip of his beer, then slowly refocuses his gaze on me. His forehead creases over his glasses, his thin eyebrows shooting up. "I noticed you."

"What are you saying?" The words spill out of my mouth before I even realize it.

The waiter comes back with a glass and a bottle of wine, which he pours so slowly I almost reach for it to speed up the process. He leaves a small bowl of popcorn on the table, and I'm equally eager for and dreading what will come next.

After the waiter leaves, the man smiles, content to have my full attention again. "A beautiful woman like you. Anyone would notice you."

My shaking breath empties me of everything I had, the shreds of normalcy I've been hanging onto all day. I get up quickly, knocking the table and spilling the wine everywhere as I do. My first thought is that I should clean it up—Good Taylor always cleans up!—but I have to get out of here more. Grabbing onto the shopping bags, I squeeze through the few other people on the terrace, mumbling apologies as I bump against them. Heat burns through my body, shame and fear all tangled up.

And then, without another look behind me, I start to run.

CHAPTER 5

Cassie

NOW

Paris is not made for walking. Those cobblestones looked pretty in the pictures, but they're vicious in real life. My high-heeled sandals keep getting stuck in the crevasses, on top of murdering my toes with every wobbly step. These shoes make my legs look extra-long and I love them, but right now I can barely put one foot in front of the other.

"Should we take a taxi there?" I say, trying to catch up to Olivier.

Turns out this place is not literally "around the corner." You'd think he could have told me that when he saw what I was wearing. Twice, I asked him to slow down and wait for me. He did, but only for a few minutes before speeding ahead, leaving me stuck behind elderly couples walking their overly groomed poodles.

He stops, letting me reach him once again. "We don't really take taxis in Paris."

He sounds like I should know this already. Like I'm so dumb to even ask. I hate that he succeeds, that I *do* feel dumb when he speaks to me like this. There's so much about this world I don't know, me, the country bumpkin.

"I can't walk in these," I say, my irritation covering up my shame.

When Olivier and I were in the city, I insisted we take Ubers every-where. He didn't complain then, just complied. He would have done any-thing for me.

"We're almost there," Olivier says with a shrug.

I glance down at my feet, letting out a big sigh in case I'm not being obvious enough. I dressed up for our first outing in Paris—a real husband would appreciate that.

"Trust me, okay?" he adds as he takes my hand. His grasp is so firm it makes the big diamond on my engagement ring twist and dig into my skin.

I've already received a few comments asking me to spill all about the surprise, so what choice do I have? We turn the corner onto a square with even more uneven cobblestones and Olivier guides me through every treacherous gap. We're walking so slowly that I catch a few people staring—laughing?—at us. I sneak envious glances at the clothing stores lining the square and debate going into one to buy a pair of sneakers.

Eventually, we make it to Les Deux Magots, a fancy café with stark gold lettering—like it means *money*—a lush green awning, and penguin-clad waiters moving around the tables with such choreographed gestures it feels like they're doing a TikTok dance.

Olivier's face falls when he notices how busy it is. Every table on the terrace is taken. While he heads over to the blasé-looking hostess, I whip out my phone. Even if we don't get a table, I can still post about this place.

But first, there's a text waiting for me:

So whats the surprise? Spill!

It's from Brianna, one of my besties from high school. Of course she'd ask. Brianna spent her honeymoon at a cabin in Vermont. For a total of three days. She kept saying they were saving for a bigger adventure in a year or two, but then those conversations stopped and she started talking about starting to "try." *Try for what?* I'd asked. The rest of our group had glanced at me funnily. It's like, as we approached our thirties, everyone suddenly wanted to get married and have babies. I felt so behind, suddenly. And then I wasn't.

I take a snap of the bustling terrace, the glossy people with their sunglasses, cigarettes neatly tucked between their fingers and outfits straight out of an influencer's feed.

But first, I write on my Stories over said picture, lunch at this fabulous spot. If you're not drinking fine wine on a terrace, are you even in Paris?

No need to respond to the text; I'm sure Brianna will check my Insta in no time. She's not the one who needs to see this anyway.

When I look up, Olivier is eagerly waving at me to come over. Next to him, the hostess eyes me up and down, and I suddenly feel naked. I mean, we're basically dressed the same, except her gold sandals have low heels and her lipstick shade is a little lighter than mine. Plus her hair is tousled in a way that makes it look like she woke up like this, even though there's absolutely no way she woke up like this.

I glance down at my outfit. Okay, so maybe I don't *exactly* look like her but hey, one of us works at a restaurant, and the other has all the money in the world to eat here. That's right, bitch. Olivier may look fancy and all but *I'm* footing the bill. I'm the one who has everything she ever wanted. Maybe not *everything*. Still, I lift my chin up and follow him to our table. The hostess slams two menus down before we're even seated and immediately walks away.

"What's her problem?" I say.

Olivier shrugs. "She's just…" He thinks about it for a moment. "French. Actually, she's Parisian."

I wait for a further explanation but that was it. Our waiter comes by with a bread basket and a jug of water, then says something I don't understand. Olivier responds. In French. I mean, obviously. It's just that I've never heard him speak French before today and it feels weird. Rude, even. Almost like they're talking about me behind my back, but in front of me.

I stare at him, once again expecting he'll clue me in. He stares back as the waiter hovers over me, shifting from one foot to the other. I sigh, try to focus on the menu which, thankfully, is translated.

But it still feels foreign. I knew about croque monsieur, but croque madame? And what even is "Poilâne" bread? Maybe it doesn't matter. Isn't bread just bread? To be honest, I'm dying for a burger, but I don't see one listed.

"You order first," I tell Olivier.

"I already did," he says.

See what I mean? Rude.

"Do you need help?" he asks now.

"I'm fine!" I scan the menu one more time. I don't know what I want. At home, lunch often means leftovers, the last slice of pizza eaten straight from the box. (Why waste a clean plate.)

Feeling Olivier and the waiter's eyes firmly on me, I let out a frustrated sigh and point at the most expensive item on the menu. "I'll have the beef fillet," I say. A spasm crosses Olivier's face. It annoys me way more than the waiter's obvious smirk. "And a glass of white wine. The best you have."

There's an awkward silence that goes on for way too long, and I'm tempted to ask what the hell is going on. The waiter and Olivier exchange a glance and, finally, my husband speaks. "Red wine goes with beef. Usually."

"Really?" I didn't mean to say that out loud. I should have known that. Honestly, what I really want is an ice-cold beer, but after I mentioned wine on my Stories, it occurred to me that that's what a chic Parisienne would drink. Plus, I feel like that should be my next picture.

The waiter suppresses a smile, but not very well.

I feel my cheeks go flush. "Red, yes. That's what I meant. The best you have. And a side of french fries." I say, handing back the menu.

"The beef fillet comes with potatoes, madame," the waiter says.

"Can't I have french fries?"

"House fries coming up." The waiter walks away but Olivier still has that contrite look on his face.

"What?" I say sharply.

"The beef fillet...?"

"What?" I insist.

He shrugs. "No one orders the most expensive item on the menu."

"I can order whatever I want."

"Of course, I..."

"This is supposed to be my honeymoon," I cut in. I feel like a petulant child. I know I sound like one, too, but I'm speaking the truth.

"Right." And then in a lowered voice, "And mine too."

I don't respond. For a while, the only sound at our table comes from his leg jittering under, making the cutlery rattle. I check my phone, subtly at first and then openly because who cares if I'm on my phone anyway. No new messages. No comments. No signs. Olivier picks up the small pot of butter from the bread basket and lathers it thickly on a piece of baguette. He shoves it a little too deep into his mouth, like he's trying to stop himself from saying something else.

When our order arrives, I can't help but eye Olivier's omelet with envy. It's runny and creamy and, though I'd never admit out loud, definitely a better choice than my beef, potatoes, and fries combo. To add insult to injury, Olivier got a beer. He catches me staring as his drink and our eyes lock. I'm not sure what passes between us. We're strangers, still now. I knew that. I *know* that. I'd just never put much thought into it until today.

I grab a fry and take a bite. "I don't know about this place," I say without really thinking.

"I'm sure the beef is delicious."

"I mean Paris. I'm starting to wonder..." I add. "Maybe we should... stop." I'm not sure what I mean. I just know that this thing between us, it's not working.

Olivier leans back, eyes wide. In shock. Or maybe pretending to be in shock?

"No," Olivier says. It sounds so stark I think it surprises even him. "I mean, please, Cassie, we're here. It'll be fun. I promise."

I roll my eyes. "Like you wanted to be here."

"I did," Olivier says. I raise an eyebrow. "I do. Of course I do."

I pick up my glass to keep my hand busy. But then I take a sip and the wine is actually quite good. Smooth and fragrant.

Olivier reaches across the table for my other hand. I watch as he rubs it. It feels more intimate than anything we've ever done. "Cassie, I want this to be everything you want it to be. Or at least for it to look like it is," he adds, glancing at my phone. "Here," Olivier adds, pushing his beer toward me.

I admit it's tempting but I'm trying to make a point here. "I'm very happy with my wine." Before he can insist, I gulp the whole thing down—the glass was only half-full anyway, what a scam—and gesture at the waiter to come over.

The stuffy elderly couple next to us—he in a tie, she with a flashy ring on every finger—turns toward me, faces twisted in poorly hidden distaste.

"I'll have another one of these," I say to the waiter, my eyes firmly on the two oldies and their judgmental attitude.

Olivier smiles at them apologetically and, for a moment, I consider storming out of here. What a snobbish place full of arrogant people. The thing is, my feet hurt. Instead I decide to check who viewed my Stories.

But before I can do that, Olivier reaches across the table again, this time for my phone. "Let me. You look great in this light."

It's hard to resist a picture on this gorgeous terrace. And my second glass of wine has just arrived. I raise it to my lips, adjust my sunglasses on top of my head, and look over Olivier's shoulder instead of straight at the camera, like my husband is so smitten with me that he takes my picture without me even noticing.

"Wanna check if you like it?" he asks, handing me back my phone.

I do; it's a good picture. And he was right, I look *great*. Relaxed, happy, even. I think. I smile as I post it to my Instagram. Paris is always a good idea, I write.

Then I take another sip. I thought I didn't like wine, but I guess I was wrong.

All along, Olivier's eyes never leave me. "Look, Cassie, I feel like we got off on the wrong foot. I want this to be a week that we'll never forget. But I know you have your own…needs as well." He glances at my phone, but moves on quickly. "If you just give me the chance…I'll make sure you have the most amazing adventure here." He looks down at his plate and takes a bite before continuing. "And maybe you could use a night away from me," he says softly. "In fact, I might catch up with some friends while I'm in town, if that's okay with you."

"Without me?" I feel like I should be offended. And I kind of am.

"Well, um, I didn't think you were interested in meeting my friends. But if you want to, of course I'd love for you to come. It's just that we'll be speaking French all night and it's a bunch of guys. It might be a little boring. But you know what, I'll text them right now and tell them that I can't leave my beautiful wife on our honeymoon."

Do his friends even know about me? I know why they weren't at our wedding—it was too rushed for that—and Olivier isn't on social media. Seriously. No one can see what he's up to.

Olivier slips his phone out of his pocket. "Thursday good with you?"

I put my fork down. I can't say I care about Olivier's friends. I only ever thought about how he was going to fit into my life, not the other way around. Before I can answer, my own phone beeps with a new text. The name on the screen makes my heart leap. Darren. *Well, hello there!*

Hey. Paris looks good on you. A little too good, if I'm being honest. Makes me wonder...

I swallow, hard. This is the text I've been waiting for. The *sign* I've been dying for all these weeks.

"Cassie?" Olivier says.

I can't look away from my screen. The three dots appear and I hold my breath.

"Everything okay?" Olivier says.

I nod. Smile. Everything is very much okay. Paris *was* a good idea after all.

CHAPTER 6

Olivier

Being laid off from Bhotel was only one of the wrong turns my life had taken. Growing up, I'd looked at the way my family dragged itself through life in total disbelief. My father was a handyman and my mother traveled one hour by train to man the phones at a used car dealership. Neither had any other ambitions or expressed interest in getting us out of our tiny, dark house in the deep recesses of suburbia. We were painstakingly average. Overcooked meat and canned veggies for dinner, no conversation. Mindless game shows on TV afterward. Rinse, lather, repeat. My older brother, Sébastien, had dropped out of school to become a plumber, the kind of manly job my father envisioned for both of us. I knew, from a young age, that a grander life awaited me. I just didn't know how hard it would be to hang on to it once it materialized.

I started my first business at thirteen, taking bets about random things in the schoolyard: which football (European football I mean, a.k.a. soccer) team would win the national championship, what song would hit the top of the charts next week, etc. What started as a fun little game went on to become the event everyone was waiting for at recess. It didn't happen overnight, of course. I hustled hard, gathered the troops, built up the hype even when I didn't believe in it myself. I was marketing my business without even knowing what marketing was. And it worked. I took a 15 percent cut of the gains and amassed hundreds of euros in a few months.

This got me noticed by the cool-slash-rich kids. The ones who hosted parties at their beautiful houses while their lawyer or doctor parents were away, who had the latest tech and only wore recognizable brands. They became my friends, sure. But mostly, they represented endless opportunities. I scoured the web for pirated movies or video games, the ones not yet released in France. I waited in virtual lines for hours to get them sought-after tickets to concerts. I got Sébastien to buy liquor for them. And I watched my commissions roll in with heart flutters.

By age sixteen, my dad started making noise about what I would do with my life. Little did he know that I'd quietly been stashing away what, to me and to him, amounted to unthinkable amounts of money. I was ready to think bigger, so I convinced Sébastien to open an investment account in his name, one that I would manage. I'd read all about shorting stocks, how the riskier moves often yielded the greater gains. I'd spend sleepless nights reading financial news and scrutinized stock exchanges worldwide around the clock, learning more English in that time than I ever did in all my school years. Sometimes, I'd earn thousands in a day. Thousands! It was such a thrill in and of itself that I didn't think about spending it. My only splurges were a new phone and laptop, better tools to keep an eye on the market.

Things took a turn when high school came to an end. My friends moved to Paris for university, something I'd never considered for myself, and my parents put more pressure on me to go out and—ironically—earn some money. When I told them I'd made close to 20,000 euros in the last month, their reaction ping-ponged between disgust and utter distrust. Neither of them made much more than that in a year. I was lying, I had to be. *I can do the same for you*, I told them. *I'll make you rich.*

Famous last words.

It would be years before I realized I was addicted to the chase, the possibility of always more money. Some would have called it gambling, but I didn't see it that way. What I did required strategy, trusting my gut, riding the highs, learning to bounce back from the lows, which was the hardest part of it. It was better than school, better than a lame job. It was the air I breathed, my thoughts on a continuous loop. My whole life.

I stayed living with my parents and began investing their money. My brother's money, too. We could have all been set, forever. Occasionally, they asked me if it was time to stop. They had enough for a new car now. Enough for a nice vacation now. Enough for a new home, even. I still remember the day I saw my bank account juiced up to the tune of seven figures. I considered stopping then, I swear I did. I called my friends and asked if they wanted to go on a trip, anywhere in the world, but they were at school. Sébastien had jobs booked. I called a couple of exes—girls I'd dated for a few months, but had lost interest in as soon as I sensed they wanted something more serious—but they had new boyfriends. Everyone else had a life. I had money. I could do anything. And I would, right after I made one more bet. Just one more.

It's obvious by now, isn't it? I lost everything. My money. My parents' life savings. My brother's rainy-day cushion. Plus money I didn't even have, which I'd somehow have to pay back to the bank. Worse, it turned out that ignoring letters from the tax office—the French equivalent of the IRS—didn't make them go away. One day I received a visit from the finance brigade. They barged into our home and seized all my tech. They needed to understand how an unemployed, undereducated twenty-five-year-old was moving so much money on a weekly basis. They had to let me off the hook—I wasn't doing anything illegal—but I'd have to pay taxes on my gains for the last few years.

My parents, broke and spooked, wanted me out. I was a good-for-nothing, a scam artist, a lazy ass who didn't know the meaning of hard work. *Real work.* Why couldn't I earn an honest living? My brother had closed on a house he could no longer afford. He and I got into a fist fight and, even as he punched me in the face, I thought: I can make it all back. I *will* make it all back.

I was still in touch with my school friends, who frequently visited from Paris on weekends. They had jobs now, in banking or consulting. Not only did they make money, but a couple of them were in serious relationships. One was getting married, even. They knew the gist of my occupation—I'd bragged about my biggest gains more than once—but had no idea I'd lost it all. I told them I was ready to move to the capital and needed a place to crash for a little while. Fabien and Alexandre shared an apartment near Canal Saint-Martin and let me sleep on their couch. Soon, I convinced them to lend me a little money. I was on to something big; they'd make it back tenfold in a few weeks. They knew I had the potential.

I got by like that for a couple of years. Alexandre got his own place and I took over his room in the apartment. I started dating a friend of theirs, Melissa. A few good stock moves got me back in the game, and I borrowed more money from anyone who would lend it to me. My next few moves were not so good ones. I'd sworn I'd never let myself get carried away again, but there I was, owing money to almost everyone I knew. On Melissa's birthday, I was in the weeds of a new deal and couldn't be away from my laptop. I never showed up to her party and she wasted no time in breaking up with me. My friends turned their back on me. I was a mooch, a loser. My antics had been impressive when we were teenagers but, come on, I needed to grow up. To man up.

So, nearing thirty, penniless, homeless, friendless, I looked for a job for the first time in my life, which is how I ended up waiting tables at Bhotel's restaurant. I rented a chambre de bonne, a shoebox of a room, a fifth-floor walk-up. I ate ramen noodle at most meals, only bought groceries on sale, agonizing over the price of a carton of milk, most often deciding I didn't need it in the end. I closed my investment accounts, vowing to never get swallowed into that vortex again. I ignored angry calls and emails from my family and everyone else I owed money to. I "failed" to give my new address to the tax office to buy myself some time. I woke up in the middle of the night, remembering what had happened—how high I had flown, how low I had fallen—and wished I simply ceased to exist.

At the restaurant, I noticed that the American tourists often slipped me generous tips as they thanked me in their loud, brash voices, and I found myself gravitating toward them. For the money, of course, but I also liked their larger-than-life attitude, how they spent seemingly without counting. Whatever I suggested—the best wines and how about some dessert—they said yes to. My sales acumen got me noticed, and within months, I was moved to the concierge desk. There, I'd recommend ordering breakfast in, booking massages at the overpriced spa, or using our car service, when calling a taxi would have cost a fraction of the price. The Americans ate it up. If I offered them ways to throw more cash at their trip, they jumped at the chance.

When I heard about the branch opening in New York, I saw it as a sign. This was where I needed to be: the land of opportunities. One day, I'd pay back my parents, my brother, my friends, my taxes. One day, I'd be this incredible success story and they'd all curse that time they'd turned on me. One day, I would show them how wrong they all were. One day, one day, one day.

It was clear Cassie hadn't planned on turning her father's funeral into a mini-vacation, and yet she had all but moved in with me after that first night. I had no idea what her stepmother believed—that Cassie had gone back home, maybe?—but every time we went out, Cassie checked to make sure Ms. Crowes wasn't around and then slipped outside like an eel.

I'd also overheard her speak on the phone to, I assumed, her mother. There were mentions of the funeral being fine and of "home," but nothing about going back yet. Cassie was in no rush to leave. I had to use that to my advantage.

At her request, I took her to the famous pizza place, the hot club, the vibey cocktail bar, mentally calculating all the money this was costing me and whether the investment would ever pay off. She kept taking pictures of everything, including us, immediately posting them on social media. Cassie wanted a good time and I was prepared to show it to her, at least until I could find a way to bring up my wacky idea. The clock was ticking; I was booked on a flight back to Paris less than a week away.

"Do you still have to deal with some of your dad's stuff?" I said, my tone light as we sat in the back of an Uber on the way home from our third night out. Cassie insisted she wouldn't take the subway but never reached for her phone, or her wallet, to pay for anything.

A frown formed between her eyebrows. "Why do you ask?"

I sensed I'd said something wrong. "I mean, um, are you staying longer? You don't need to be back at work?"

She fired off a text on her phone. I leaned over and tried to read the screen, but only caught a glimpse of the recipient's first name: it began with D.

"Are you trying to get rid of me?" she said sweetly.

Every time she acted all flirty, I was reminded of how little affinity there was between us, let alone chemistry. Could she feel it, too? But then I remembered she was my best shot. I couldn't let her go.

I chuckled. "Not at all! The thing is…I'm going to Paris soon." I'd already told her I was "taking a break" from my job at Bhotel but I didn't think she'd been paying attention.

"Oooh," Cassie said, excitedly. The streetlights filtered through the car window and created strange shadows on her face.

"I wish I didn't have to," I added.

She sighed, then: "So what do we have on tomorrow, monsieur?"

"I'm leaving soon," I said. "Like, very soon."

She looked miffed. "So you *are* trying to kick me out."

The car parked in front of my apartment and Cassie stormed out.

"It's not like that," I said, catching up to her, slightly taken aback by what seemed like an oversized reaction. Why did she care so much? "But I *have* to go back to France."

"Yeah, okay." She rolled her eyes as I opened the door. For two people who'd known each other a few days, our arguments were already fiery.

I took in a deep breath. "But I'd kill to stay here." I didn't realize how true it was until I said it. "Here, some people get rich and successful overnight. You can do anything if you really put your mind to it."

"So why go back?" she asked, curling up on the sofa.

I leaned against the wall across from her. "I'm not really taking a break from my job. I lost it. No job means no visa."

"Can't you get another one?" She sounded like she was talking about a sweater I might have left behind at the club.

I didn't bother hiding the snark from my tone. "You haven't met many immigrants, have you?"

Her face turned into a puzzle. "You're not exactly—"

"I'm still a foreigner here. Different rules apply to us. So, no, I can't get another visa, which means I can't get another job. Trust me, if I could, I would. Now I have to give up the life I started building here for the last nine months and leave. And if I don't, they'll deport me and I won't be allowed to ever come back. Vacation time is over. For me at least."

"That sucks," she said, meaning it. "I was thinking I'd stay with you for a while."

"Really?" So there *was* hope. I came to sit on the couch next to her. Any opening I saw, I had to take. "Don't you have to go back to work?"

"I'm taking a little break, too."

"From...?"

Cassie made a funny face. "Lots of things. I had a candle-making business for a while. I did event planning. Parties, that sort of stuff. I like to switch it up." She paused, thought some more. "I have this big house which we run as an inn. Sometimes I think about renovating it. You could say I'm an entrepreneur."

I felt my heart race. "And you want to try something new here, in New York?"

This was good. We could convince Ms. Crowes to let us live rent-free for a while. Cassie was her stepdaughter, after all.

"I want more," she responded. "And I feel like if you want to stay, then you should. Do they *really* deport people who don't have a visa?"

I nodded. There were plenty of undocumented immigrants in New York, but I wasn't going to live like that: scraping by with no health insurance, unable to apply to well-paying jobs, watching over my shoulder, always, because ICE *did* deport people like me every day.

Now Cassie seemed upset, like she genuinely cared.

"There *is* one way I could stay in the States," I heard myself say. "And it's not even that risky if we do it right."

The "we" felt so strange in my mouth. I'd never been part of a "we."

"Do what?" She seemed intrigued, a good sign.

I took a deep breath. "I'd need to marry an American citizen."

She laughed. "Like they do in the movies?"

"Like they do in real life, too."

"Huh," she said, sounding much less interested. She picked up her phone and started scrolling.

But I couldn't let the moment pass. Not yet.

"It's simple," I said, feeling my pulse quicken. "You document your relationship thoroughly—I'd do all of that, of course—and go to the appointments with the immigration officers. You'd have to come, but it wouldn't take too much time." I spoke faster and faster, struggling to hold her gaze, which was unreadable. "After two years, I'd get a permanent green card, and then we'd be free to do whatever we wanted. It'd go by so fast."

I clicked my fingers to emphasize just how fast, and surprised myself with how clearly I'd laid out my case. I'd done my research. People *did* do that. And they got away with it. A lot of them did. Probably.

"You like it here that much?" Cassie said at last.

"I've never felt more like myself than in New York." I'd never thought that out loud, but it was true. I could become someone here. I could be the person I was always meant to be. But enough about me; I had to make it worth her while. Besides, it wasn't hard to guess why she kept posting photos of us. "Don't you want to show your ex what he's missing out on?"

Cassie perked up, her eyes drilling into mine. It was a stark change, a clear warning that I'd gone too far. I mean, obviously I'd gone too far: I'd suggested that she marry me, a total stranger.

Trying to save the moment, I leaned over and kissed her. "He's a mad man, letting you go."

I thought she might push me away, but something ignited within her and soon we were full-on making out, only stopping to tear each other's clothes off. There was always tomorrow, I told myself. It wasn't over yet.

But the next morning, as soon as I opened my eyes, I sensed that something was off. The air was too still in the room, the spot next to me empty.

"Cassie?" I called out.

Silence.

I got up, checked the bathroom, the living room.

"Cassie?"

No response.

No, no, no, no, no.

She was gone. Could she report me for suggesting we get married for the green card? Could she make my life even worse than it already was?

An hour passed, and then another. I stared at the front door and still no Cassie.

Fuck, what had I done?

CHAPTER 7

Taylor

NOW

I need help."

I grip onto the edge of the counter so hard my fingers hurt. On the other side, the red-haired attendant opens her mouth in a neat O, her eyebrows knitting together. She's clearly a little shocked at my bursting into the lobby and rushing to her, but professional enough to keep her reaction in check.

"Yes, madame," she says, releasing the computer mouse to pull down both sides of her black blazer. "What can I do for you?"

When I ran from the terrace, I was convinced the man from the next table was on my heels, that he'd gotten up to follow me. After I'd been racing down the street for a few minutes, ignoring the strange looks of everyone around, I attempted a quick glance behind me. There were women carrying shopping bags, people strolling leisurely, none of whom I recognized. He wasn't there, so I slowed my pace to a power walk, turning around every ten steps or so.

When I reached my hotel—surprised that I even remembered where it was—I checked one last time that the coast was clear before entering. I even waited until two young guys in tracksuit pants and chunky gold neck chains turned the corner.

"Madame?"

The redhead is eyeing me. It's possible I've been staring into space since she first spoke.

I clear my throat and force myself to stand straighter. "Um, yes. I would like some help with…the safe-deposit box in my room."

"Oh." She pauses, expecting more.

"I think something went wrong when I tried to lock it."

She smiles a little brighter now, reassured that this is a problem she can handle. "I'll send someone right up to fix that for you." She pushes her red locks off her face, glancing behind me at the woman who just walked through the door.

"We will take care of it, madame," she adds when I still haven't moved.

She gives me a slight nod. It might be meant as encouraging, but I read it as, *Now if you could please get the fuck out of here…I have way more important things to do.*

My heart jumps at the sound of a knock. I'm lying on the bed, and I must have fallen asleep.

"Yes," I say, or at least I try to. My mouth feels so dry. I look around for water, anything to relieve the discomfort, when another knock comes. "Je viens!" I call out.

On the other side of the door, Amir, the guy who checked me in yesterday, leans in with a sheepish smile.

"You need help," he says. A statement, not a question.

I do, but I don't really want to let this stranger inside my room and be alone with him. Then again, I'm itching to check my phone, so I move out of the doorframe to let him in and follow his gaze as he scans the space. Since there is no wardrobe, I've stacked up my new purchases in piles on the floor: cotton bras with delicate lace trims, tops with different types of stripes, another pair of jeans, the ballet flats, a straw hat, and a plain baseball cap. The dresses and skirts dangle from the exposed rail. To an outsider, it might look like I've been enjoying the benefits of the most fashionable city in the world. Like I'm actually a thirty-year-old newlywed on her honeymoon.

"Your safe is locked?" Amir says.

"Yes. I think I remember the code wrong. I'm a little tired." I attempt a chuckle, then shake my head. What was I thinking before? I was never going to last without my phone. My lifeline. My only way to check on…

"Jet lag," he says, pulling up his dress pants and kneeling down in front of the safe. "It happens."

I sit on the bed while he retrieves a key from his pocket. Moments later, the door opens with a creak, revealing my phone, tucked in with all the cash.

I don't owe him an explanation, but the silence between us as he gets back up is killing me. I'm sure he thinks it's weird that I put my phone inside the safe, but he doesn't let on.

"I thought it might be out of battery," he says. "People seem to forget their chargers all the time. So I brought you this."

He takes a phone charger out of his pocket. The relief on my face must be obvious as I snatch it from him.

"Thank you," I say, getting down to plug it by the side of the bed.

"So no news on your…luggage?"

I shake my head, hoping that will be enough to get him to leave. Then, I press the home button on my phone, which only flashes with the recharge battery sign, as it does when it is fully flat.

Amir walks over to the door and turns around. "How is…" He trails off, then swallows. "Your hon…your holiday, I mean?"

"Great," I say, my throat tight. His eyes drop to my ring finger, which I start rubbing mindlessly. Of course it's bare. I'm not the marrying kind. Never was. Never will be.

He glances at my left hand once more, then grabs the door handle, ready to leave. "If you're free," he says, emphasizing the "free" and all of its meanings, "we could go for a drink, one night."

I like that he doesn't say that he'll take me for a drink, that women aren't something he gets to parade around and dispose of however he wishes.

But I haven't responded, so he says it again, "If you're free."

There's a spark in his eye. In another life, I would have said yes before he'd had time to finish his sentence. If a man wanted me, I let him have me, wondering how he could possibly be interested. I would go for the drink, and then I would putter around while he pulled out his wallet, pretending to be flattered when in fact I was too broke to pay for it myself. And way too ashamed to admit it. I worked multiple jobs and I had so little to show for it.

"I need to…" I say, pointing at my phone.

"Of course. I hope you enjoy Paris. Most people think it can be lonely to travel alone but I disagree. In a foreign place, no one's there to judge you. You get to be whoever you want and do whatever you like. I like your new hair, by the way. It suits you."

He looks deep into my eyes, smiles, and then he's gone.

When my phone comes to life, my heart does a little jump at the red circle above the green call button. A voicemail, from a number I don't know. This is bad. I hold my breath as I press Play.

Taylor? Hello? Is this working?

It's the tentative voice of Ms. Richardson, a family friend who lives three streets down from us. She usually calls our landline and I've never had to save her number in my contacts.

Hello Taylor, it's Madeline. I… Well this might seem strange but I went on my walk early this morning, and I noticed your car wasn't there. Then I remembered it wasn't there yesterday, either. At least I think so. My memory is not what it used to be. I thought I'd check in on you. It's not like you to disappear.

She pauses, like she expects me to jump in and agree. She's right. I have almost always been there in that house. Good Taylor, forever present.

Well, um, so I went to ring the bell, and I guess you really weren't there. That bothered me a bit, so I went for another walk after lunch, and that's when I saw a man.

My hand clenches around the phone, my heart in knots.

I was far away so I couldn't see who it was... Anyway, he stood by the door for a while.

She clears her throat, and the wait feels excruciating. Get on with it, Madeline.

He had a suit on, but that doesn't mean anything these days. I watched... You know I wanted to make sure you were okay now that... Well, I know what it's like to be all alone.

It's not exactly the same situation though, is it? Mr. and Ms. Richardson were happily married for something like forty years before he died a few years back. They had three children, some of whom now have children of their own. Sure, Madeline will chew your ear off about how her family doesn't visit her anywhere near as much as she'd like them to—they live so close! No excuse!—but we're not the same kind of alone.

Anyway, he searched around for a while, and then I saw he was holding something.

I press the phone harder against my ear, like that will make her speak faster. My heart stammers in my chest, trying to picture this man loitering around the house. Suddenly it hits me, how far away I am, how quickly I left. And I can't explain any of it to anyone.

He had the keys! To your house!

Ms. Richardson pauses for effect, as if she knows how much this will startle me.

And he went in.

She's whispering now, like she's afraid of the man coming after her. I am too, and I'm on the other side of the world.

He didn't try to hide or anything. I'd say he was in there for ten, maybe fifteen minutes. It felt… Well, I don't know. With all the changes your family has gone through… Call me back, okay?

I put down the phone, my mind running a million miles an hour. There's only one man who has the keys to the house, and there's no way in hell he was there this morning. He's gone, forever.

My brain buzzing, I check my social media feeds. I never post on there; I have nothing to show, but I can't help checking on other people's lives. Pictures of Paris fill my screen as I scroll. Happy people having fun in this beautiful city. Drinking wine at the terrace of a famous restaurant. Taking in the view of the Eiffel Tower. Posing on the sidewalk of a charming little street. Maybe it's all for show, snippets of fantasies that don't come close to reality, but I buy it all.

I can't call Madeline back. Deep down, she means well—I still wear the emerald-green scarf she knit for me many years ago—but she'll be full of questions and I'll have none of the answers. Maybe I should go home, forget about my past, forget about what my future could have been. I brush away the thought as quickly as it comes, Amir's words ring in my ears.

No one's here to judge you.

But that's not true. Because *I'm* here to judge me. And maybe this guy thinks this is all just a bit of fun to me. Some kind of self-empowerment crap about how women can have it all, even a solo honeymoon. And I can't tell him how wrong he is, because no one would understand what led me here. I got in with the wrong family, the wrong person. I believed the lies fed to me, when I'd sworn nothing would hurt me anymore.

So maybe that's why I'm here. For closure.

One last hurrah. And then I, too, will go away forever.

CHAPTER 8

Cassie

NOW

No amount of staring at the three dots on my phone changes the fact that Darren doesn't text again. Olivier and I finish our mains, and still nothing.

"What's up?" Olivier says, pointing his chin at my phone.

"It's Brianna," I say, putting it facedown on the table. I shake my head, like she should know better than to bother me right now. Even though she's my friend and it would make sense for her to check in on me during my honeymoon, especially after my whirlwind wedding. The look on her face when she clocked the size of my diamond and I told her about the sudden proposal… No one expected things would turn out so well for me. Hot husband, lots of money, and now this: Paris in the summer, wining and dining like the best of them.

I turn my phone up again. "I should text her back."

Makes you wonder? I type. I hit Send too fast, then silently curse myself. *Rookie mistake, Cassie. If Darren really wanted you back, he wouldn't have waited until you were on your fucking honeymoon.*

What kind of text was that anyway? The furthest Darren ever took me was an Italian restaurant in Albany, where we brought down the average

age by twenty years and he talked me out of ordering dessert because he had to get up early the next day. Can't he see how much I stepped it up? Or have I still not shown him enough yet?

I let out a sigh. "Did you really mean it earlier? About making this trip special?" I ask Olivier.

"Of course, I—"

I don't let him finish. "Good. Because I want this honeymoon to be perfect. Amazing views, lots of shopping, great food, and a lot more wine."

I never understood why people think French wine is better—booze is booze—but I can actually taste the difference. It goes down so nicely.

I check my phone again. Darren hasn't responded. His silence feels like a slap in the face. We were good together. Not always, but a lot of the time, and then he decided he could do better than me. It's taking him way too long to realize how wrong he was.

"Who cares about them," Olivier adds, glancing at my phone. "You deserve the best, Cassie. And I'm going to make sure you get it."

I nod, unsure how to respond. *Up to five years jail time*, the lawyer said. That's what I risk if this whole thing with Olivier goes pear-shaped.

When the waiter comes to clear our plates, Olivier seems giddy about the dessert options. I let him choose the chocolate profiteroles to share. A house specialty, apparently. They arrive a few minutes later and we each dip our spoon into the short tower of puff pastries, breaking them down to get to the cream inside. For a moment it feels like we're goddamn Lady and the Tramp, eating from the same plate and making gooey eyes at each other. And I don't care how Olivier looks—with his perfectly ironed baby-pink shirt, his squeaky clean sneakers, and his cropped hair—or how well he blends with all the Parisians. *I'm* Lady. He's just a stray I picked up in a weak moment.

After lunch, Olivier makes good on his promise. Not only that, but he gets us an Uber so I don't have to walk any further in my high heels. I didn't even need to ask him. We drive to the embankments of the Seine, past forest-green stands selling vintage books, all lined up on the edge of the river. It's summer in full swing. Sunny and bright. Girls in pretty floral dresses carrying straw baskets—I should get one of those—and guys eyeing them up and down. Couples riding bicycles next to each other while chatting away. It makes my heart swell; such dreamy Instagram content.

But that's only the start of it.

Olivier reaches for my hand as he leads me down the path to the water, where a boat is docked. It's double-decked and open on top. Dozens of people are already lined up to get on, their phones out so they don't miss a moment of it.

"It's called a bateau-mouche," Olivier explains. "They sail down the Seine, past all of the most iconic spots in the city."

"I can read the sign." I sound like a surly teenager, but deep down, I'm impressed. We're going on a cruise. How whimsical. He understood the assignment, finally.

For the first part of it, I'm so busy taking it all in—through my screen—that I almost forget why I'm here. But as I lean over the railing, Olivier's hands wrap around my waist, startling me. He smells good: clean and woodsy.

"Cassie, can you look at me for a minute?" he says, motioning for me to turn around. I do. Now our heads are almost touching. "I know things haven't always been easy since we met, and the wedding was… It's not the fancy affair you had in mind. I know it was rushed. Too rushed. But I've been thinking about this a lot and I want this to work. This marriage—"

The boat sails underneath an ornate bridge, shadows covering Olivier's face. His eyes seem a little shiny, like he's tearing up.

He waits until we're on the other side, nearing the Eiffel Tower, to continue. "We could be something more. So much more."

I raise a dubious eyebrow.

"I'm serious," he adds. "I mean, look at us. There's so much potential here." Olivier runs a hand through my hair, which is blowing in the wind.

So freaking romantic. "For one, I can't help thinking about what the inn will look like when we're done with it," he adds.

Ugh, he won't shut up about that. Upstate New York is booming (his words), and New Yorkers are more than happy to pay through the roof for a chic room in the country. We already own the property—well, I do—and the upgrades he has planned will do wonders: repainting the walls, retiling the bathrooms, and purchasing new furniture from local artisans for that rustic flair city people expect when they come to our neck of the woods. He even has plenty of marketing ideas, from his time working at a luxury hotel. It will cost a lot of money, of course, but according to my dear husband, we'll make it back tenfold. Sometimes I wish I'd never told him about my family inn. Sometimes I wish…a lot of things, actually.

"There's still plenty of work to do, but it'll so worth it in the end." Olivier must have been rambling on about the plans for the inn, which is usually when I tune him out. "Everyone you know will envy us. I can make you happy, Cassie. I *want* to make you happy."

My first instinct is to laugh. Where is this coming from? And why now? This was never about happiness. But what if… I mean, if I stop to think about it, Olivier did seem very excited when I told him I'd booked tickets to Paris. Not at first, maybe. At first he was stunned, silent. But then he was the one who suggested it should be our honeymoon and that we make our wedding happen ASAP before jetting off here.

"You're lying," I say. I know he's good at it. A pro, even. I need to remind myself of this game we're playing.

"I'm not," he replies, gently grabbing my chin. "The truth is, things have changed, Cassie. I feel… I mean, we're married. We live together. Soon, we'll have a successful business, something we built together."

I shake my head. Look away. What if he's not lying?

Olivier tightens his hold on me. "Your ex had no idea what was good for him. That's his loss. I don't want to change you or for you to be anything other than who you are."

I never told Olivier what happened with Darren, why we broke up, right before my father died. But it's like he knows, instinctively. He saw the weakness within me, used it for his own benefit. Didn't he?

The breeze picks up and the cool air makes my skin tingle. Olivier caresses my cheek, and when he comes in for a kiss, I don't pull back. I mean, I'm squeezed against the railing anyway, and there are people all around us, but I don't *want* to pull back.

"Je t'aime," he whispers in my ear after our lips part. "It means 'I love—'"

"I know what it means," I say. It comes out harsher than I intended, so I soften it up with a smile. I was never good at languages at school, but even a moron would know that. We've seen the movies, Olivier. We've all heard these words before, spoken to other people. "Take a picture with me."

If he's disappointed that I didn't say it back, he doesn't let it show.

He hesitates. Then: "Of course."

Or maybe I imagined it, because when he leans against me, he presses his face to mine, like he wants to be as close as possible. Lit by the orange hues of the afternoon glow, with the water and the Eiffel Tower as our backdrop, we look pretty damn good. Like we're in love.

Olivier *wanted* to marry me. I called the shots and he went along with all of it. And he's right; he never tried to turn me into someone I'm not.

He leans over to check out the picture. "We look right together," he says, beaming. "Like it was all meant to be."

My throat catches. I don't know what to say, which never happens.

Once again, Olivier stares deep into my eyes. "I love you, Cassie. 'Till death do us part.' That's what we said. That's what we swore."

I open my mouth to respond but close it again. The thing is, Olivier doesn't know me at all. Because if he did, he'd understand that I didn't think too hard about what we swore. I had other things on my mind, other people. And, to be honest, I'm not exactly the best at keeping promises. Never was, and probably never will be.

CHAPTER 9

Olivier

THREE MONTHS BEFORE THE HONEYMOON

When Cassie walked through my door again three hours later, her demeanor had changed. She was wearing her funeral dress, the short little black one, her hair brushed nice and straight.

"You're here!" I said, dropping my cool act. I'd been anxiously checking the time, running nightmare scenarios through my head. "You're back."

I got up and went to hug her, I was so relieved. "I'm sorry if I scared you about the whole marriage thing. I completely understand if you want to forget I ever said that."

Panic made the words tumble out fast and furious.

Cassie made a strange face. "You were serious about that?"

"Of course I was." Had she not heard the desperation in my voice? Had she not listened when I said I was about to be forced out of the country? "I'd marry you in a heartbeat, if you'd have me." I chuckled, like wasn't this all so very sweet?

She studied me in silence, half-amused, half-confused. I didn't know what else to say to convince her but I was willing to try anything. "We're having fun together, aren't we? Think about all the great things we could do. So, yes, I'm serious, Cassie. I want to marry you. And if it's about money..."

I drifted off. I'd have money again. I'd pay her, one day. I was just about to promise that when she cut in.

Her eyes lit up. "That asshole," she said, as she went to the coffee machine.

"I'll do that," I said, jumping to take over and pulling out two coffee mugs. I'd have done anything she wanted me to.

She went to sit on the couch. "That little rich asshole."

"What happened?"

She shook her head. "*Millions* he had. Plus the house. *Houses*, I should say. You won't believe how much *this* is worth," she said, circling the air with her index finger.

I already knew, of course. I'd looked it up when I moved in, thinking of the day I'd have my own brownstone in one of Brooklyn's finest neighborhoods, instead of living in the basement.

"I'm so sorry your father treated you that way," I said, thinking I knew where this was going. "It's not right."

Cassie took the mug I offered her and sipped slowly. "Turns out his parents had money and when he inherited, after he left us, he made a few smart investments or whatnot. She, his 'wife,' said he had every intention of leaving me something in his will. That he'd planned to amend it someday. I am his child, too, and he didn't mean for me to have nothing at all, but he never thought he'd die so suddenly. I mean, duh, obviously."

"Oh, Cassie!" I put on my most compassionate air, ready to hug her into oblivion, whatever she needed.

But then she continued. "Turns out the house, *my* house, wasn't my mom's after all. It belonged to his family. He just let her live there after he left. She never said anything."

"You could ask her about it," I said, treading carefully. I wanted to show that I was on her side, *by* her side, when no one else was.

Cassie stopped midsip. "She's dead." She said it like I should know this, like it had come up before. Had it? "Anyway, it's mine now."

She nodded fiercely, nostrils flared and jaw clenched, nowhere near done with getting all this off her chest. "She thought giving me the house would be enough."

Every time she referred to her stepmother, Cassie said "she" or "his wife" with such loathing it was almost comical. Or maybe it was pain. My landlady had never seemed like such a bad person to me, but she must have known her new husband had conveniently left his daughter behind to go live this lovely life with his new family. I liked the guy a lot less now than when he was alive.

"Well," I said. "Owning your house is pretty nice."

Cassie shook her head, like I wasn't following. "I wasn't going to only take what I was given. At first I was going to throw out a number, but that felt kind of crass. So I waited. And oh my god, I thought I heard her wrong. Like what, a couple of million is nothing to her?" She seemed to think about that, her face beaming with a new insight. "Maybe it *is* nothing to her. Shit. I bet the boys, her 'sons,' are getting much more. Plus she gets this house. Ugh, I hate them all. How she almost made me beg…"

Had Cassie just said "a couple million"? I held my breath, wondering if I was hallucinating.

It was too much all at once.

"That's incredible," I said. I think my eyes may have been watering, the stress from thinking I'd lost her, my ticket to freedom, to the shock of her whirling back in here with all that new information.

"You're sweet," she said.

"I mean it, Cassie. You're really *something*. Going after what you want. Getting your due. You're fearless." Sometimes I wondered where that stuff came from. *You're a smooth talker,* my dad would say. *Lots of pretty words, that's how you tricked us.*

Cassie studied me, excited now. "Come home with me. I'm done here.

64

Really glad I stuck around until they read the will. She's having the paper-work drawn up, and I'll get the money in a few weeks."

"The two million dollars?" I said, still trying to make sense of it all.

She nodded, still partly sour from not wringing even more cash out of the widow. Finally, it hit me. Cassie hadn't stayed in New York for fun. Or for me. She was strategizing, staying away from her stepmother until she felt ready to finagle something out of her father's death. She wasn't leaving without her slice of the cake. And it had worked: now she was inheriting two million dollars and her house upstate. See, *this* is the American dream. And it had fallen into her lap.

"So, are you coming with me?"

I felt my mouth open, words forming in my brain, possibilities shaping in my mind. But now that she had money, I had even less to offer her. "I'd love to be with you. But I can't say in this country unless we get married. I know it sounds crazy. You barely know me. But is there any way you might consider it?"

She laughed. "So you're, like, proposing to me?"

"Yes!" I said eager. Hungry.

"You want to marry *me*?"

"It would make me so happy." I mean, it was the truth.

She smiled strangely as she looked me up and down. It took me a moment to understand what she was waiting for. I felt my mind and my body dissociating as I clumsily knelt in front of her and grabbed her hand. "Cassie, will you marry me? I'll get you a ring," I added quickly, just as I remembered cubic zirconium was all I could afford.

"How does that even work, the green card thing?"

I paused, not wanting to sound too keen. Then I tried to steady my voice before launching into it. "I know someone who did it; it's easy. He used an immigration lawyer who handled everything." That was a lie—the first part, anyway. I had *read* articles about people who'd done this. It was pretty common, apparently. America was so good at putting a shiny bow on itself that many looked at it and thought, *I want a piece of that.* "In New York, you can easily apply for a license and get married twenty-four hours later. I don't really have friends in the city, and you have no family left, right?"

She grimaced, like she was disappointed I hadn't been paying attention. But I *had* paid attention, and I could tell how much she craved it.

I forced a smile. "Just you and me then. Feels even more special, don't you think?"

Marriage fraud, they called it. For me it meant immediate deportation, banned from re-entering the country for life. For her there was imprisonment, up to five years, and a $250,000 fine. The U.S. government knew all too well how valuable American citizenship was, and it didn't like when its people attempted to sell it. But that was only if we got caught.

My only other option was to go home quietly until I figured out a way to come back to New York. But no, that wouldn't work. I'd managed to keep my tax debt at bay while I was here. I owed a lot of money for me, but I guess not enough for the French government to come at me in another country. But if I moved home, there would be nowhere to hide. They'd find me, maybe not right away, but soon enough.

Besides, I had no idea if I could ever come back here. It was getting harder and harder to obtain work visas for the United States. Many international companies were giving up on trying to bring in employees from their foreign offices; the hassle wasn't worth it anymore. I'd already had to go through months of paperwork before I could move here. Between the new immigration laws, being let go from my current job, and having no college degree, it'd take a miracle to make that happen again.

"I want to go home and do it there," Cassie finally said. "The wedding, I mean. With my friends and everything. I want a white dress, drinks, dancing, the whole shebang."

I should have asked myself why she was even considering helping me. Was it only about making her ex jealous? Did she expect anything of me? I should have been full of questions. Two years of my life were in the balance, as well as my entire future. But I felt so desperate, the ticking time bomb of my departure ringing louder and louder in my ears.

"That sounds wonderful," I said, getting off my knee. I felt ridiculous staying down on the floor. She hadn't said yes. But she hadn't said no, either. "And you'd look so beautiful. I can picture it." She smiled. "But I couldn't wait that long. My visa expires next week. I'd have to get married as soon as possible. I could get in a lot of trouble if I stayed after it expired."

Cassie pouted. "You mean like, at City Hall?"

There was no time to go upstate, meet Cassie's friends, and start planning a wedding.

"We'll get you a dress," I said quickly, coming to sit next to her and looking deep into her eyes. "And flowers. We'd have photos taken, obviously. I'll book a restaurant with a nice view of the city." I tried to make it sound romantic, when in fact I knew I had to make it look genuine. "And we could have a big wedding later on, if that's what you want. It'll be double the fun! You know, people do that in France sometimes. They do the marriage thing first at City Hall, and then have the party with everyone. You'd get to wear two different dresses."

She pondered this silently for a while. Was she just waving the possibility in front of me like a stuffed toy dangling from the top of a carrousel? I felt the urge to grab her by the arms and shake her. *Say something!*

But she didn't, so I went on. "If you do this for me, I'll owe you forever. I'll do anything for you." She perked up and opened her mouth, but nothing came out. "And of course, as soon as my green card application is in, I can get another job. I won't ask anything of you." And then at last, the words I meant the least came out: "You're an amazing woman, Cassie. I know it's only been a few days, but meeting you has been the bright light I needed."

Finally, she put her empty coffee mug on the floor and leaned close to me. "So you're coming home with me?"

I couldn't help looking down at the cup. I knew she wasn't going to pick it back up or put it away. Over the last few days, I'd felt a bit like her servant, making coffee, washing her mug after she was done, picking her stuff off the floor, unclogging the drain after her shower. I couldn't imagine the state of her house. Was I really going to live there with her? For two whole years? No, of course not. I'd convince her to come back here, in New York, where great things awaited me, especially with Cassie's fortune. I'd just go along with it for now.

"Of course I'll come home with you. Like I said, I'll do anything for you. *Anything.*"

I sounded so pathetic. It felt like an eternity before she rolled over and straddled me, her face so close that her coffee breath felt like it was mine. "I *would* look good in a wedding dress."

It all happened in a flash. Cassie chose a light-pink fluffy dress, even though I wished she'd gone with the traditional (and more legit-looking) white. At City Hall, we picked a witness out of the assembly and exchanged *I do's* with strained smiles. Pictures pictures pictures. Evidence for the immigration officers. Cassie never suggested sharing those on her Instagram account, and I'd assumed she was holding back for the bigger wedding I'd mentioned. Then, the deal done, two quasi-strangers husband and wife. No going back.

The minute we returned to my apartment—after an expensive lunch during which she only picked at her food—Cassie made a beeline for the bedroom.

"All right," she said, collecting her clothes off the floor. "Let's go."

"Now?" My voice was high-pitched; I couldn't keep the surprise out of it.

I was at her mercy. We *had* to live together. I had to do what she said.

Cassie threw her things in her weekend bag. "Did I tell you it's my birthday next week?"

She hadn't. In fact, I had yet to realize how little I knew about my brand-new wife.

A couple of hours later, we were making our way through Penn Station. It was all so rushed, but soon I'd have a green card and, let's be honest, access to two million dollars. I'd booked an appointment with an immigration lawyer along with our slot at City Hall and had already filled out the forms that allowed me to stay here temporarily until my application was processed. It would all work out.

During the train ride, Cassie typed angrily on her phone, her nails clicking on the screen even louder than normal, while I stared out of the window. It was early May, but gray and misty. There were fields with cows roaming and farms built in dark-red wood just outside of Manhattan. Who knew?

When we arrived at our destination over two hours later, Cassie sent a few texts, grunted with obvious frustration, and asked me to get us an Uber. I was still too rattled by the sudden dash to wonder what that was about.

The ride through town did nothing to appease me. There was hardly anyone on the streets. Many of the shops were closed with faded FOR RENT posters taped to the inside of windows, one lone bar was announcing cheap lager for happy hour, and everything felt kind of muted. Bland. Half-dead.

We neared Cassie's house, the inn. Maybe she could sell it. I'd handle the whole thing for her. I bet she'd like that.

It wasn't a big shock after seeing the town, but the house seemed beyond tired. Some of the palings around the porch were broken, the shutters hung unevenly on each side of the windows, and a tree drooped so low that it obscured the whole left side of the house.

The front door opened as we got out of the car, and a woman about our age appeared. She stood on the porch, staring at us with narrowed eyes and pinched lips.

"This is Olivier," Cassie said, wrapping an arm around my shoulder and beaming at me. She'd never pronounced my name so well before. "He's from France. Funny, no?"

The woman nodded, then forced a smile. "Hmm. Funny, yes."

She was tall and looked shapeless in her baggy jeans—but not the fashionable kind New York girls wore—and sweatshirt. Her mousy-brown hair and lack of makeup reeked of country.

Cassie left me with our bags and went inside, not bothering to introduce us. She must be Cassie's employee, if she ran the inn in her absence, though the place looked so desolate I couldn't imagine anyone paying money to stay here.

At the top of the steps, I put the bags down and held out my hand.

"Hi!" I said. "I'm Olivier. Well, Cassie already said that."

A bitter smile formed on her lips. "She hasn't mentioned me." Her tone was all snark; it wasn't a question.

I had to make a good impression with Cassie's circle. They had to believe us when we announced we were married or getting married, whichever way Cassie chose to handle it. We needed witnesses. More proof. A solid case, or as solid it could be when we got married a few days after meeting, and so close to my visa expiring.

"How's business?" I asked, to make conversation. "I bet spring is a busy season."

She frowned.

"The inn?" I clarified. "Do you have many guests staying here at the moment?"

"The inn's been closed a long time," she said blandly.

Then, to my surprise, she reached down to grab Cassie's bag. No time to recover from the fact that Cassie had lied about running an inn. Or had I misunderstood? The events of the last few days were muddied in my mind.

"I can carry that," I said quickly.

I tried to take it from her, but her grasp was firm. Then, she headed back inside.

I followed her. "So you are?" I was after a name, something to break the ice.

She didn't bother turning around. "I'm Cassie's sister."

She looked *nothing* like Cassie. Her face was angular, with sharp cheekbones, when Cassie's was round. Cassie was petite with brown eyes, and hers were dark green. I was aware that siblings didn't necessarily share the same eye color, but that's not what confused me. Cassie had said she had no family left. So where the hell did the sister come from?

"I look forward to getting to know you," I said, a little too upbeat.

Geez, that sounded creepy.

She was in the doorframe and turned back to me, a blank expression on her face. "I don't think that's going to happen."

I stared at her, waiting for a laugh. But there was none. It wasn't a joke.

Well, fuck, that was weird. But that was only the start of it, because then I walked into the house, where everything was dark.

CHAPTER 10

Taylor

NOW

'm not going to fool myself: my days in Paris are numbered. I had to book a return flight when I was at the airport and chose five days later. I should be back early enough so I wouldn't rouse suspicion. Two days in, it's clear that the honeymoon will be over before I know it.

But for now I have money, a new look, and more clothes than I can wear. It's time.

The bathtub is cramped and I ran the water too hot for a summer day, but a few minutes in, my muscles feel like they're melting. My head rolls against the edge as I try to keep my eyes closed, letting my mind run adrift.

I have so little left over from my childhood—before my mother was taken from me—but my few possessions told me all the stories I wanted to believe: a copy of *Le Petit Prince* in French and a fine knit blanket with the words "Pour les doux rêves de" embroidered above my name. *For the sweet dreams of.* There's also this lullaby that echoes in my head sometimes, though it has faded to almost nothing over the years.

Dodo, l'enfant do
L'enfant dormira bien vite

I open my eyes. I never really thought I'd find my father based on some meager scraps, did I? It was such a Good Taylor move to hope. Reaching up, I wipe my hand on the towel hanging from the rail and grab my phone, immediately clicking on the Instagram app. On my screen, the city stares back at me in all its splendor. Pictures of half-eaten croissants on tiny bistro tables flanked by wicker chairs. Views of the Eiffel Tower from a bateau-mouche cruising down the Seine. Quaint cobblestoned streets on which chic girls teeter on high heels.

I zero in on one picture, posted yesterday. She's in a lacy black dress and platform sandals. An outfit that smells new, worn for the first time. @ cassieny looks like she's having a blast: sitting front and center at the terrace of Les Deux Magots restaurant, bent over halfway as if laughing too hard to stand straight, the sun caressing her bare legs, her cat-eyed sunglasses giving her that whiff of celebrity, someone who doesn't really want to be seen, even though she's posting endless selfies on Instagram.

Technically they're not selfies because she has someone to take them. New wifey to Olivier, her Instagram bio reads, her husband's name followed by a French flag. Then, In Paris for our honeymoon, followed by the bride-and-groom emoji and a heart. We get it, Cassie. Your life is picture perfect.

I flick through a few more pictures, all signs of the perfect French honeymoon. Does it look as good in the flesh as she makes it seem? There's only one way to find out.

Cutting my bath short, I dry myself and rip the tags off the flowing red dress I bought yesterday. I slip it on and stare at my reflection in the mirror, unsure what to think. It's so visible, so loud. So not me. I put on the straw hat as well as sunglasses that eat up half my face. The kind of things I'd never wear. When I'm ready to head out, there's nothing left of Good Taylor. Maybe this is the French version of me, who I was always supposed to be.

Outside, the air is damp and still a little cool for the midmorning. I check the latest on @cassieny: her Instagram tells me she's finishing up breakfast at a café near her hotel. The geotag function is handy like that. It's a bit of a walk to get there, and as I head south toward the Seine, I make sure to take in everything: the wrought-iron Juliet balconies, the chipped paint of the wooden shutters, and the advertisements at the bus stops, which I try my best to decipher.

The crowd thickens as I edge closer to the water, groups huddled up on the bridge looking at and snapping pictures of Notre-Dame Cathedral. A young woman with brown hair down to her waist approaches me.

"Do you want me to take your photo?" she says, glancing at the phone in my hand.

The woman's smile seems so genuine that I nod in spite of myself. Afterward, I stare at the result on my screen. I wouldn't say I look happy, but I definitely feel lighter than I did when I got on that plane. Maybe it's the Paris effect. I run a quick calculation in my mind. I could move to a cheaper hotel, and then to an apartment. The money might last me six months. More, if I'm careful. I'd keep learning French. I'd find a job. I'd change my name, obviously. There could be a life for me here. Maybe. For now I delete the photo, my heart twitching as I hit the trash-can button.

My first destination is on the other side of the river, after a walk down the windy streets of Saint-Germain-des-Prés. Les Deux Magots restaurants is one of the city's most famous cafés—nothing is too good for @ cassieny—but since it's still morning, the lunch crowd hasn't invaded the place yet. On a corner of the sprawling terrace, a woman twice my age reads a book with a cream cover and red lettering, a small espresso cup laid out on the table. She looks so chic in a crisp white dress and black suede high-heeled pumps, and oozes enough elegance to eclipse everyone around her.

My stomach twists in a knot as I eye the empty table next to hers. Let's try this again. Soon a waiter comes over and drops off the world's tiniest glass with a water jug that's not much bigger. Both are streaked and stained by what must be years of dishwashing. I like that worn feeling; I've never aspired to anything too shiny.

I order breakfast—tartines with butter and jam, orange juice, black coffee—and for a while I sit there watching the world go by: people strutting along, talking on their phones, carrying groceries, talking animatedly with their companions. They're going places, meeting others. Living.

I've never had friends, even at school. I was the shy girl who always felt out of place—who *was* out of place, literally bounced around many homes until I could be squeezed into another life for good. Trying to make myself as small as possible, I sat in the back of class or in the quiet corner of the lunch room and only spoke when spoken to. And even then, I was so startled by the fact that someone would willingly interact with me that I would stare at them, wondering why, oh why. My whole life, I dreamed of the day I would have *somebody*, someone who wanted to be with me, who would make me whole again.

An anxious glance at my phone tells me that @cassieny is on the move, leaving Le Bon Marché department store with a straw basket in the crook of her elbow—so French of her—and arms full of shopping bags. Back to the hotel to drop these off! And then, heading to the Luxembourg Gardens, she announces as if we should all care. Truth is, I do. I want what she has. I always have, even if I would have never admitted it to anyone. I count my euros—I'm still getting used to the thick two-tone coins and the colorful notes—and get up.

A few minutes later, Cassie's Instagram history leads me to Ladurée, the French temple of pastel-colored pastries. The window display looks sickly sweet, all fluff, pink, and creamy. The mint-green facade and the gothic lettering feel all too familiar, even though I've never seen them before in real life. When it's my turn to order, I let the salesperson in a black apron pick an assortment of macarons.

A short walk later, I find myself on the edge of the Luxembourg Gardens. It's big enough that you can forget you're in the middle of a big city, with lots of green metal lounge chairs scattered around a pond. Today is the perfect weather for it: sunny, bright, breezy. I sit down, taking notes of the crowd around me. I'm surrounded by couples. Love on display everywhere. My heart collapses onto itself, like it's trying to obstruct the view.

I'm munching on a rose macaron when I spot @cassieny, lying on one of the chairs, her skirt riding up her thighs as her husband snaps a few more pictures. She looks down at her legs and yanks the dress a little higher. Then, she shifts her Chanel handbag so it's clearly visible in the picture. She must have gotten it during her earlier shopping spree. Meanwhile, he moves around and even crouches on the ground to get a different angle. Then, she takes the phone from him and studies the screen. A smile forms on her face. He must have gotten a good one, the dutiful husband.

Sure enough, @cassieny has a new photo up a moment later. Almost like being at the beach, but better, she wrote, adding an umbrella emoji. Back in real life, she's wrapping an arm around her husband's waist, holding her phone above their faces. I'm too far away to see his expression, but he seems a little tense, his shoulders too close to his ears. As if to prove my instinct, he turns his face to the side, away from the phone, like he doesn't want to be in the photo. Or not like this. Maybe not even with her.

His gaze turns in my direction and my mouth goes dry. I drop the now half-empty box of macarons at my feet—these things are addictive—then bend down to retrieve it, going as slowly as my limbs can move when my heart beats louder than a marching band.

I count to three, then allow myself to glance up. They're gone. I swallow hard as I scan the park, each of the chairs, down the alleys, scrutinizing every tree in case they're hiding behind it, the wifey on her Paris honeymoon and her French husband. There are no new posts on her Instagram. I hit Refresh again and again, my throat closing at the idea that I might not get to know what comes next. I'm not going to let her get away so easily.

I stand up, readjust my sunglasses and my hat, and start walking toward where they were. When I reach the chair she was sitting on, a sigh of relief escapes me. There they are, walking in the direction of the northern exit of the park, Cassie staring at her phone, not paying attention to where they're going, and him walking a few steps ahead. It's almost as if they're not together.

I fall in step behind them, far enough that they won't feel my presence, but not so far that I might risk losing them. For a while I feel confident about my chances of not being seen, at least until they stop in the middle of the sidewalk. She says something to him. He smiles but his shoulders are still crunched up. Then she wraps her arms around his neck, hanging off her husband like she wants him to carry the whole weight of her. That's her thing, isn't it? To expect the people in her life to just take care of her.

Time stands still as I watch them watch each other. Is this the look of love? Something feels off, but maybe I'm imagining it. In some ways he reminds me of an older, jaded husband, the one who has three kids and a double-mortgage-shaped noose around his neck, along with a two-hour commute to the office. I used to see those types of guys all the time at work. I pitied them, and at the same time, I would have killed to have some of their problems.

But on the other hand, this husband looks like a brand-new boyfriend who's still not sure how to behave around his girl. Should he hold her hand? Offer to carry her shopping? There's a tentativeness to his moves. Almost like he worries about what people will see. What they will think.

And while there are plenty of passersby on the street, I'm the only one paying attention to this: his face moving closer to hers, the slight lift of his eyebrow, a question in his eyes. But then he comes to an answer, pressing his lips against hers, pulling her body closer until they are only one, his hands in her hair. I'm several feet away, but I can practically feel the heat emanating from their bodies. The want. The love. *This* is a honeymoon. And as I stand there watching what I'll never have, I can't contain the feeling growing inside of me: my life is so still, so insignificant, it might as well be dead in the water.

CHAPTER 11

Cassie

NOW

A beeping sound jolts me awake. My head pounds as my eyes adjust to the thin ray of light filtering through the shutters. It's eerily quiet in here; it must be early in the morning. Next to me, Olivier grunts in his sleep. He stirs and rolls toward me as I pick up my phone, the glow of the screen revealing my husband's naked body.

We had sex last night. Shocking for newlyweds, right? It wasn't until we were catching our breaths that I realized it had been a while. We definitely hadn't done it since the wedding. In fact, it was way longer than that. Weeks, maybe even a couple of months. Maybe that's why he was on edge.

I flick off the duvet and slide off the mattress, my feet landing quietly on the plush carpet. The sleeping pill hasn't fully worn off yet and I feel unsteady as I try to stand up. Gripping my phone, I head to the bathroom and don't turn on the light until I've closed the door behind me.

Hey

It's Darren. Sitting on the edge of the tub, I contemplate the three letters, wondering. We're six hours ahead, which means it's midnight over there.

Darren isn't much of a night owl. It was a thing between us when we dated. He liked to get an early night so he'd feel fresh and rested for his new job at the governor's office. I thought going to bed early was for old people. I wanted friends over, drinks, music. If we didn't live a little at our age, then when would we? *Some of us have jobs,* Darren would reply between yawns. I'd storm off and slam the door behind me. But then we'd make up. We always did.

Hi there, I text back, my heart pumping in my ears.

Is he with u?

Darren doesn't like to say Olivier's name. Most people back home went straight to "Oliver" or "Olly." Olivier let them, but you could see the defeated look on his face. We country folks weren't sophisticated enough to pronounce his French name correctly. For Darren, though, I secretly hoped it was more about the fact that I'd gone to the city and came home not just with a guy, not just with a boyfriend, but a handsome one. A successful one. One with a fancy accent and shit. A rich one. Though that, of course, was a lie.

He's asleep
It's 6 am here

I feel the need the remind him that I'm in some faraway place, in a different time zone. Darren hasn't been anywhere, done anything. But I couldn't resist his clean-cut baby face, with a jaw so square and a nose so sharp it just oozes masculinity. He's the kind of guy who can drive a stick, fixes things around the house, and makes dad jokes. Who's so ready to become one, too.

I miss u

Before I can even process what I'm reading, the door to the bathroom bursts open. I let out a yelp as I jump.

"You've been gone a while," Olivier says as he stands there, naked.

He catches me looking up and down, and smiles. I might be blushing. That level of intimacy between us feels weird. Unnatural.

Yesterday, Olivier took me shopping at Le Bon Marché, the chic department store near our hotel. He waited patiently as I tried on armloads of designer clothes, giving me his opinion with a smile plastered on his face, even when I ignored it. I walked out with more clothes than I've bought in an entire year before, as well as a Chanel handbag: the classic black quilted one with the two interlocked C's and the chain strap. The same bag you see dangling from the shoulders of all the cool girls and celebrities alike. I didn't do the conversion from euros to dollars but it would have been close to seven grand. For a bag! A simple black bag. But I can do that now. I thought Olivier might balk at the price, but he agreed I should treat myself.

Afterward, I took my new Chanel out for a spin at the Luxembourg Gardens. There, Olivier insisted on taking pictures of me. He held my hand any chance he got. Kissed me on street corners. I wasn't sure what was happening to him, but I didn't hate it.

"You coming back to bed?" He glances briefly at the phone on my lap.

"Yep," I say, getting up to follow him.

But I can't fall asleep again.

I waited for Darren to cave for so long. The first time we were together—in high school—it was me who broke things off. I had dreams of going places, getting out of our basic little town and that dark house that felt so miserable. The mother I grew up with was a broken woman, one who could only bring herself to go through the motions: making just enough money to get by, keeping me clothed and fed. Even that took a lot out of her. I know she didn't want to live like this, depressed and lonely. But she did and it meant that I had no choice but to suffer through it, too.

Mom had been single forever and, when she finally met my father, she thought her luck had turned around. She was desperate for a family, but I took my sweet time to come along. A complicated pregnancy led to a difficult baby—me—who spent her first few years in and out of doctors' offices. I never slept at night, apparently. Never stopped crying. Never went more than a few weeks without catching an illness of some sort. I was so hard to take care of. So much harder than I should have been.

My father didn't want a family anywhere near as much as my mother did, or at least he didn't want *this* family. He shed us like dead skin by the time I was four. That's when Mom turned the house into an inn—there was so much space for the two of us. She'd stopped working when I was born, so instead of trying to figure out a nine-to-five job as a single mother with a young child, she set up the spare rooms for guests and reached out to travel agents.

Growing up, I hated it all so much. Not just the strangers in the house, but the feeling that she couldn't stand to be alone with me. She'd finally met someone, had a good husband. Her life had taken a great turn before I came and messed it all up.

I was barely a teenager when I started sneaking out at night. I wanted to meet boys, to try anything, to *live*. To do the exact opposite of what my mother was doing. I'd disappear for the weekend, coming home smelling like weed and tequila, my hair knotted with leaves. She'd scold me, half-heartedly tried to ground me, but I could tell she didn't care enough to follow through. So the next time I'd up the ante, curious to see what would make her snap. Turns out, you can't break someone who is already shattered.

You could say that Darren and I weren't the most obvious match from the start. Not with his classic American family—a mom, a dad, a boy, a girl, and a sweet golden retriever to boot—his straight As, his dreams of a house, a yard, and a secure job. To me it felt both exotic and vanilla at the same time. I wasn't exactly sure what I wanted, but that wasn't it.

Or maybe *that's* why we were drawn to each other. I broke up with him half a dozen times, but I always came back weeks or months later, all too happy to nestle myself in his safe, strong arms again. He'd always been open about the fact that he wanted marriage, kids, the works. And I'd always said, *No thank you. Not for me.*

But after years of seeing that the grass wasn't greener elsewhere, and as my friends settled down into vanilla lives of their own, I started to wonder. After Brianna got engaged to her high-school sweetheart, I noticed she beamed brighter than a Budweiser neon sign for weeks. By the time of the wedding, Darren and I had been back together for six months. Brianna had decided to keep her bridal party to her sisters only, and once the sting of being left out had dissipated, I had picked out a bright-red satin dress that made me feel sexier than ever.

When we got home that night, I jokingly told Darren that if he proposed to me now, I might say yes. He'd laughed awkwardly, which I'd put down to him being drunk. Or maybe he didn't think I was serious. So, a few weeks later, I casually pointed out an ad for engagement rings while scrolling through Instagram. When Darren barely glanced at it, I figured it was because he planned on surprising me. So then of course I *needed* to know. I texted my friend group that I felt "something" was coming and that—hint, hint—I'd appreciate a little warning from my dear gals. They all sent cute emojis back but no intel.

Months went by as I dropped more not-so-subtle hints. Nothing. By then I was even looking up baby names—me, who had always felt like having children could only be a death sentence. I'd left my tablet open before heading out to the bar. When I came back, Darren was still up, looking upset. He sat me down and told me he couldn't keep going like this. He'd gone to visit a cozy three-bedroom house and was going to put in an offer. His boss saw great things in him. He felt ready to get married and have a family. But it wasn't going to be with me. I liked to party too much. I drank too much. I couldn't cook. I'd never hung on to a job for more than a few months and I was always asking for money to spend on frivolous things. Surely even I could tell that I wasn't marriage material?

Oh, he didn't say it exactly like this, of course. But the gist was there. He wished me all the best, really. Three days later, I got the call from my father's wife. When she asked me who would join me at the funeral—it was clear she knew nothing about me—I couldn't bring myself to say that I had no one. I told her my fiancé would be there. Then I traveled to the city, alone, and told that stuck-up bitch that Darren had been held back at work. It's not like he knew my father anyway.

I shouldn't be saying that

Ur married

But I don't know what I'm doing without u

Darren kept sending texts throughout the night and I'm still not sure how to respond. Did he really mean it? Is it too late now?

By the time Olivier and I head out for breakfast, the mood has turned. We order coffee and a basket of pastries but it seems like neither of us is hungry. We spend most of it on our phones, barely glancing at each other across the table. Darren didn't just send endless texts; there's also a video in the thread. Now, certain that my husband is paying me no attention, I hold my breath as I hit Play, making sure to put the video on mute.

Two pale, naked bodies are on a bed, their limbs so intertwined that at first it's hard to guess who is where in what position. Then it hits me. It's us, I mean: Darren and me. Filming ourselves having sex had been my idea. Obviously. I found it so sexy, that I could watch us from anywhere, get off on it when he was at work. But Darren always said no. *What if somebody got ahold of the video? You can never delete anything off the cloud.*

I didn't let it go. It was after one of our louder arguments, another one of those about what I was going to do with my life, when I would start acting like a grown-up, blah blah blah… Eventually we'd made up, and when I'd pulled out my phone and hit the red button, he'd watched me silently. I kept waiting for him to stop me as I placed it on the bookshelf but he never did. It was the best sex we'd ever had. I'm full of good ideas.

"Your face has gone all flush. Are you having an allergic reaction or something?"

I look up to find Olivier staring at me.

"Um, yeah… I mean no. But, um, something happened."

I don't know where I'm going with this, but I can't be here with Olivier right now. Not when Darren is making a move. A real one. At last.

"Back home?" Olivier's voice is laced with concern. "What is it?"

When Olivier and I arrived at the house, he'd seemed pretty annoyed to find out that the inn hadn't been running for a few years. It's not like I'd lied to him, exactly. It was true that we ran an inn; I just hadn't felt the need to clue him into the actual timeline. He reminded me that I'd talked about renovating it. Had I? I didn't remember that—and soon he'd become determined to make it into one of these chic places in Hudson or Kingston. He could turn it into a profitable business, he said. The poor guy was looking for work left, right, and center, coming up empty. Back then, I was still convinced it would only be a matter of days until Darren realized his mistake. In the meantime, if Olivier wanted to fix the draft in the windows or clean up the yard, I wasn't going to stop him. He'd been planning the bathroom remodels when I'd announced we were going to Paris.

"Don't worry about it," I say. "I just need to return a call. I'll be right back."

I'm up before I finish my sentence. The cloth napkin slides off my lap, my thighs knocking on the table as I push back my chair. Stepping out into the aisle, I bump into a waiter carrying a tray full of hot drinks. The cups clink loudly against one another, and for a moment, it seems like it might all come tumbling down. Luckily he manages to steady the tray, giving me the space to practically run out of there.

Worried that someone could listen in, I head out of the café, feeling the soft summer breeze in my hair as soon as I'm outside. I let my mind race as I turn around the corner to the side street. My first instinct is to call Darren but my instincts aren't always right. It's only a few texts. An old video. If he wants this, he has to try harder. *Then* I'll have to figure out what to do about Olivier.

Shit, what could I even do about Olivier? I need to know. My brain feels like it's on blast as I flick through my contacts, stopping at the name of Erica Min, the immigration lawyer Olivier hired to handle his green card application.

She picks up after a long while, her voice sounding sleepy. "Hello?"

"It's Cassie," I say, assuming this is enough of an introduction. "I have a question for you." I start pacing down the street. "I mean… It's kind of… private. If I ask you something, will you tell"—the word remains stuck on my tongue for a second—"my husband?"

"It's three in the morning," the attorney replies. "I guess I didn't put my phone on Silent."

Whoops. I'd forgotten about the time difference. "It's an emergency."

"Ms. Laurent, I—"

"Please!"

It was her idea that I go by Olivier's name. She said it made the marriage look more real, which meant the Department of Homeland Security was less likely to dig deeper than they had to. If we hadn't already been married, that's probably when I would have walked away. I didn't want to change my name. But mostly I didn't want any funny business with the Department of Homeland Security.

I push through before she can protest again. "Hypothetically, let's say I didn't want to be married anymore. What could be done?" If Darren wants me back, I need to be ready. I have to show him I can be a responsible adult, after all.

Erica Min lets out a big yawn, taking her time to respond. "People divorce every day."

I've only had one interaction with the woman before, but I found her so dry. I mean, I know she's a lawyer, but life is not that black and white.

"Right," I reply, trying to keep the annoyance out of my voice. "But in our case—"

"Your case is no different," she cuts in. "You're free to do whatever you want. I'm not a divorce lawyer, but you and your husband have no shared assets. My guess is it would be fairly simple. And probably quite fast, too." How fast, I want to ask. "But," she continues, "it would obviously have implications for your husband. If you got divorced before his permanent green card was granted, his application would be canceled. That would be the end of the road for him in this country."

"Even if he found a job and could support himself?"

"We've gone through this before."

Have we? It's possible I wasn't paying enough attention. When Olivier said he would only go home with me if we were married, I didn't see the big deal. It was a quick trip to City Hall. We didn't tell anyone. It didn't really count, you know?

When I don't say anything, the attorney continues. "The only way your husband is allowed to work is through his green card, meaning through his marriage to you. Right now, he's been granted a temporary authorization while his paperwork is in progress. But if that were to be stopped, Mr. Laurent would have to leave the country immediately. The Department of Homeland Security doesn't look kindly on immigrants who overstay their welcome. And if he did try to stay, he could be deported. He might never be allowed back in the United States. Obviously you know your husband better than I do"—she pauses, as if expecting me to confirm that—"but I got the sense that he was determined to continue living here. Which requires you two to stay married, for now at least."

The thing is, I'm feeling ready to be done thinking about Olivier, about what's good for *him*. "Right, but say we didn't stay married, what would happen to *me*?"

A loud cough startles me and I whip around to find an elderly man whose path I'm blocking. *Sorry*, I mouth, moving out of the way. He only shakes his head in response. Rude.

"You're the American citizen, Ms. Laurent. You hold all the cards here. Most likely, you'd be completely free from the moment the divorce papers were signed."

"Most likely?"

She clicks her tongue. "As we've discussed before, and I'm not saying you did that, we're talking in hypotheticals here, but entering into a marriage for the sole purpose of supplying a green card to an alien is a federal crime and carries a sentence of up to five years in jail. However, if you were to willingly stop the fraud before the process was completed, the Department of Homeland Security would be unlikely to find out, which means there's not a lot to worry about on that front."

A couple of well-dressed women go past me, eye my new shoes, and nod approvingly. Yes, yes, my sandals are gorgeous, but I don't think they'll let me keep those in prison. Except I'm most likely not going to prison, is what I'm hearing. Still, it feels like one of these things I should be certain of.

"So I *can* get divorced?" I say, when the women are out of earshot.

Darren wouldn't go for an affair; I'm sure of it. He wouldn't touch me until Olivier was well and truly out of the picture.

"Of course. People fall out of love. It happens. Especially when they get married as quickly as you and Mr. Laurent did."

"But?" I continue for her, because I don't need this woman to sugarcoat it for me. Besides, Olivier is going to wonder where I am.

"But things might get a little complicated if the decision to divorce is not mutual. Disgruntled ex-spouses are a breed of their own. Ask me how I know." She chuckles.

"Right, so I can get divorced and I probably won't get in trouble for the whole thing. But if I did that, hypothetically, what could Olivier do to me?"

At least I already know he's not getting any of the money.

"Was that your emergency?" When I don't respond, she lets out a deep sigh before speaking again. "Let's put it this way: you might not want to be with him anymore, but for your husband, divorcing now means a significant life change. You might be faced with a man who has nothing left to lose, and those are the most dangerous people."

After I hang up with Erica Min, I stand there frozen. Olivier loves me. He wants to be with me forever. So what happens if I destroy his entire future, his dream, and his whole life? I'm not sure I want to find out.

CHAPTER 12

Olivier

TWO MONTHS BEFORE THE HONEYMOON

I took me two weeks to accept that Cassie was not coming back to New York City, not even for a few days. First there was her birthday party, at which I'd expected her to announce to her friends that we were engaged. Surprise! Wedding incoming! Instead, she'd barely spoken to me all night, at least not until her ex, Darren, arrived. Then she was all over me, bragging loudly about how successful I was, turning me into a work acquaintance of her father rather than a lowly tenant living in his basement. Her group of friends listened eagerly at how much fun we'd had in the city. Cassie gushed about how "generous" I was, how I'd wined and dined her all over New York.

Then she moved on to how I'd wanted to come here to spend more time with her, because it was all about Cassie, Cassie, Cassie. At some point, her "best friend," Brianna—who even has best friends at our age?—started making eyes at me, and far from being ticked off, Cassie low-key glowered. So this was how it was going to go. With a twist of Cassie's imagination I'd become this rich guy who had fallen so deeply for her that I was more than happy to leave my fancy job and glitzy city life behind. And still, she made no mention of our situation, the wedding, the engagement, whatever she wanted to call it.

And then there was the appointment I'd set up with the immigration lawyer, Erica Min, back in the city. I reminded Cassie half a dozen times, and even then, I felt like I practically had to drag her there. She complained about taking the train but wouldn't drive, either. In the end, she handed me her car keys, begrudgingly.

Inside, Cassie plugged in her phone and played a pop playlist on extra-loud as she stared out the window, barely saying two words to me. She looked like a lovelorn teenage girl, and me like a dad who was taking her to school against her will.

Still, crossing the George Washington Bridge, I felt a jolt of joy. My body thrummed with want as the skyscrapers came into view. As I drove down the West Side Highway, I thought about the first time I went to Times Square, almost a year ago now. I'd stared at the neon lights with total awe, the wind knocked out of me by the greatness of it all. After all the setbacks I'd gone through, my darkest times, I found myself living in the most exciting place on earth.

Today was different. I had to scrape the bottom of my bank account for the lawyer's fees, and I was only able to afford a woman who worked out of a mildewy basement office in Midtown East. There were dubious stains on the orange carpet, and the coffee Erica Min offered us was spit-out disgusting.

"So, let me get this straight. You two barely know each other, and you got married just as your visa was about to expire," she said, after consulting the folder I'd carefully put together.

Online, her full smile and short white hair made her look approachable, but in the flesh she seemed weary, her eyelids droopy, and her maroon skirt suit was clearly too big for her frame.

"It was love at first sight," I explained. "Cassie's my landlord's daughter. We met in front of my apartment. Isn't that funny?" I left the heart attack and the funeral out to give the story a sweeter quality.

Cassie smiled blandly, like what we were discussing didn't concern her in any way.

"Sure," Erica Min said with a bite.

This was not going well. "Look, we're in love, we're married, and you already agreed to take our case." She'd also said we could do this over video call, but I'd lied and told her I had to be in the city anyway. It felt like truth enough. Any excuse to get out of that sad house.

"That's why I must insist you have a proper wedding. It doesn't have to be fancy; it just has to *be*." She flicked the folder closed and crossed her hands over it, her gold pinkie ring on full display. Then, she turned to Cassie. "I understand your parents are deceased, but you've told your sister you're married, right? Because, honestly, it doesn't look too good that she wasn't there for the ceremony."

"We're not close," Cassie said. "I don't see why I need to tell her."

I'd barely seen her sister since we'd been upstate. To be honest, I hadn't seen much of Cassie, either. She got up late, spent hours on her phone, and then would leave to hang out with her friends, who I tried hard to keep track of. One—Julie?—was a department manager at Walmart and could, quote unquote, mix a mean cocktail. Harper, a barista, mentioned her numerous tattoos—their meaning, their location on her body, their birthday—any chance she got. Brianna, the more approachable of the lot, was an admin at a dentist's office. I got the sense that the others only somewhat tolerated Cassie, and Brianna was the connection that kept them friends.

As to what Cassie did with her life: well, not a whole lot. She didn't "currently" work. Talking to people at her party, I'd pieced together a clearer picture of my wife: that candle-making business hadn't gone very far. Cassie had talked about setting up a stand at the local markets, but had never followed through. The event planning she'd mentioned had been to help organize Brianna's bachelorette and another friend's birthday party. And the inn... Well, they had stopped operating it when their mother got sick and it became too hard to manage it all. Cassie had lied about everything. *Everything.*

The lawyer nodded slowly, her expression bland. "Well, tell your sister. Ask her to be your maid of honor or whatnot. We need something to work with."

Cassie shrugged and looked back at her phone. I'd checked her Instagram after parking the car: she'd posted a video of us going over the bridge, captioning it, In town for business! I'd rolled my eyes so hard. Cassie wouldn't know the meaning of business if it hit her in the face.

"I'd love to have a wedding!" I said, so chipper I jumped in my seat. "We talked about that, didn't we?" I placed a hand on Cassie's thigh. She didn't react.

Erica Min raised a thin eyebrow. "I'm going to be straight with you," she said, wagging her bony index finger from Cassie to me. "The Department of Homeland Security sees people attempting to commit marriage fraud every day. I don't know what kind of deal you two have, but since you're already married, you better work on making it squeaky clean, and fast. Or else, I'd give up now."

Cassie's eyes darted to me. It was not the time to point out that I hadn't given her money—hadn't offered anything other than a reason to make her ex jealous—and I wasn't sure how much longer I could fake it. But of course it was obvious now that I was going to pay for this in other ways. Nothing was ever free, a lesson I apparently still needed to learn.

"We're in love," I said. "That's why we got married. Right, Cassie?"

She looked startled, like I'd awoken her. "Uh-huh. What do you mean, give up?"

"Nothing," I said, jumping in. "No one's giving up anything." The last thing I needed was for Cassie to find out she could divorce me at any moment and just move on with her life.

An awkward silence followed.

Ms. Min cleared her throat. "Okay, well, if we're going to do this, you need more pictures of you two with your families and friends, whatever you got. Vacation photos would be good, too." She paused but neither of us had anything to say about that. "What's your husband's date of birth?" she said to Cassie, who had moved on to staring at her chipped nail polish.

She pouted. "Umm, January...something?"

I swallowed hard. Not even close.

The next question was for me. "How does your wife take her coffee?"

"Black," I answered quickly, hoping it would make me sound confident.

Cassie shook her head. "That's only because there was no milk at your place. And sugar, two teaspoons." She glanced at the lawyer like, *Can you believe this guy?*

But Erica Min didn't indulge her. Instead, she rubbed at her temples. "This is not good at all. Plan a wedding. Get to know one another. Have a honeymoon, maybe."

Cassie perked up suddenly. "We could go to Paris!"

"Yes!" the lawyer said, sounding way too enthusiastic now. "Take her to your home country, show her your culture. She could meet your parents."

"No," I said without thinking. "That won't work."

I was pretty sure my parents knew I'd moved overseas but they hadn't tried to contact me. I'd disconnected my French number and hadn't given my U.S. one to anyone back home. Mom still sent me perfunctory emails for my birthday—March third—and Christmas, to which I always planned to respond before the shame and guilt held me back.

The lawyer shot me a shady look. "Well, you gotta do *something*. And be faithful to each other, okay? The last thing you need is for someone to come blabbering about how y'all are having sex with other people."

I did my best to look offended, but Cassie simply blushed. Could this day get any worse?

It could. Because after we left the lawyer's office—armed with instructions for our upcoming meeting with the immigration officer and more paperwork to fill out—Cassie said she wanted to drive home right away.

"I'm tired," she said with a shrug as we bumped against the masses of workers on their way to lunch.

From doing what? I wanted to ask, but of course I bit my tongue.

"What about my apartment?" I said instead. "What do you want to do about it?"

Erica Min had been clear: we *had* to live together and be able to prove it. But it didn't matter where, so I'd casually brought up the idea of splitting our time between the city and upstate. I'd been scared of asking Cassie and it felt easier doing it in front of a third-party. In response, Cassie had scrunched up her nose.

Now she shrugged. "You should keep it. It's your place, your stuff. Don't you want to have your own space?"

Did I want to? Fuck yes. Could I afford to rent an empty apartment in Brooklyn if Cassie didn't want to live there? We all knew the answer to that.

"I should move out," I said, my voice a whisper. "I should go there now and pack my things."

"I don't want to see her," Cassie said, meaning her stepmother, Ms. Crowes.

I wondered, again, what exactly Cassie had said or done to get that two million dollars. It frightened me to think that she and I weren't that different after all: we always found a way to get by, no matter what it took.

Before I could protest, she added, "Can't you sublet it or something?" Huh, that actually wasn't a bad idea. At least until she finished her thought, "This way you'll have it for…whenever."

That "whenever" sounded horribly bad. We were going to live together for two years. Had to, had to, had to. And yes, it would have been nice to have a place to crash in the city, to get away for a few days here and there, but I'm pretty sure that wasn't what Cassie meant.

But fine, I'd sublet it for now. I'd started this whole thing, and I needed to do what it took to make it work. Cassie waited at a nearby coffee shop while I packed the rest of my clothes and toiletries.

Then we drove back. Drove *home*. To the only home I had now.

What an utterly depressing thought.

CHAPTER 13

Taylor

NOW

Blood rushes to my brain the moment the newlyweds are out of sight. It's like there's an invisible string between us that I can't bring myself to break. I'm in too deep now. I don't know where this honeymoon ends, but I *need* to find out. They, I mean we, wander through the streets of Paris for hours on end, stopping at ice cream shops on Île Saint-Louis and designer stores on rue des Canettes, in the fifth arrondissement. Of course, I don't get to buy my own cone with two scoops—the hazelnut flavor sounded pretty good—and I can't see what's in her shopping bag as she exits the glitzy Saint Laurent boutique, but I know this: life seems pretty sweet when you have a rich husband treating you all over this dreamy city.

For dinner, they have a reservation at a little abode in the tenth arrondissement, opposite a tree-lined square. Google tells me the restaurant offers a surprise three-course menu, which means they'll be there a while. After watching them walk inside—her in brand-new block-heeled sandals, which turned out to be her purchase from this morning, per Instagram; his hand on the small of her back—I wander a few streets over to get a tomato and cheese crepe from a street stand. My fingers burn through the greasy paper as I come back to eat it on a bench, in full view of the restaurant. The wife doesn't post anything until dessert, and that's only to rave about the lavender crème brûlée. Not the kind of detail I'm interested in.

I've long finished my own meal when the newlyweds emerge, their faces shiny and their legs wobbly. I spotted an empty bottle of champagne in the picture, and that may not have been the only one. Nice for some. Suddenly, the wife trips on a cobblestone—she's clearly the drunkest of the two—and he yanks her sharply, catching her before she falls. What a good man, a loving husband.

I walk them back to their hotel in Saint-Germain, even though that's the opposite direction from mine. I'm too far behind to listen in to their conversation, if they're talking at all. We did a lot of walking today and my feet are killing me, but I still manage to discover new things about them: he stands straighter when she's looking, like he wants to be on his best behavior, and she's not taking as many pictures anymore. She only stops when we go over Pont Neuf to snap Notre-Dame all lit at night. It shows up on her Instagram Stories a minute later, but that's it.

Not willing to take any more chances, I drop them off on the corner before they arrive at their hotel. Of course, I already checked it out online. Two thousand dollars a night for the honeymoon suite, I nearly choked on my water when I saw that.

That night, I sleep in fits and turns, my mind buzzing with images of the happy couple and so many questions. Are they really happy, or just good at pretending? Is it true love I saw or can anyone fake it that well?

When I wake up, my muscles sore and my eyelids still heavy with sleep, I'm tempted to sink into another long bath. But curiosity gets the better of me, so I pick up the newlyweds after their breakfast. Lucky for me, her posting habits are regular enough that I could guess when they'd be heading out for the day. Cassie can't get enough of the flaky croissants and the smooth "café"—as she calls it—at the place down the street from their hotel.

Today, she is in a skin-tight heather gray dress she bought on this trip, along with her Chanel bag and matching logoed ballet flats. He really is sparing no expense. I can't imagine why he thinks she deserves that. Who is she, really? A country girl who tries way too hard. Meanwhile, he blends in among other well-dressed Parisians, as dapper as ever in skinny navy chinos rolled up at the ankles. He wears them sockless with the same sneakers he's had on all trip, which are curiously still bright white. He's that kind of guy. Always cool, always put together just so. Freakishly handsome.

To my surprise, our day begins with a trip to the Musée D'Orsay. These two aren't the museum-going type; I bet she read a list of places to visit in Paris and is dragging him there against his will. Though of course he chose this. Chose to marry her, chose to go on the honeymoon. No one forced him. At least the museum is crowded enough that I can follow them inside, after letting a group of Japanese tourists go between us. I pause to admire the grand hall bathed in the sunlight shining through the large curved windows. Black statues elevated on white pedestals line both sides, making me feel small and so much less sophisticated.

I find her first, sitting on a bench on the other side of the main hall, completely absorbed in her phone. A few minutes later, I watch him browse the Impressionists wing on the top floor, where he glances at every painting, paying attention to none. The fact that they split up is not enough to draw conclusions—even the happiest couples might want alone time.

An hour passes before we leave the museum and walk down the twisty streets of Saint-Germain. It's a beautiful day out and there're always a few people in between us. More than once I worry I'm pushing it, getting too close. Three's a crowd; I'm well aware of that.

It's not until they make a right onto a little alley that I feel the change of air between them. He's walking a little behind her now, hunched over his phone, which is new for him. She doesn't notice at first, but when she turns around a moment later, the look on her face is not only one of annoyance at him lagging behind. Her jaw is tense, her eyes bulging. She stops and crosses her arms against her chest.

Something is off. I hide in a doorway just a few feet away from them, holding my breath as the bronze door knocker digs into my back. A quick glance tells me it's shaped like a snake.

"I want to do what I want to do, okay?" I hear her saying. Screaming. "It's my life! MY LIFE! And *my* money!"

The last part stuns me the most. Cassie doesn't have any money. Against my better judgment, I risk a look in their direction. His chest rises and falls as he stands in front of her. She moves her arms up in the air with wild gestures, so much so that her Chanel bag almost hits him in the face. He flinches and steps back but he seems oddly stoic in the face of her tantrum.

It takes all my willpower to peel my eyes away from them and lean back. At least I can still hear her. I don't make out all the words, mostly the fact that she's real mad and he's still taking it, in silence. When she stops grumbling, the distinct sound of steps coming from inside the building startles me. Someone is about to open the door, and I'm going to have to walk onto the street. I'm screwed. The only thing that might save me is a distraction. Without thinking too much, I grab my phone, flick through my contacts, and press Call on the all-too-familiar name.

Strangely, she picks up immediately. "Hey," Cassie says.

"Hi!" I say as quietly as I can, without raising her suspicion. Crossing my fingers that neither of them is looking this way, I leave my hiding spot and walk quickly in the other direction. Seconds later, I reach the corner and turn down the next street, out of sight. "How's the honeymoon going?"

My heart is beating a million miles a minute but there's no way she saw me. My sister has always complained about how I suffocate the air around her. It wouldn't take her that long to ask what the fuck I'm doing here. Yes, okay. Cassie is not some random newlywed I discovered on Instagram. But she so often feels like a stranger that it's kind of all the same.

"Paris is just the most amazing place *ever*." She sounds light and upbeat, nothing like she did a moment ago. "You know."

I do. Growing up, Cassie would always tease me about my belief that my parents—my *biological* parents—had some sort of French connection. I only cared about having something that might bring me closer to them: my mother was in prison and I knew so little about my dad, just a few vague memories, like those of French lullabies whispered in the dark. All my hopes were cast onto him, this stranger. But Cassie thought this was my way of feeling superior to her, more sophisticated. We all knew what happened with *her* father. He had every opportunity to see her if he wanted to. But mine…he could be anywhere, from any place. I could make all sorts of excuses for him, and I did.

One time—when she was nine and I was ten—Cassie stole my embroidered baby blanket, one of the only items I got to bring with me when her mother, Rae, took me in. I cried for hours, feeling like Cassie had ripped a lung straight out of my chest, while Rae and I looked for my beloved heirloom. We found it behind the toilet of one of the guest rooms on the top floor of the house. Cassie had doused it in bleach and hidden it in the tight spot. The smell never went away, the embroidery destroyed. It was ruined, forever.

"I love all of your pictures," I say, cheerfully. I know what she wants and I give it to her, always.

"Well, yes," Cassie says, like she's so pleased with herself. "I saw your comments."

Of course I left comments. I needed to pretend that everything was normal, that I hadn't actually followed her and Olivier to Paris, right after dropping them off at the airport.

"It looks dreamy. I'm so happy for you."

"Oh yeah?" Cassie sounds suspicious, but it won't last long.

This is how it goes between us. I let her walk over me because, in her mind, I did the unforgivable: I stole her life, her childhood, her mother. I didn't have my own anymore, so I took it all from her. She doesn't care that I would have done anything to stay with mine, that I didn't want any of this. I was only seven; it wasn't my choice. But it wasn't hers either to get a big sister, practically overnight. Cassie felt the constant need to remind me that she was the real daughter. That it was her mother and her house and her toys and her clothes. How could I have forgotten? They were always too small for me.

"You got the perfect Paris honeymoon," I say, infusing my voice with envy. It's not hard.

It was about eight years ago, on my twenty-first birthday. My mother had been dead for years, but I'd never let go of the idea that I could find my father. My possibly French father. All I dreamed about was a trip to Paris. I'd been talking about it for so long and Rae surprised me, surprised all of us. She'd saved up some money and the three of us were going on a vacation to France! How amazing was that?

It was not. Cassie threw one of the biggest fits I'd ever witnessed. Why would I—the burden—get anything I wanted? Rae had already applied for our passports. She'd found a good deal on flights and a cheap little hotel. We were going. Except that the day before we were supposed to leave, Cassie disappeared. Rae and I canvassed the whole town, drove around for hours, worried sick. Cassie came back two days later. She took one look at our suitcases, still packed and ready in the entrance, and smiled a big wicked smile. Rae lost all the money she'd spent on the bookings, and we never discussed it again.

That summer I worked harder than ever—early mornings cleaning rooms at a local motel on top of the inn's, afternoons at the local bakery— and bought myself a car. A piece of freedom. I jammed my brand-new passport deep inside the glove box, the only space that was truly mine. Of course, as soon as I got the car, Cassie demanded I drive her every- where—to her friends', to Darren's. She could have used her mother's car, of course, but she never liked driving. I should have used the money to go to Paris on my own, but by then I was much more focused on escaping her grasp, and not just for a few days.

"It's so beautiful here. Much better in real life," Cassie says.

I'm two streets away now. Suddenly, Olivier walks past me, looking dejected and furious at the same time, his hands deep inside his pockets, his gaze down. Does he know I stole the money he stashed away at home? Does he realize that I see him for who he is: a liar and a cheat? I lower my head, grateful I wore my hat again, that I had the wherewithal to change my appearance before going after them. He doesn't even glance up anyway.

"So what are you two doing now?" I say.

Cassie doesn't miss a beat. "Oh, we're just about to head to this rooftop for lunch. Olivier managed to get us in at this super-exclusive place. He knows everyone in Paris. It really makes the trip much more special."

My mouth goes dry. "You're on your way there now?"

"Uh-huh."

"The two of you?"

Cassie sighs. I don't usually push her that much. Growing up in our house, *her h*ouse, I quickly learned to be the quiet one. The easy one. Rae was my mother's only living relative—a cousin a few times removed. Child Protective Services managed to track her down and told her that I'd been through three foster families in over a year and that a more stable situation with a relative would be preferrable. Rae had agreed and taken me in out of the kindness of her heart. At least that's what I thought. Cassie was just six years old, but she despised me from the moment I stepped through that door.

Later, she'd blame me for the fact that her father never came back for her. It makes little sense now, but back then I believed it. I believed everything. My presence had threatened the balance of this already fragile family, and I could be kicked out just as quickly as I was brought in. So I did as I was told. I studied and got good grades. I helped around the house after school. From age ten, I made the rooms for the few guests we had, and by twelve

I was preparing breakfast for everyone. I needed to pay my dues. Cassie only hated me more; my good-girl behavior made her look even worse.

"Yes, Taylor, the two of us. I'm on my honeymoon, remember? The whole point is to have a good time with my husband. This is what people in relationships do. Though of course you wouldn't know."

"You're right, I'm sorry."

The words come out of habit. Still, I crumble on the inside. How do I let her do this to me over and over? She lays down traps and I get caught. I bought it all: every perfectly framed Instagram picture, every video in which she quipped about how much love was in the air. Fucking bitch.

"I gotta go," Cassie says.

I'm overcome with so much rage that I want to hang up on the spot. Then I remember there's something else I need to ask her. It might sound suspicious, but I don't care anymore. "Wait. A man came by the house. He had the keys. Do you know what that's about?"

She lets out a deep sigh. "He told me you weren't there."

"Why does a random man have the key to our house, Cassie?"

She's silent for such a long while that I almost give up. Cassie won't be honest with me anyway; she never is. "He's a Realtor. And he doesn't have the keys. I told him where we hide the spare set, since he said there was nobody home."

"Why do you need a Realtor? I thought you and Olivier were renovating the house?"

"We were. We are. I don't know. I'm thinking I might sell it instead."

"You can't do that!" My voice comes out like a squeal.

It's not that I like it that much, not like I haven't thought a hundred times that I needed to leave. To get away. For good. But something always stopped me. A bad breakup. Rae's terminal cancer diagnosis. Trying so desperately to save money while Cassie always demanded I invest in one of her new ventures, like that candle-making business. I knew it would fail, but as always, I chose the easier way out. Saying no to her was so much worse. If I did, she was never out of ways to make my life harder.

"Of course I can."

"No, Cassie. Even you can't have everything you want." I've never spoken so harshly to her, but I'm right. "Your mother adopted me. She left what she had to *both* of her daughters."

It's something we never speak about because I know how much it upsets Cassie. Her mother loved me, too. Maybe not in the best way, but she did. And I *was* a good daughter to her. I drove her to chemotherapy appointments, picked up her meds, made her smoothies—the only thing she could keep down. Meanwhile, Cassie would just flail about, say this was too much to handle, and then head out to Darren's, not to be seen for days.

"Oh sure," Cassie says, her tone dripping with sarcasm. "My mother loved you. Her little extra daughter. The good one. So yes, she split everything evenly in her will. She didn't give a crap about how that made me feel."

"That's not true." I can't help but comfort Cassie, to prop her up. Because as hard as I tried to ignore it growing up, Rae and Cassie's relationship was fraught with conflict. Rae had wanted children, but not at the cost of having them alone. She'd never recovered from her husband leaving, from how the family she'd dreamed of had imploded. *Call your father*, Rae would say. *Ask him if he wants to come for Christmas, your birthday, your graduation. Find out about "her."* But Cassie never did. In fact, she swore up and down she *didn't* want him there. She didn't remember him and she certainly wasn't going to beg for his attention, especially if that's what her mother wanted. Rae would read the cards Cassie occasionally got from him, searching for mentions of her. You could see the pain on her face when she found none. I think Cassie never responded to them because she knew her mother was desperate for that connection.

"Yeah, well, whatever, Taylor. It doesn't matter because the house didn't belong to Mom. It was my dad's and *he* definitely didn't put you in his will."

I feel like all the air has been punched out of me. The house is dark and damp and in so much need of repair, but it's also the only home I remember, the only place where I've felt safe. The one thing I thought was at least partly mine.

"Cassie…" I start, breathless.

She can't do this to me, not after everything I've done for her. Who pays the bills and buys the food and cleans the place? She's never kept a job more than a few months and hasn't bothered trying to get one since her mom died a year ago. Grief is convenient like that. That day she came back from the city with Olivier was one of the first times I ever stood my ground. She texted me from the train, demanding I pick her up. It took everything I had to say no.

"No, I'm speaking," she cuts in. "Here's the deal, Taylor. You've been mooching off my family for long enough. The house belongs to me. ME! Which means that, right now, you're living on *my* property. That bed you sleep on? Mine. Those rooms you always complain about cleaning? Mine. The driveway in which you park your shitty car? It's all mine. And I think it's about time you get the hell out of there."

CHAPTER 14

Cassie

NOW

'm still fuming when I get back to our hotel room, alone. This isn't the first time Olivier and I have had an argument, but it *will* be the last. Because I'm done. I call the shots here; that's what the lawyer said. If I want to text with my ex, he can't stop me. If I want to sell my own goddamn house, I can just do that. I know Olivier has decided to focus on renovating the inn because he's struggling to get a job, but he'll have to find something else to do. Haven't I already helped him enough?

And what was Taylor's deal? She sounded weird on the phone, and there was so much noise around her, cars honking and people. I lose track of all the little jobs she does to survive, but one thing was certain: she wasn't home, or anywhere near it.

Sitting on the bed, I scan the room as if it's going to tell me what to do. I know I can't get rid of Olivier with a click of my fingers but I need some time away from him. I need to go home and figure things out with Darren without my "husband" hovering over me.

Olivier had suggested we use our wedding date for the safe's code, but I can't remember which day that was exactly. I have such fuzzy memories of that trip to the city—meeting Olivier, my father's funeral, feeling wild and spontaneous as we walked into City Hall, dying to see the look on Darren's face. And Taylor's face. Sometimes I wonder if these few days—just over a week!—were all just a terrible nightmare. You know, aside from the part where I came away with two million dollars and the deed to my house.

Lucky for me, my phone knows everything. Flicking through pictures of that day, I find the date easily: April 27. I type in 0427 on the key pad but the door doesn't open. In fact, a beep resonates as a red light flashes. What the? I try again; same result. Fuck.

I can't ask Olivier, obviously. He stormed off after our fight. He was so mad to learn I'd been making plans to sell my house while we were here. Couldn't I sit still for a minute and enjoy this perfect honeymoon? I'd be more than happy if he never showed his face here again. But he will. He has to. I don't have much time. And then it comes back to me. It was a comment Olivier made when we were in the city, how he never understood the date system in America. *It makes no sense, putting the month before the day. The rest of the world does it the right way: day, month, year. Why do Americans have to do everything differently?* It struck me because it was the first time—the *only* time—Olivier had a bad thing to say about his new country. Everything else was perfect: the job market, the economic growth, the can-do attitude. There were so many reasons he *had* to stay there and couldn't fathom moving back to France.

I kneel back in front of the safe, this time typing 2704. The door unlatches with a much softer buzz, unveiling my passport. I slip it inside my Chanel. I can leave now. I'm free. I can divorce him, not right this minute, but soon. I'm free. So why does it feel like I'm not?

I'm about to lock the safe again when I see Olivier's backpack against the wall. I remember now: we were at the airport, waiting to board. Olivier went to the restrooms and asked me to watch it. But then I realized I had to go, too. I didn't want him to know I was nervous. I'd never been on a plane before, never left the country. I only had a passport because Mom planned that stupid trip to Paris for Taylor all these years ago. For *her*, she could close the inn. For *her*, she could plan a vacation. Anything for Taylor, the daughter she actually wanted, the one who didn't drive her husband away.

I wasn't going to carry Olivier's big backpack to the restrooms with me, and I wouldn't be long anyway. When I came back, Olivier was livid.

"You left my bag here?" he said.

I shrugged. "I was only gone a few minutes."

He exhaled loudly. I'd never seen him so upset. "My wallet is in there. What were you thinking?"

I did *not* like his tone. "You don't have any money." I loved to remind him of that. *He* didn't have money; *I* did. "And who would want to steal that?" The bag was nylon, nondescript.

"My passport's in there. Remember what the lawyer said? This temporary green card I have is linked to it. If I lose my passport, it will set back my case by months while I apply for a new one. And I couldn't even get back in the country!"

People were starting to look at us. "Everything's fine," I said. "Nobody stole anything. Just chill, okay?"

I don't close the safe. Instead, I grab Olivier's passport, which was in there with mine. I hold in my hand his most precious possession. Without it, he can't fly home with me. Without it, I'll have plenty of time to figure things out with Darren while Olivier is stuck here. I look around the room for a sharp object. I find one a few minutes later, a Swiss Army knife that doubles as a corkscrew, in the drawer next to the mini fridge.

Slicing through the burgundy leather-like cover feels better than I could have imagined. Then, I rip up the passport page by page. Soon it's in pieces around me and I can't contain the gleeful sigh that comes out. Brushing my hands along the carpet, I gather all the pieces together, then stuff them into the pockets of my denim jacket to discard later. I don't want to be here when he finds out what I did.

And I won't be. I flick through my phone and look up my flight details. I'm going home. Today, if possible. But the app won't let me do anything.

An error message appears every time I click on the Change Flight button, telling me that no changes can be made online and that I should call customer service. Gah!

My eyes firmly on the door, I call the Delta hotline. A robotic voice announces that the wait to speak to an agent is around three hours. I choose the option to have them call me back instead of staying on the line, and hang up. Then, I pace the room, wondering if I should start packing. I bought so many things—that Chanel bag and ballet flats, the Saint Laurent sandals, a mountain of clothes, that cute little straw basket—and I don't know how it will all fit. I should get started now, but if Olivier comes back and sees what I'm doing, there's no telling what he might do. The lawyer's words ring in my ears. People who have nothing to lose are the most dangerous ones.

So maybe I won't leave today. It's midafternoon now, and if I have to wait that long to change my ticket, I might just have to stay another night. In fact, maybe it's better this way. If I run away from my honeymoon at the first sign of Darren wanting me back, he might find it a little too easy. But he does want me back, right? That's what this was all about, isn't it? I stare at my phone. There's only one way to find out. While I wait for him to pick up the phone, I step out onto the balcony, my fingers cramping more with every ringtone.

"Well, hello there!" he says, his voice soft and honeyed. "Did you like the video?"

My skin tingles everywhere but I need to keep my head straight. "What are you doing?"

He sighs, waits a beat, then says, "I don't know."

The pain is sharp, slicing through my heart. "Okay, then bye," I say sharply, like I'm going to hang up.

"No, wait. I always thought we wanted different things. When I talked about marriage before, you'd scoff, saying it was for boring people."

He's not wrong about that. My parents were married and look where that got them!

"Your life doesn't seem so boring now," Darren adds.

I smile but something bothers me. Why didn't he try to win me back before the wedding? I waited. I would have gotten rid of Olivier. No one knew we were already married, and it would have been easier to explain it all away. I got engaged to someone else, Darren realized the big mistake he'd made, he won me back, engagement over.

But then he undoes me. "I know he has money and everything, but I miss you, Cassie. We were good together. Maybe I didn't realize what I had at the time but…I wish we could do it all over again."

We can, I want to scream. *We can and we will.* "You didn't say anything before."

"We broke up so many times. And then you turned up with him."

"You never said anything," I repeat, wanting to sound strong and resolved when, in reality, I know my willpower is shredding like Olivier's passport did a few minutes ago.

"I'm saying it now."

"What *are* you saying?"

He ponders it for endless seconds before speaking again. "I don't want to play games anymore. At the wedding, I thought… I don't know. I still didn't really believe it. This guy is a stranger and it all happened so fast. But now…you look so happy with him in the pictures, almost *too* happy. So tell me, is it real between you two?"

Maybe one day I'll explain why I took all of these pictures, how much I needed to rub them in his face. Actually, I probably won't. If we get back together, if I get everything I want, then I will learn to let things go. To move on from whatever happened before. I'll forget about Olivier, will never mention his name again. Darren and I will be happy together. We will be happy and that will be it.

But we're not there yet. When I came back home with Olivier, I thought Darren would be jealous. I figured he'd fight for me. I wasn't going to dump Olivier until he did. Is this what he's doing now? Is it enough?

"It's not that simple," I say, cautious.

"I thought he was the perfect guy. Handsome, rich, ambitious."

"He was. He is."

"Okay," Darren simply says.

He sounds so sad that I want to hug him. I hate Paris and everything about it.

"What if I wanted to come home now?"

"What about him?"

When I announced our wedding—our *surprise* wedding, with three days' notice—I thought that would be it, Darren's last chance to make a move. He had to act or risk losing me forever. And he did do *something*. He came and even made sure we had a moment alone before the ceremony. He told me he was sorry for not being there for me at my father's funeral. He really wished he could have come, if only I'd told him. We both knew what it meant. If he had, I wouldn't have met Olivier. But he didn't say that out loud. I waited for something more. A declaration of undying love. A plea to not go ahead with the wedding. Him getting down on one knee, saying *he'd* marry me instead.

But none of that happened. I was already standing in a white dress. I'd bought three turquoise chiffon bridesmaid dresses at a local store, the only color left over on the sales rack. I'd begged Brianna to put together an extremely last-minute bachelorette party for me. I'd paid for the flowers, the fucking cake. Almost everyone I knew—all thirty of them—were in my living room, waiting for me to walk down the aisle and marry a man they thought was so much better than me.

What was I supposed to do?

In the moment, it felt like there was only one answer. So I married Olivier for the second time. I told myself I'd drown my sorrows in Paris. By the time we were on the plane, I found a renewed urge within me. I'd rub it all in his face. I'd rub every moment of it so hard that Darren would cave, eventually. I had more tricks up my sleeve: the French honeymoon might do it.

"Let's pretend Olivier doesn't exist for a second," I say, my heart twitching. Why is this so hard? Why is everything always so fucking hard?

In truth, the Paris trip wasn't only about Darren. That prissy little bitch who pretends to be my sister always thought she was French. When we were kids, she talked about nothing but going to Pareeeee, where her daddy would be. She carried that embroidered blanket with the French lettering everywhere, claiming he had given it to her. People thought it was so endearing, that little girl who dreamed of her foreign family, after all she'd gone through. In truth, we all knew her mom was a junkie and her dad was French like I'm Kim freaKing Kardashian.

It wasn't until much later, when she was on her death bed, that Mom told me snippets about Taylor's family. She was barely coherent by then, whispering half-formed sentences in between extended breaks of loud breathing.

Wish she could have met him

Denis, his name

No current address

In Paris, maybe

Didn't want

Her hopes up

I was angry then, angry *always*, when it came to Taylor. Mom was dying, and that's what she was thinking about? That's what she wanted to waste her breath on? I never knew if she told Taylor this, or just me. I'd never admit out loud that Taylor was maybe—probably—right about her dad all along.

When I met Olivier outside my father's house, all I could think about was that Taylor would keel over with jealousy when she found out that I'd met a handsome guy from Paris. I didn't care if he was actually from there; he would be in my version.

Darren sighs, bringing me back to our conversation.

"I can't tell if you're messing with me," he says. "Please tell me, because I think I'm still in love with you."

My heart melts. This is what I've wanted to hear all along. Below me, cars honk and bicycles swirl in and out of traffic. It's rush hour, and I keep an eye out for a dark-haired man dressed in navy slacks and the ridiculous white sneakers he cleans every night with an old toothbrush. He tries so hard with the little he's got. He tries and he fails.

And then I admit it out loud: "I love you too."

"Cassie?"

It's like I'm hit with a Taser. A few seconds pass before I accept the fact that it wasn't Darren's voice, and it was definitely not coming through my phone. I turn around and there's Olivier, all smiles.

"Hi!" I press the phone against my thigh, hardly breathing.

"Who were you talking to?" he says.

"Taylor."

Even if he only heard that last part, Olivier has lived with us long enough to know that Taylor and I don't exactly "love" all over each other.

"What did she want?" Olivier asks, closing the balcony door behind him.

It's a tight space up here, and we stand a few feet apart from each other, while below us the world moves on.

"She was freaking out because she thought there was someone in the house."

He rolls his eyes. "And how does she think you're going to help from the other side of the world?"

"Right?" I shake my head. "She needs to get a life."

"She's a special one, your sister. I know you feel for her, but it might be time she move out, don't you think? We need our own space, you and me. We're married and we have to think about *us*."

I swallow hard. He still thinks this is all going to work out, that we'll stay in Paris for a few more days and then go home to start our husband-and-wife life. All I can think is that I need to *not* be here when he finds out that none of this is going to happen.

"Let's not worry about her right now. We're on our honeymoon." I try to sound casual as I push past him to head back inside the room. I want to check my phone, but I'm sure Darren has hung up by now.

I'm still in the doorframe when Olivier grabs my wrist a little too hard. "I think we have more talking to do."

"Ouch!" I say loudly.

He immediately lets go of my hand and I make a big show of rubbing it, my face contorted in manufactured pain.

"Sorry." He sits down in one of the chairs. "Please. Let's talk."

My mouth goes dry, my legs wobbly. He knows it wasn't Taylor on the phone. I could tell him I'm too tired, not in the mood, but then he'd follow me inside where we'd be all alone. Out here there are passersby below and people in the building across the street, their shadows occasionally moving behind the windows. Witnesses, just in case.

I lean against the railing, as far away from him as possible.

"I know things have been off between us over the last few weeks," he starts. "And if that made you think twice about being with me, then I'm really sorry."

What if he checks the safe? I need to get him out of here.

"I don't think I can ever thank you enough for what you did for me," Olivier continues, giving no indication that he senses the turmoil inside me, "and I know you've probably regretted marrying me at least once."

He waits for my reaction, but I'm too confused to even make one up. Are we supposed to be honest with each other now? His eyes go red and start brimming with tears. He pinches the bridge of his nose with his fingers, rendering me even more speechless than I already was. I was so close to getting out of here. Out of *this*.

"I really believe we could have a great life together." His voice is shaking now. "I was surprised that you'd called the Realtor while we were here. Why now? But if that's what you want, of course that's fine with me. Every couple has to make compromises."

The words spill out of me. "We're not a real couple."

Olivier jerks back, like I slapped him. If he's acting, he's really good at it. "Please don't say that. I love you, Cassie."

He gets up and starts coming my way. A nervous laugh escapes me, sending hurt all over his face. He stares at me, breathing deeply, his fists clenched. I step away from the railing, like I burned myself.

"I'll take you on a honeymoon here every year," he says, waving at the air between us. "Or anywhere you'd like. Maybe we got married for the wrong reason, but that doesn't mean we can't make it right." But I don't want to make it right, not with him. "Please, Cassie. Say something."

So I do. I say the first thing that comes to mind. "Let's go get a drink." I reach for his hand. "I'm sorry about our fight, too. There's so much of Paris I haven't seen yet."

His face breaks into a smile, all the tension diffused. I need to get us away from this room, from the safe and the missing passport. The airline will call back and I'll change my flight. I'll be gone long before Olivier knows it. One more drink won't kill me. All that really matters is that I'm not here when he realizes I've ruined his life.

CHAPTER 15

Olivier

TWO MONTHS BEFORE THE HONEYMOON

On the drive home from our appointment with the immigration attorney, I tried to give myself a silent pep talk. Maybe I'd look for a job around here. Or I'd convince Cassie to go ahead with what she'd vaguely mentioned in the city: we'd renovate the inn and would reopen it, with prices to match its new standing. It could be a viable business, maybe? It would be a lot of work: the house was dark, smelled of mold, and desperately needed a fresh coat of everything. I wasn't built for handywork. My father would laugh if he knew I was even considering taking up this kind of project. There was always Cassie's money, which could pay for a contractor, but I couldn't imagine wasting it on this hellhole. And Cassie kept changing her tune about when the money would come or what she wanted to do with it. The sad truth: whatever she did decide, I would have to go along with it. She had me by the collar, could drag me along as she wished.

By the time we arrived back at the house, I felt completely lost, worse than ever. I couldn't even bring myself to go inside.

I grabbed the rusty bike I'd found in the shed adjoining the house. Daylight waned as I cycled down the main road out of town. Trucks honked, then took over, nearly running me off the road more than once. It didn't matter. After the meeting today, I was dead. This thing with Cassie would never work. We'd conveniently bumped into her ex a few more times since the birthday party, and Cassie would wrap an arm around me and get all gooey. But, when no one else was watching, her interest in me seemed to fade a bit more every day.

I wasn't sure what to do—redeclare my undying love for her? Remind her she'd agreed to this and she better hold her side of the bargain, or else? Or else, what? Then there was the way she'd perked up when the lawyer mentioned giving up. We wouldn't be able to fool an immigration officer. Couldn't keep up this act for a full two years. I'd get deported. I'd thought having to go back to France was bad, but now I was going to be forced back there as a criminal. And still with no money. I was so very fucked.

Reaching the next town, I went down a few roads in near darkness, until I got to Main Street. There was a bar, a dive-y sort of place with a shattered window. I could use a drink. Inside, the place smelled of lukewarm beer and fried everything. A few men were gathered around a billiard table in the back room, while a lone woman played darts nearby. I claimed a seat at the counter—they were all empty—and waited. A bearded guy was stacking plastic crates in the corner and proceeded to royally ignore me.

"Excuse me?" I said after a few minutes had passed. "Can I get a drink? Vodka tonic?"

The guy grunted. Then, without looking at me, he yelled, "Reese! You there? Someone at the bar."

I was silently grumbling to myself about the amazing service when the flap doors swung open from the other side. Out she came: with wavy hair that brushed against her shoulders, eyes rimmed dark and lips so red they brightened her whole face. She wore a black top so fitted it seemed like two sizes two small, and I became mesmerized by how her hips swayed as she walked toward me. She took me in, casual disdain all over her face, and I shook my head, trying to be sure I wasn't hallucinating. Who was this woman?

"Reese?" It had been a long, messy, and gut-wrenching day. I couldn't handle anything more.

"That's my name." Her tone was all snark, but with a touch of kindness to it, like she wanted to have a little fun with me, in good spirit. "Gin okay? We're out of vodka."

I nodded, speechless.

A minute later, she handed me the glass without a word and stared at my hands as I gulped it down, trying not to wince. Before the City Hall wedding, I'd bought three rings from a pawn shop in the Financial District, one with a small fake diamond and two wedding bands. They were the cheapest ones I could find on such short notice, and mine left a black mark around my finger. We hadn't worn them since getting upstate, but I'd reminded Cassie to put her rings back on for the appointment with the lawyer. She'd taken hers off as soon as we'd stepped out of the building. I'd waited until I'd parked the car in front of her house, for all the difference it made.

Now I looked at my finger too, rubbing where the ring was, removing any last trace of it. And then I was back to staring at her; couldn't help it.

"You have an admirer," the bearded guy said to Reese.

She answered with a chuckle as she wiped the counter with a shredded rag that looked like it'd seen the war.

"You got this wrong, Jack," she said. "This guy is the infamous Cassie Quinn's new French boyfriend. Moved in with her and everything. He even has the accent to prove it."

"Fancy that," Jack said.

They laughed and I felt like the butt of some private joke.

Reese turned to me and looked deep into my eyes. "Cassie is full of surprises."

My stomach dropped, and there wasn't one ounce of saliva left in my mouth. I should go home. All hope was not lost yet. I could try harder at wooing Cassie. I'd seen the look in her eyes when I'd told her I loved her.

I'd faked so many things in my life. Surely affection could be fabricated, especially with someone like Cassie, who needed it so much. Otherwise, she wasn't going to keep me around, was she? But deep down I already knew that whatever I did, it wouldn't be enough to salvage the situation.

I glanced up again at Reese, who had moved to the far end of the bar. It made me feel uneasy. Wanting more. I *needed* to look at her.

"So, um, you work here?" I said. What a dumb fucking question.

She pressed her lips together. "Some of us gotta work, you know."

I looked down at my well-fitting polo shirt, my clean nails, my white sneakers—the off-duty style I'd adopted since spending all day in a uniform at Bhotel—and I wanted to tell her, *I know. I don't want to be like this.* I'd gone along with Cassie's story that I was this rich guy who was spoiling her. Now, for the first time, I wondered what people around here had said when I'd turned up with Cassie. I'd hoped to make a good impression with her circle, and it occurred to me now that I had no idea how I'd fared. I needed to prove to Reese that I was a good person. Sure, I'd done lots of shitty things, but I'd meant well, always.

"Have a drink with me," I said. "Please."

She looked around the room, but there was no one else in sight. She debated for a moment, then grabbed the gin bottle on her way back to me, along with another glass. She poured both of us some, splashed in some tonic, and clinked her glass to mine.

My hands shook as I took a sip. There was so much hurt in her eyes and in her slumped shoulders, wounds on display. In that moment I couldn't explain what I felt about her. Attraction, yes, but mostly: kinship.

"I feel like we haven't been properly introduced." I rubbed my hands against my jeans, getting rid of the dampness from the glass. "Hi, I'm Olivier. I just moved here."

I held out my hand.

She rolled her eyes. "I think you already know everything there is to know about me."

"On the contrary, it seems I don't know anything at all. Tell me, what do you do for fun around here?"

She grunted.

I didn't touch my glass, couldn't take my eyes off her. "You don't like it here?"

At that, she laughed. It was deep and cool and sexy. I couldn't believe I hadn't heard it before. That laugh was going to derail my life even further. I think deep down I already knew that.

"It wouldn't have been my first choice."

"Where would you go? If the sky was the limit."

Her eyes narrowed. "The sky is never, ever, ever, the limit."

"What if it were? Can't we dream, for one night?"

She took a deep breath, then slowly unscrewed the cap on the gin bottle again. "I guess so."

So that's what we did.

We dreamed aloud.

That's how it started between us anyway.

I immediately felt comfortable around her. With Cassie I always had to be on my best behavior, to watch myself. But Reese saw me for who I was, from the start. At least that's how I felt as she leaned over the counter, resting on her bare forearms, her eyes firmly on mine.

I talked about my childhood in the suburbs outside Paris where, every day, I dreamed of a different life. I explained how I started making money, how quickly things got away from me. I opened up about how I alienated everyone I knew, how low I fell, how desperate. And then, the job at Bhotel, the opportunity to come to New York. How alive I'd felt there, a most thrilling second chance. I told her things I'd never said to anyone else.

Reese listened. I asked about her, too, eager to uncover her secrets. When she talked, it felt like the words took a lot out of her. She alluded to her deadbeat parents—my word, not hers—how lonely she'd been growing up. How weighed down she was by that feeling of unbalance, of knowing from a very young age that she was always on the brink of something even more terrible than what she had already gone through.

Tears filled her eyes, and without thinking, I reached over the bar to rub my hand against her cheek. She flinched and I started reversing course, but the look in her eyes showed surprise more than anything else. She didn't expect kindness, especially not from me. She didn't actually share what her dreams might be, and after pressing her on it to no avail, it occurred to me that even thinking about your dreams is a luxury for some. It broke my heart a little. I put my hand on hers again and this time she didn't react. Her skin was smooth. So soft. Next, I ran my thumb against her bottom lip. She flinched again but not as hard, and a current coursed through me.

"I wish I knew you before," I said. I hoped she heard what I meant: I wished I'd met you before I met Cassie.

"You don't even know me now," she replied, taking my hand and placing it back on the sticky counter.

"What if I want to?"

"Oh, because wanting something is enough to make it happen?"

What first came to mind: I want you.

"Quite the opposite," I said. "I thought if I just put my mind to it…but look at me." I glanced around the room and then down at myself. "Nothing has worked out how I wanted it to."

Part of me felt pathetic, admitting that to her. But it was freeing, too. I couldn't remember ever letting my guard down like this.

We didn't even drink that much; I can't blame it on the alcohol. Over the next few hours, she poured us two more gin and tonics, and only stepped away a handful of times when a patron came to order a drink. It was past midnight on a Tuesday and the bar had emptied fast. Even her colleague had gone. I couldn't tell how long we'd been alone. Since we'd started talking, it had felt like there was no one else in the room.

"I have to close up," she said when the clock ticked over to 1:00 a.m.

Her voice was laced with sadness. At least that's how I heard it. How

I wanted it to be. Right then, I wasn't in a smelly bar, drinking cheap gin, beholden to a shitty wife, who at this point seemed to care so little about our marriage that it felt like I'd made it up in my head. I needed this night. Couldn't let it end.

"Don't," I heard myself say. "Can we stay here a little longer?"

She shook her head as she stared at me. A loaded moment passed before she said in a whisper, "We can't."

Then, not taking her eyes off me, she came out of behind the counter and slowly walked toward the restrooms, which were down a hallway behind me. I turned around and watched in silence. She'd switched off the music, and I could hear the sound of my own heartbeat. I felt entranced. Cassie didn't exist anymore. In fact, we hadn't talked anymore about her all night. Already she couldn't get between us.

I peeled my eyes off Reese to down the last of my drink, then made a decision. If she turned around before reaching the door, it would mean something. An invitation, perhaps. I wasn't sure what I would do, but the air was starting to feel stale again, the tension in my shoulders coming back. Reese was only a few meters away, and I missed her already. That made no sense, but I did.

She turned around.

Her eyes were already trained on me, though I couldn't read the expression in them. In that moment, I'd have given everything I had to find out what she was thinking. She stood still, watching me. I knew that if I got up now, there would be no going back. I was with Cassie, and Reese was well aware of that. There was a clear line in the sand. Getting up meant crossing it.

I got up.

I got up and the corners of her red lips turned up ever so slightly. Not a smile, exactly. An encouragement. That's how I took it. I had no idea what I was doing. What *we* were doing. Because she was in this, right? She'd turned around. The way she looked at me...deeply and without blinking. I walked over to her, watching her chest rise and fall, an exquisite feeling running through me. I had never felt this way before. Over the years, I'd grown more certain that the life I hoped for—the success and the glitziness and the money—I had to pursue it alone.

And now I was about to fuck it up for good. But it already was, wasn't it? In that moment, it didn't matter anyway. I couldn't stop my legs from bringing me to Reese. All night I'd inhaled her perfume, something earthy but subtle, and now it was filling the air between us again.

She didn't move, away or toward me. I was close enough to notice the freckles on her cheeks, and I still couldn't have said how she felt. It had fascinated me all night, how unreadable she was, even when she shared the most intimate details of her life.

We were centimeters apart now. I opened my mouth to speak, then closed it. She did the same. No words came out. Instead I ran my hands through her hair and pressed my body against hers, our chests touching, her warmth becoming mine.

Her own hands wrapped around my waist. She pulled me toward her as she leaned against the wall. My nose gently rubbed against hers. Her sweet breath melted into mine. I wanted to cherish the moment, but was too eager for the next. Our kiss was hungry, winded, our bodies almost still. Because if we moved, if we made any noise, then this would feel real. It was a small world. Anyone could see us. Small-town folks knew everyone around. Cassie could easily find out.

It was risky, so very risky. And it was too late already.

We still hadn't said a word when Reese glanced toward the restrooms' door. A jolt of anticipation raced through me.

And then…she pushed me away.

"I can't," she said.

I opened my mouth to protest. She felt what I was feeling, too. Right? I wasn't imagining it. But also, I couldn't—shouldn't—do anything to lead her into this. I couldn't be the one who made it happen. I wasn't going to screw up everything for no reason.

"Please," she added.

"If that's what you want," I whispered.

She swallowed hard, but didn't respond. So I did what I had to do.

I let her go.

CHAPTER 16

Taylor

NOW

A year ago, a few weeks before Rae died, I was bringing breakfast to her room when she asked if I could close the door behind me. She'd been a plump woman before, but she'd lost a lot of weight and was barely recognizable. Her frizzy grayed hair was matted, and her complexion had turned dull with a yellowish tint. She was also coughing so much by then that talking, even for a few minutes, took a lot out of her. But that day, she knew her time was near, and she had things to say.

"When I go..." she started.

I shook my head, unwilling to think about that. I'd never been set in my feelings about her. On one hand, she'd rescued me. Who knows what would have happened to me if she hadn't come forward after I was placed with Child Services. She gave me a home, a safe enough space. It took me years to understand why she'd done it, how a mother could love her child so much that she'd take in a stray like me just so her little one could have company. The next best thing to a real sibling. A family of three, again, even if it would never be the same since her husband had left. I knew Rae loved me, in her own broken way. But she wasn't *my* mother, not the one I wanted.

And I'd blamed her for taking me in, too, when my own mom could still come back for me. I kept waiting for her. I would have done it forever but she died when I was thirteen, a couple of years after she was released from prison. She never responded to the letters I sent her, never tried contacting me. And now I was about to have no one left. The idea of more loss, more loneliness, felt crushing. I had tried all I could to keep the inn afloat, dreading any moment I'd have to spend with my own thoughts. But taking care of Rae had become a near full-time job and we had stopped taking bookings. Soon it would just be Cassie and me. No buffer, only grief. Thinking of that made my head spin.

"I'm worried for Cassie," Rae said after a coughing fit. "I know she hasn't always been kind to you, but I hope you have it in your heart to still be there for her."

My heart twisted in a dozen directions. I couldn't remember a moment in our childhood when Cassie and I played together for more than a few minutes, not one instance when we talked without dread running through my veins. I knew she'd use whatever I said against me later, how she'd make fun of me with her friends at school, refusing to let me eat lunch with them, leaving me out of their circle, like the pathetic little loner I was.

Rae kept talking about how Cassie would be alone, how hard it would be for her. I was about to be orphaned all over again, but Rae didn't see it that way. In the end, she only thought of Cassie. No one cared what would happen to me.

I've just sat on a bench opposite my darling sister's hotel when my phone rings.

"Miss Quinn! I'm sorry I couldn't get back to you until now. Is this a good time?"

"Yes, of course. Thanks for calling me back."

A week after Rae's funeral, a local Realtor named Martin Beckmann came by the house and asked to talk to the owner. I said that was me. One of us anyway.

"I hope you don't mind me taking a tour the other day," he says now, sounding as slimy as he did back then. "Your sister told me you'd be okay with that. In fact, I'll need to come by again. Would now work by any chance? I just wrapped up an appointment nearby."

I guess I should feel glad he's asking me now, since he wasn't so considerate last time.

Just then, Cassie and Olivier come out of the hotel. I get up too fast and blood rushes to my head.

"Miss Quinn?"

"Yes," I say, starting to walk a little behind the happy couple.

At the time, Martin Beckmann had seen the obituary in the paper and wanted to ask if we might be interested in selling the house, now that our mother had passed. *Truly sorry for your loss*, he'd said. *So you own the place with your sister, is that right?*

"I called earlier to ask you something, if that's okay?" I say, ignoring his previous question.

"Um, yes, sure."

"My sister is traveling at the moment. I don't want to bother her with this."

Definitely not when she's walking ahead of me. She and Olivier both look tense, going fast, staring straight ahead. Not talking. After our phone call, I followed Cassie right back to the hotel. Then I wandered the streets for a while, unsure what to do. I grabbed a sandwich, called the Realtor, and waited.

"Anything I can do to help."

He *really* wants that commission.

"It's a bit delicate. The truth is, my sister and I don't always see eye to eye." I force a smile, hoping he can hear it. "And as you know, we own the house together since our mother passed away…" I pause, letting him jump in. He doesn't. "The thing is, we're not blood sisters, Cassie and I. Her mother adopted me. But it's all the same now."

"And your question is?" he says, sounding colder now.

"Well, I guess, I was wondering…since you've been in touch with Cassie lately… I mean, I wanted to check that we're all on the same page here."

"Hmm," is all he says for a while. But this time I'm not going to fill the silence, so I wait until he continues. "I don't want to get in the middle of anything. Family dynamics can be tricky." Again I bite my lip. "I think you should speak to your sister."

"Right, maybe we should all hit pause for a while. You don't really need to come back to the house until she returns from her trip, do you? I'd rather not have any visitors this week."

"Well, hmm, I have some interested buyers and I was hoping to show them the place sooner rather than later. But I'd like to come by before then to make sure it's in tip-top shape."

He pauses then, and it hits me, the state we left the house in. The wedding had just wrapped up; I'm not even sure I put all the leftovers in the fridge. I picture the empty beer bottles strewn about, the torn wrapping paper from the gifts the happy couple received. I was supposed to drive back home and clean it all up. I definitely *would* have cleaned it up, if I hadn't jumped on that plane. The flowers must be starting to wilt now. Did he say anything to Cassie? Could she know I haven't been home since?

"Look, like I said," he continues, "it's not for me to discuss, but the fact is, I saw the deed. I'm sorry you've been led to believe otherwise but your sister inherited the house from her father. It's all in her name."

I can't breathe. I heard what Cassie said earlier, but she says lots of things and most of them are complete bullshit. She'll talk about how she created a candle business when in fact it was me who designed the labels to stick on the jars and paid to get them printed. Me, who continued to buy the ingredients because Cassie insisted it was such a great idea, and that all her friends were already placing orders. She'd sold one-tenth of our stock before she decided she was bored with that and wanted to do something else.

And it was *me* who first thought selling the house would be a good idea. I'd originally suggested we spruce up the inn and reopen it, but Cassie had scoffed. *I can't see myself running a business with you,* she'd said. Martin Beckmann had left me his business card after giving his pitch—the town might be a little run-down but there was so much opportunity in the region and developers called him all the time. That night I brought it up with Cassie, fear pooling at the bottom of my stomach. I offered her what I thought she'd wanted this whole time: to be rid of me.

We'd sell the house, split the money, and go our own ways. I had no idea what I'd do, but I knew I didn't need much. Half the money from the house would be a huge leg up to start over elsewhere. That would be my way of taking care of Cassie, as her mother wanted, and to relieve her of me. Of course, as soon as I finished speaking, Cassie threw a fit, called me a gold digger, and stormed out of the room. I'd left the business card on the console in the entrance and noticed it was gone the next day. Cassie must have thrown it out. Case closed. Or so I'd assumed.

"You're certain about that?" I say, trying to keep my voice light. I'm homeless but it's okay!

"I'm sorry Miss Quinn, but yeah. Your name doesn't appear anywhere."

"Right, well, thank you for your help. One more thing, if you don't mind. Did she tell you why she's interested in selling the house now? I'm not sure if she told you, but Cassie and her new husband were planning to renovate and reopen the inn. In fact, he spent the last few weeks peeling off wallpaper, fixing up leaks, and working on the yard."

"Oh! I don't think I knew about a husband. Your sister's married?"

"She certainly is."

In fact she and her handsome French husband are walking inside Café de Flore right now. Another Parisian hot spot, renowned for its star power

129

and its awning overflowing with lush plants. I keep an eye on them as they sit down inside. It's been overcast all day, but now the clouds have turned a dark shade of gray. It's going to start raining any minute.

"Huh, well, I don't know what to tell you," Martin Beckmann says. "She called me about two months ago, asking if I could value the property. Then she canceled an hour before our appointment. She called me again last week saying she was interested again. I asked to set up an appointment but it turned out she was out of town this week. Said I could come by when she returned. Then she texted me the next day that I could visit it by myself and use the spare key if you weren't home. Doesn't really know what she wants, your sister. So I called her. You know, I wanted to make sure I wasn't wasting my time. She told me the whole story and now I get it. Most of us think we'd love to be in her situation, but it can't be easy."

Startled, I bump into a trash can on the street corner. "How so?"

"All of that money she inherited…on top of the house. It's kind of like winning the lottery, you know? No disrespect to your family, of course. She's right to think long and hard about what to do with it. A couple million seems like a lot, but between taxes and everything, you could be one bad investment away from losing it all."

I clear my throat, trying to steady my voice. "I'm sorry, I don't follow. What money?"

"From her father. Sounded like a real piece of work, that one. Leaving her as a child to go live the high life. My old man did the same, though there's no way he's not spending every last cent before hitting the grave."

I'm stunned into silence. The money. Cassie has money, and so much of it. And it all fell into her lap, just like her husband. Because of course she'd never work for it. She just waits around for things to bend to her satisfaction, while the rest of us play an endless game of Tetris, trying to make every unexpected bill and every setback fit within the already messy constraints of our lives. How did I not see this before? The new clothes. The renovation plans for the inn. The wedding dress. The house filled with flowers. The freaking honeymoon. I couldn't understand why Olivier would go into debt for her when he kept saying he was desperate for work, willing to do anything to make ends meet.

"Um, wait. I'm sorry," the Realtor continues when I haven't spoke for a while. "I shouldn't have said any of this. I don't even know why she told me. That's really none of my business... It's just, like I said, I have an interested buyer and your sister isn't returning my texts today. I want to make this happen, you know? In fact, maybe you could slip in a word to her? I'll help her find somewhere new, with less repairs and not so many stairs. Actually, I listed a home last week that'd be perfect for a couple looking to start a family..."

I hang up. He's right about one thing though. He really should have kept his mouth shut. Growing up, money was always a problem. The inn brought in enough to cover the basics, but Cassie made impossible demands—a new phone, cash to go out with friends, more clothes. Rae gave everything she could but it was never enough.

Cassie was nineteen when she earned her first penny, and even then, she only lasted six weeks working as a cashier at our local grocery store. She was always late and her boss quickly got tired of it. Meanwhile, I'd lend her whatever she asked for, always. *We gave you a roof,* she'd say, when Rae wasn't around. *My mother took you in when she could barely feed us both.* It was the truth; I couldn't deny it.

So I'd work any job I could find, and with my earnings, I'd pay Cassie's phone bill. I'd buy the drinks she'd have with her friends on her nights out, even though I was never invited. I let her have the secondhand tablet I'd gotten my hands on, which I snagged for a great price, considering it was almost new. I'd stolen her mother from her. I had to pay for that. Again and again.

But last week, I was cleaning on top of the kitchen cabinets—Surprise, Cassie and Olivier were getting married! The house had to be spotless—when I found the old porcelain cookie jar Rae had bought at a yard sale.

She often hid cash there, her own little savings nest. The money sometimes went missing, and Cassie would point the finger at me before Rae had even gone down the stepladder. I don't think Rae believed her, but fighting with Cassie was exhausting, and she usually gave up. Once, when a thousand dollars went missing, Rae grounded us both for a month. I never went anywhere so it didn't make much of a difference to me. Cassie kept sneaking out after we'd gone to bed and we all pretended we didn't notice.

The jar should have been empty. I'd looked through it a year before, when I was struggling to pay for Rae's medical bills, guilt twisting my insides at having to stoop to Cassie's level. But as soon as I pulled up the lid last week, bills burst out of it. It was full to the brim. So much money! Cassie didn't save. She spent anything she had as if it burned a hole in her pocket. The only logical explanation: it was Olivier's money. I had no idea why he would hide it up there, but there were only three of us in the house. The man had been full of contradictions. Cassie spoke endlessly about how generous and successful he was, but from the moment he'd arrived, I'd watched him on that rusty bike, which no one had used in a decade, and wondered if he enjoyed playing poor country boy, or if something else was going on.

I keep staring at the café. Cassie and Olivier have each ordered a glass of wine and she's clutching her phone tight. I'm her sister, whether she likes it or not. After my mother died, Rae decided to file the paperwork to formally adopt me. She didn't tell Cassie until it was done. She ran it past me, suggesting we change my name, so we'd be a "real" family. I think it was the guilt talking, of taking me in for the wrong reasons, of letting me suffer at her daughter's hands. She went through the legalities to make herself feel better. It was only after it was done that I realized I didn't *want* to change my name. Didn't want to erase my past or to make it even harder for my father to find me, if he ever tried. But I was so used to going along with whatever was dictated for me that it hadn't even occurred to me to speak up.

I don't care how much money Cassie has; that house is my only home. I have a right to know. I'm so sick of her treating me like a pest invading her space, when I never asked to be there and did everything for her. And now she has it all: the house and the money and the husband.

When I have nothing.

And nothing to lose.

I catch a glimpse of my reflection in the window: the shorter blond hair was the right call and my cap ensures they won't recognize me. Pushing it further down to cover some of my face, I walk inside. It smells like peanuts and red wine. Cassie and Olivier's table is in the middle, flanked tightly by several others on every side. My heart beats a little faster with every step. I don't know what I'm doing, just that I don't care anymore. I'm halfway across the room when Cassie gets up, her phone pressed to her ear. She shoots Olivier an apologetic smile before walking off to the back of the café. Olivier interlaces his fingers, nervously playing with his wedding band. He glances at Cassie a few times as he bites his bottom lip. That's when I see the Chanel bag dangling from the back of Cassie's chair. I make a snap decision. I want to hurt her. A little. To start with.

She's still on the phone, her back to me and to the door of the restrooms. Olivier takes a sip as I near her chair. It's so tightly packed in there that he might not see me even if his gaze wasn't drilled on his wife. I kneel down, pretending to look for something on the floor. The waiters are too busy running around to pay me attention. My palms go clammy as I tug on Cassie's bag, releasing the strap, which clinks at it hits the black-and-white-tiled floor. No one else hears it. No one comes running to me. Clutching the buttery-soft leather to my chest, I get back up halfway and, in a few quick strides, I'm inside the restrooms, panting and sweaty.

I must have lost my mind. No, that's not true. I lost it a while ago, ever since I offered to come with her to the city for her father's funeral. *This isn't your family. I don't need you.*

Still, I drove her to the freaking train station. I gave her money for the ticket. I texted and called her to make sure she was okay. But of course she was. Just a couple of days later, her new French boyfriend popped up on her Instagram feed. Her father had died and there she was, having a grand old time in the city.

My heart in my throat, I unclasp the bag, which is lined in dark-red leather. There's a Chanel lipstick in a slick gold case, sunglasses, a bunch of crumpled receipts, Cassie's passport, and her wallet. A new wallet that matches the bag. The leather is smooth, and it smells of all the money it must have cost. I guess it's easy to throw cash around when you didn't have to lift a finger to earn it. I grab the wallet and slip it my own bag. Now I have to walk out the way I came.

Though I'm keeping my eyes down, I immediately notice the commotion—Olivier on his knees, searching between the legs of other patrons, and Cassie clutching her phone.

"Where is it?" she whispers-screams. "Excuse me! Have you seen my Chanel?"

My heart pulsing, I crouch down and let the bag drop at my feet, where it falls against the brown satchel of the man sitting at the next table from the newlyweds.

Then I slip outside, my whole body buzzing. I never tried to hurt Cassie before. I was never vindictive or, rather, I knew *she* was, and I was always too scared of the consequences. But she can't blame me for what she doesn't know.

As I walk across the bridge to my side of the river, there's no denying the lightness within me. The relief. Maybe this is what I needed to do all along. To stand my ground. To fight for what's mine. What *should* be mine.

By the time I reach my hotel, everything feels clear to me. This is a trial run. I'm not done with Cassie yet. Not done at all.

CHAPTER 17

Cassie

NOW

Remember how I made plans to catch up with some of my ex-colleagues while I'm in town?" Olivier says, slowly swirling his glass by the stem and bringing it to his nose. "Well, I thought maybe you'd like a night to yourself. I feel like you could use some space."

"Oh." I do remember, vaguely, though I've lost track of the days since we got here. "Thursday, you'd said," I say more to myself.

He takes it as a question. "Yes! I wouldn't be out late, just for a drink or two—"

"You should go! I mean, *definitely* go."

"Unless you want to come—" He takes a sip, his Adam's apple bulging in his throat as the liquid goes down.

"No!" I say a little too loudly. "I mean, I'm feeling kind of tired anyway."

This is perfect. Even more perfect: my phone rings. It must be the airline, calling back early.

"Sorry, I have to take this," I say with a coy smile, getting up.

I walk toward the back of the café, out of earshot from Olivier, who keeps glancing at me as the customer service agent asks how he can help me. I explain my situation—I want to fly home early, no big deal!—but he tells me that I didn't book changeable flights. If I want to fly back on a different date, I'll have to pay for a whole new one-way ticket.

"I can do this right now for you," the agent announces gaily, like he's being so helpful.

"I already paid for that flight. What does it matter if I come back earlier?"

"I'm sorry, ma'am. I can't make changes to your current ticket, but it will only take a few minutes to book a new one. When would you like to fly?"

I'd have to go get my wallet; Olivier might ask questions. He keeps biting his lower lip as he tries to discreetly look in my direction. I still can't tell if he bought my lie about speaking to Taylor earlier on the phone, and I shouldn't push my luck.

"I'll do it online, thanks for nothing."

I hang up and return to our table, downing the rest of my wine without sitting down.

"Taylor again?" Olivier says, an eyebrow raised.

I nod, then place my empty glass on the table a little too forcefully. "We should go, no? You don't want to keep your friends waiting."

That's when I notice that the shiny strap is no longer dangling from the back of my chair.

"My Chanel!" I say, my mouth going dry.

"What's wrong?" Olivier says.

"My bag's gone."

"I'm sure it's somewhere around here."

He gets up, then starts looking around on the floor.

"I can't believe this. Someone stole my bag!" I raise my voice, commanding attention.

"Um, excusez-moi?" the man at the next table says a moment later. "You're looking for this?" He lifts his hand to show us what he's holding: my Chanel.

I let out a huge sigh of relief as I snag it from him. I can't believe I almost lost it right before going home. It's got to be a sign: time for me to leave. I never should have come here.

The man points at his feet. His own satchel is resting against the table's leg. "Il était là."

"Merci beaucoup," Olivier says. Then, to me, "It probably fell when you got up. The tables are so tight. If one person moves, everything shifts."

My jaw is still clenched as I hook the strap over my shoulder. I could make a bigger fuss, but I want to get out of here more. Unfortunately, Olivier says he'll walk back to the hotel with me before going out. He wants to get changed, even after I assure him that he looks great as he is. I force a smile all the way down the street, through the lobby, up the elevator, and as we enter our suite. I'm so close to be rid of him. *So close.*

"You're sure you don't mind?" Olivier says as he kicks off his shoes and starts unbuttoning his shirt.

"Not at all. Go! Come back as late as you'd like."

I nestle into one of the armchairs and study him.

He pulls another shirt from the closet. "How about I order you some room service? And then maybe run you a bath. You could have a little self-care night, and then we'll do something fun tomorrow."

"Sounds great! Thank you, Husband."

Can he hear how fake I sound? Of course I don't plan on being around tomorrow, but this suite is amazing and I've barely enjoyed it. It's probably too late to leave tonight anyway. I'll book the first flight out in the morning and slip out while Olivier recovers from his hangover.

"It's the least I can do," Olivier says, retrieving the iron and board from the closet. His voice is sickeningly sweet.

"Aww, you're the best."

He walks over to his side of the bed, grabbing the room phone. "They make a really good burger here. And how about a nice bottle of wine? You liked the one from earlier, right? I'll ask if they have the same red."

"Um, sure. But how do you know the burger is good here? We never ate at the restaurant."

Olivier's hand grips tighter around the phone, and it takes him a moment to respond. But when he does, he's all smiles. "I read the reviews online."

"Right. Yeah, a burger is great," I say, getting up.

I go out onto the balcony while Olivier places the order and finishes getting ready, ironing his shirt and spraying himself with his woodsy fragrance. Meanwhile, I get to enjoy this view for a little while longer. Paris really is pretty in that old, antiquated way. I don't know much about its history, but you can feel it in all of the old monuments, the churches everywhere you look. Maybe Darren and I will come back here on our own honeymoon. Or will he think that's weird? Obviously we'll get married now. I've shown him proof that I do pretty well as a wife. But first, I should focus on going home. Olivier can't stop me if he doesn't know.

When I get back inside, he's wearing his freshly ironed shirt and lacing up his dress leather shoes. A tray of food has appeared on the bed. The bottle of wine has been uncorked, some of it poured into a big, round glass, and the plate is covered by a metal bell. I lift it up to find a cheeseburger and fries, all juicy and crispy, with a side of ketchup. It makes my mouth water. I never got to have lunch.

"You have a good time, okay?" Olivier says, giving me a peck on the forehead. "I ran you a bath."

A delicate scent of lavender escapes from the bathroom and, peeking inside, I notice that the tub is covered in a thick layer of bubbly foam.

"Can't wait!" I say, walking him to the door and waving goodbye before slamming it shut.

Finally, he's gone.

First things first: I need to book that flight. But when I look inside my bag, my wallet is not in there. I topple its contents onto the bed to be sure, but only my passport, my lipstick, and crumpled receipts fall out. *Shit.* I look everywhere around the room, under the bed, on the nightstand, in the bathroom, and even on the balcony, stopping only to take sips of my wine to calm my nerves.

It's the same wine we drank at Café de Flore, where my bag went missing for a short while. I never thought to check inside.

No wallet means no credit card; I can't book a new flight.

Shit shit shit shit.

Reaching for my phone, I fire off a text to Darren. Hey

Hey babe, he responds right away. *Babe*, it's like we're back to our old selves already. It's all working out perfectly. Well, almost.

Just want to let u know Im leaving. Coming home tmrw

For real? U told him?

Yep

Hes okay with it?

Dont worry about him

I take another sip, trying to focus on the fruity taste of the wine. Darren hates lies, but he wouldn't understand the truth.

Wow! Sorry but can't talk rn. At work

I just told him I'm leaving my husband for him and that's all I get?

Wait a second

I need u

Something happened

Boss calling me into his office, **Darren replies.**

Please!

But I can't bring myself to say why I need help, because I know how Darren will react. There I was, asking for money again. I should have paid more attention. I should have been more careful. It's my fault. A seven-thousand-dollar bag? What was I thinking? I'm a grown-up now. I need to sort myself out.

Sorry babe

Text me what time u arrive at the airport. Will try to come pick u up

I pour myself another glass of wine, waiting for more, but nothing comes. *Fuck.*

I gulp down my drink as I scroll through my recently called numbers.

"Hello?" Taylor says as soon as she picks up. "Cassie?"

Like earlier she sounds funny, awkward.

"I need your help."

I'll give Taylor that: she *can* be helpful. When we were younger, she'd do my homework better than I could do it myself, and so fast, too. One time, I got caught shoplifting at Walmart and the security guard held me hostage, saying I had to have a parent pick me up, or else he'd call the police. I texted Taylor and she arrived fifteen minutes later, armed with a bunch of reasons why he should let me go. I'd never do it again; she'd make sure of it.

Of course I did it again.

"What's going on?" she says.

There's a forced breeziness to her tone. Taylor is all nerves, always watching her back, watching *me*. From her point of view, I'm having the most fabulous time in Paris with my most fabulous husband, while she never got to come here. Never found her father. Never even learned what Mom told me about him. So why is she trying so hard to sound cheerful? What am I not getting? But I have more important things on my mind.

"I lost my credit card," I say casually.

"Oh gosh, Cassie! I'm so sorry. What happened?"

"I was having too much fun. These French wines are good…" I take another sip, as if to prove my own point.

"I'm sure they're amazing!" Her voice sounds shrill, like she's drunk. Maybe that's it. She's seeing me, the amazing life I have now. And she's drinking to numb the pain.

"Can you give me your credit card details? I need to book something." There's a pause at the other end. Maybe I was a little harsh with her earlier. I do that sometimes. "I'll pay you back."

Seeing the good times I was having with Olivier in the city, my friends assumed I'd hit the jackpot. It sure looked like it on the pictures I posted on social. Olivier was handsome, polished, and he was taking me to the greatest spots around the city. He had to be rich, right? I mean, that's what I thought when I first met him; everything I wanted to do, he agreed to. In the end I didn't need to correct my friends. I was coming home a brand-new person. Loved up and loaded. I liked that version so much better, that a man like Olivier wanted to take care of me. And then, when the money came through weeks later and I started spoiling myself, no one batted an eyelid.

"Right, you'll pay me back," Taylor says.

"I promise I will. And I didn't really mean it about you having to leave the house right away. There's no rush."

"Um," she says softly. "But it makes sense, right? You and Olivier are married now. You want your own space. Maybe you'll have kids soon…"

Here's the thing: I don't actually have to play that game with her anymore. I'll be home tomorrow, without Olivier. She'll find out soon enough that we're over. But I'm not ready to explain to her that I'm getting divorced. I'm not ready to sound like a failure, like I couldn't keep up with this, either.

"Hmm, I'm more focused on enjoying the honeymoon right now," I say, lifting the cover over the plate to grab a french fry. It's salty and crisp.

"So why do you need my credit card details then? Can't Olivier help you?"

Nosy little cow. It was easier when Mom was alive. Taylor always felt stuck in the middle. I would ask and she would obey, no questions asked.

"He's out with friends. I don't want to disturb him." And then, realizing how that must sound, I add, "We decided to do this fun thing I read about online. Spending a night apart every now and then is meant to spice things up in a couple. So he's seeing his Parisian friends and I'm having a decadent night in: expensive wine, room service, and Olivier ran me the bubbliest bath you've ever seen."

She doesn't respond. Maybe I overdid it. I think the wine is starting to get to my head. I'm feeling woozy, like I can't quite focus.

"Taylor? I need that credit card number. Seriously, okay?"

"And Olivier is gone. All night?"

I let out an angry sigh. "Yes."

There's only silence for a while, and I'm about to ask again when she says, "I'll text it to you."

She hangs up before I can tell her to hurry up already.

I bring the tray of food over to the bathroom, along with my refilled glass of wine, and set everything down on the stool by the tub. *Come on, Taylor!* When she doesn't text right away, I try to call her again, but she doesn't pick up. And she doesn't answer the text I send her, either.

I'm feeling sweaty now, my heart pumping. It's been a rough day. The bath is starting to cool down, so I turn on the hot water tap as I take my clothes off. Pulling my dress up overhead is a struggle—my arms are cramping. Even my screen looks blurry. Stepping into the tub, I knock the tray of food, and the metal dome falls to the floor with a loud thump. The fries go everywhere and the burger lands by the toilet. Great. My mouth feels pasty; I'm not sure I could eat anyway.

The water soothes me instantly. As I sink in deeper, everything starts to feel good and right. I pour in more of the bath salts and watch as the lavender flakes dissolve over my legs.

Still no text from Taylor. Flicking over to the Instagram app, I hit Record, making sure to capture everything.

Self-care night! I caption the Story. How about this cloud of happiness!?

Taylor better be watching. But of course she is. That's why she sounded funny on the phone. She can't stand it. I picture her at home, in the dark and dreary room she hardly leaves when she's not working.

Alone.

Lonely.

So very lonely.

She hasn't had a boyfriend since that guy who took her away somewhere up north when she was twenty-six. Over a year later, she heard Mom was sick and came home, and it was like she'd shrunk even further, her head almost always bowed down. As far as I know, there hasn't been anyone else since. Poor Taylor. No one ever wanted her.

I rest my head on the edge of the tub. All I can think is that I have everything. *Everything.* Especially everything she'll never have.

CHAPTER 18

Olivier

ONE MONTH BEFORE THE HONEYMOON

For the next few days I thought of nothing else but Reese's slim waist, the mole at the top of her chest, the raw softness of her voice. My mind ping-ponged endlessly. We could never do this. We couldn't *not* do this. Every time I tried to push that night out of my thoughts, Reese came back with a vengeance. I swore I smelled her perfume everywhere I went.

When I walked into the bar again the following Monday, her face brightened with the warmest, most stunned smile. It disappeared just as quickly, but I saw it. I saw it.

"What are you doing here?" she said, wiping down the counter.

I took a seat on the far edge, away from a group of three men. "You must know," I said, making sure they weren't paying me attention.

"People will talk," she said, casting glances around.

"Tell me to leave you alone," I whispered. "Tell me to never come near you again. Is that what you want?"

She stared deep inside me.

"Is that what you want?" I said again with much more conviction than I felt. Slowly, I got up and watched as her throat tightened. "I'll do whatever you say. Do you want me to go?"

She shook her head ever so slightly and then, speaking so low I wasn't sure I was hearing it right, she said, "I close up at one. My car is parked two streets back. Don't show your face in here again."

I did as told, heading out into the cool spring night. A few blocks away, I stumbled into another bar and waited for her. When time came, I found the old Chevy easily; the street was empty. For the next few minutes, I paced back and forth on the sidewalk. If I kept my body moving, my mind might leave me alone.

Then she was there. Immediately, I pulled her to me and kissed her. It felt like we were a couple going home from a night out but with the thrill of the first time. Of the unknown.

"Is this okay?" I whispered, scared to the bones that she was going to say no. She nodded. I kissed her again. It was even better than the first time, maybe because I'd been so unsure it would happen once more. A few minutes later, we got into the back of her car, T-shirts flying over heads, limbs banging into windows, knees digging into the fake leather seats. I had a condom in my wallet and took my time retrieving it, giving her plenty of opportunities to say, *Stop. Wait. No. We can't. This is all wrong.*

She grabbed it from me and ripped the packaging open.

Afterward, I held her in my arms and breathed in her soft neck as I lulled her, keeping her as close as I physically could.

"I don't want to leave you," I said after a long while.

My left arm was numb from the uncomfortable position, and it was late enough that Cassie might wonder where the hell I was. I had to go home. I couldn't go home. Not yet.

"But you will," Reese said.

I didn't respond. Couldn't lie to her. Couldn't tell her the truth, either.

We met again and again and again, often at roadside motels neither of us could afford. When I was with her, I didn't care about anything else. I held her tight, every part of our naked bodies touching, our skin in permanent contact, sharing our most intimate thoughts into the early morning. In those moments I felt truly at peace, like I never had before.

Of course, we could have gotten caught. We probably almost did, several times, but Cassie wasn't even that much of a problem. The money arrived, *finally*, and she was constantly out shopping or drinking with her friends. Sometimes they'd drop her home only a few minutes after I'd left Reese. I probably still smelled of her. How reckless we were.

I was still technically looking for a job in the area, but my focus quickly turned to being with Reese whenever she wasn't working. I worked on the inn, taking the rusty bike to the closest hardware store to get tools and supplies, which Cassie begrudgingly paid for. I fixed squeaky doors, ripped up the wallpaper, and battled with a leaky faucet until I conquered it. I had plenty of free time and YouTube taught me new skills I didn't want to learn every day. At first it was the perfect cover: it gave me something to do, something that would please Cassie, with all the flexibility to fit into Reese's life. Soon, I started thinking further: the new and improved inn could be good for me. It was a new purpose, a potential new career. Something worthwhile to fill my time for the next two years.

I also worked on the next steps of my green card application for the immigration lawyer, filling out documents, answering questions about my parents' birth places and the addresses of my previous employers. When Erica Min asked about whether we'd set a wedding date, I replied with a vague *Working on it!*

Life was good, considering. I daydreamed of the next moment when I could hold Reese in my arms, and everything else faded into the background.

The words came out about six weeks after that first night. "I think I'm falling in love with you."

Reese was putting her underwear back on and swung around, her eyes shot wide open, like she'd never heard that before. And then it hit me: she'd never heard that before. She'd mentioned a guy she'd dated for a while, a toxic relationship in which she got attached too soon. Since then she'd stuck to one-night stands, sometimes with guys she picked up at the bar, but never locals. She didn't like the gossip.

"Reese," I said, reaching for her waist. "I'm in love with you."

She flicked my hand off and started to pull on her jeans. "No, you're not."

Her voice was cold, her body stiff all of a sudden. I had sensed the darkness within her before, had guessed the deep wounds that kept her at that dirty, smelly bar when she was clearly smart, with so much potential. In that moment it felt like I'd barely scratched the surface—that there was a lot more pain she was grappling with. It made me want to rub her hair and tell her that everything would be okay. I was there now and I wouldn't let anyone hurt her.

"I'm dead serious," I said. "I've been thinking it for a while, but I was scared to admit it out loud. I love you. Please, look at me." She did. "I love you."

She breathed deeply, in and out. In and out.

"Would you ever come to the city with me?" I continued. "There's nothing keeping you here. Maybe you just need a fresh start. I know you'd love it there."

"And Cassie?" Reese said.

She didn't wait for my answer and went back to getting dressed, clasping her bra with swift moves before adjusting the straps on each shoulder.

I swallowed hard. It's not like I forgot, exactly. I just didn't want to have to think about her. Of course I wouldn't be going back to the city anytime soon. "I don't want to be with Cassie. I never did."

Reese's head whipped around with surprise again. For a split second, the immigration lawyer's face filled my mind. I could answer all the questions she asked, and I was still completely screwed.

"But you're still with her," Reese said.

It wasn't a question. We'd both gone into this with our eyes wide open and the situation hadn't changed. I was with Cassie. An old family friend of the Quinns, Madeline Richardson, had put in a word for me with an art gallery owner two towns over who might need a part-time manager, though it wouldn't be until the fall. The inn was looking a little better every day. My life could fall into place, if I let it.

Reese retrieved her shoes from the other side of the room. She was about to slip out of here, and I couldn't let her leave. She had to know my feelings were real, but the only way to do that was to give her the truth. The scary one.

I shuffled over to sit on the edge of the bed and took a deep breath. "Cassie and I aren't actually dating. I'm not her boyfriend, I just...*have* to be with her. Fuck, it's so much more complicated than that." I buried my head in my hands, dread filling my lungs. "Cassie and I, we're married."

Reese jerked back, her eyes bulging. She looked like she'd been shot in the heart.

"You're married?" Her tone was flat. Resigned.

"I can explain."

"Since when?"

"We did it at City Hall, in the city, before we came back here."

I worried Reese would storm out then, but she stood there, frozen.

So I kept talking, starting from the beginning: losing my job, my visa, booking my flight back to Paris, and feeling so depressed about it all. I spared no details about meeting Cassie, how aloof she'd been, how easily convinced at the same time. How I thought, right until the moment the civil servant asked the questions, that she was going to change her mind. How weird it felt when she didn't. We were married. In it together now.

And then, the most important thing of all, the fact that I'd been mulling over for weeks now: "I would give anything to have met you first."

Reese chortled, then shook her head, like she wanted to push away that part of the story, to make sure it never touched her. "You're married," she said in a whisper.

I got up and started to walk toward her, but she recoiled in such an obvious manner, her hands raising in front of her chest in protection, that I stopped. "And I can't divorce her. I have to be with her for two whole years and pretend to be happily married until it all goes through. I can't do anything until then."

Even as I said it, I no longer believed these things would happen. Two years was a long time to feel hopelessly miserable, even before I fell for Reese. The truth was, I *could* divorce Cassie and marry another American citizen, if Reese would have me. But doing so before my permanent green card was granted would be like throwing my application into the trash. I'd have to start all over, losing months in the process. Worse: it would raise a huge red flag with the Department of Homeland Security. Marrying one woman you barely know is one thing, but marrying two, back to back? It would never work. And then, of course, there was the money. Cassie was already pissing it away. These two million dollars were wasted on her.

"If I could choose," I added, "I'd choose you. I want to be with you."

Reese's jaw went slack. "I'm so freaking stupid. Every time! Every *single* time. I don't know what I was thinking. Don't ever come near me again."

She stormed past me, fury seeping out of every pore. For a long time I stood there, staring at a brown patch of humidity where the wall met the ceiling. The situation with Cassie was already headed for a complete disaster. Soon I wouldn't just lose Reese, but everything.

I didn't know if there was a way to fix this, to be with Reese and get rid of Cassie. To get rid of Cassie and keep her money. To have everything I could possibly want: Reese and the money and the green card and the freedom to go back to the city and start all over again.

But if there was a way, I would find it. And if I did, then that's exactly what I would do.

CHAPTER 19

Taylor

NOW

I want to throw my phone against the wall and watch it break in a million pieces. What stops me is that if I did, I could no longer watch Cassie drink her expensive wine in her expensive bubble bath inside her expensive fucking Parisian suite.

There are many things I hate about myself, but I despise this one the most: Cassie has that power over me. Most of my life I've stood by as she gets *everything*. Her mother's love until the very end, the kind I would have killed for, even if it wasn't perfect. A roof over her head. A safe space, always. The freedom to make mistakes, as many as she felt like making. A perfectly nice boyfriend, Darren, who always ran back to her no matter how she treated him. And now her dreamy French husband, her father's inheritance, so much money that she'll keep wasting away on stupid things.

But it's never enough. She always wants something else, something more.

I pour myself a glass of Bordeaux—you paid for that one, too, Cassie!— and hit Play on her videos. By now I've seen every corner of that suite a dozen times over: the sprawling bed with the sharp edges of the frame. That balcony just high enough that one would probably not survive a tumble over the edge. The depth of that freestanding bathtub, like it's straight out of Versailles. The marble tiles of the bathroom floor, so shiny they must be slippery, especially if one was to drink too much wine.

Stop it, you're hurting yourself.

But what if...

The truth is I never loved Cassie. I tried. Not because she was my sister, but because I felt like I had to. I owed it to Rae.

I wanted a family, not just the two of us, a real family, Rae told me two weeks before her death. *I'm going to have to hope you girls become closer when I'm gone.* She'd never had much of a family herself, and after her husband left, she couldn't accept that it was going to be just Cassie and her. Even if she'd met somebody else one day, it probably would have been too late to have another child. How convenient that she happened to hear about a girl in need—me—to fill the void. I never quite got the full story, but Rae and my mother were distant relatives. They'd met maybe once before. Yet, that was enough for Child Services to contact Rae and ask if she might find it in her heart to take in a little girl who'd lost everything.

But Cassie and I never became sisters. I was her sidekick, her punching bag, her emotional support animal, a human pet. I still remember the day I came to live with them on a freezing November morning. A week later, I joined the local school midterm. Cassie wasted no time in telling the entire class what happened to me. *This is Taylor! Wanna know why she's here?* That story never left me. From then on, I was always Poor Taylor.

Sometimes I wish they never found me in that car. Deep down I always felt that my mother would have come back for me. She would have remembered, eventually. She would have saved me before it was too late. It was a mistake. An honest mistake.

But of course I could never know for sure. What if she really had left me to die? From day one, Cassie sensed the insecurities within me. The doubt. Did my mother love me, despite what happened? Did anyone? What about my father, did he want me? Would he ever rescue me? Cassie found every little wound and picked at the scabs. Scratched them until they got infected all over again. If someone couldn't immediately remember my name, or if Rae forgot to sign a slip from the school, Cassie would run around the house and scream, *Taylor is so forgettable!* I never said anything. Even as a child I understood it was the price I had to pay for safety. For having survived.

Back on my screen, Cassie is soaking deep in the bath now, a nearly empty glass of wine perched on a marble shelf next to her. She looks glowing, her eyes shiny, somewhat empty. She's staring at the camera. At me. I take a sip of my own wine and stare back.

The fog clears, at last, and I accept what I must have known from the start. She's doing this for me. *To* me. For a while I told myself it was about Darren. Cassie was so mad when he dumped her in the spring. Breaking up had been her thing; *she'd* called the shots all these times. And then her father had the nerve to die right after that. When she turned up with Olivier, when he stuck around despite looking miserable, when she stayed with him even though they spent less and less time together, I tried so hard not to take the bait. Even when she bragged about him being French, even when she joked, repeatedly, about how she couldn't wait to go visit his family in Paris. I took deep breaths and buried myself deeper into work, taking any new hospitality job I could find, staying out of the house as much as possible.

Eventually she'd move on. She always did. It was the same with all her boyfriends. When Darren wasn't in the picture, there was always a new one, and they knew instantly that I didn't matter. *You have a sister?* they'd say when they came to pick her up and saw me lurking in the shadows. Cassie would shrug like, *Oh, her?* Then she'd check that her mother wasn't listening before adding, *She's not my sister.*

On the rare occasions when a guy actually paid me attention, Cassie's radar would light up. She'd make sure he knew what happened when I was a child. She'd bump into him everywhere, all suggestive smiles and low-cut tops.

My first kiss happened junior year with Bobby—a sweet but awkward boy with thin lips and bad acne. We went out for three blissful weeks. Suddenly, he started avoiding me at school, ignored my text messages, and didn't answer the door when I went to his house, even though I could see him through the window. It had to be Cassie's doing, though I never found out for sure.

I didn't lose my virginity until I was twenty, to a coworker at the restaurant where I waited tables who only spoke to me when no one else was watching. I wish I could say I was proud enough to stop seeing him, but soul-crushing loneliness makes you do strange things.

My first—and only—real relationship started a few years later with Jayden, a guest at the inn who was passing through, from Buffalo. He was a writer, staying with us until the beginning of a three-month creative retreat in the Catskills. He had wavy hair and wore only plaid shirts. Cassie was with Darren then, sleeping at his place most nights. She didn't notice Jayden's interest in me until it was too late to sway him.

I'd visit him at his retreat any chance I got—I'm not sure he got much work done, and the other writers looked at us with a mix of disdain and envy—and I counted down the days to the end, tears streaming down my cheeks. But right before he was due to leave, Jayden asked if I'd ever thought of getting out of town. I could come back with him to Buffalo, see something different. A blink and I was driving off with him and the two duffel bags I'd packed in a hurry.

I got a job at a bar, rented a room above it, and spent my free time waiting for Jayden to call, which, after the first month, happened less and less frequently. He was always writing, always working, and yet always asking to borrow money.

Over a year, that's how long it took me to discover he had another girlfriend, and that she had a toddler, his child. One might think that would have been enough for me to leave. It wasn't. I continued to pretend, to accept any scraps of attention he was willing to give. I'd gotten out of that house, away from that family where I never belonged. I had my own life. I called Rae most weeks but I must have spoken to Cassie all of three times while I was there.

And then, one day, it was Rae who reached out. She'd been diagnosed with lung cancer. The doctors estimated she had months to live, a couple of years at most. She could use a little help at home, both of her daughters by her side. It was my choice to go back, but it didn't feel like one.

I pour myself another glass of wine and put my phone facedown on the tiny nightstand. Taking a long sip, I try to focus on the warm notes, the fruitiness. I can still walk away. I can be here, but not with Cassie, not *because* of her. I can put that life behind me and look forward.

Except I can't.

I've lost everything. *Everything.* Family and love and even my home. I shouldn't have gotten on that plane. I shouldn't have started following them. Shouldn't have stolen her bag.

But there was nothing to stop me. *No one.*

So I grab my bag and retrieve Cassie's wallet. I'd give a million dollars to see the look on her face if she found out that I'm the one who stole it, that *I* have the credit card she so urgently needs. Of course I don't have a million dollars; Cassie does. But, emptying the contents on my bed, I discover something else: her hotel key card, in a paper sleeve marked with the room number. Maybe it doesn't work anymore. Maybe she reported it as stolen and the front desk issued her a new card, deactivating this one in the process.

Or maybe it does.

And maybe I'm done watching her live this grand life of hers through a screen.

Maybe I'm done with Cassie altogether.

I gulp down the rest of my wine and put the card in the back pocket of my jeans. After slipping into my ballet flats, I pull my hair into a low ponytail and cover it with my cap.

I worry about her, Rae whispered to me before she died. *I don't know how she will look after herself. Promise me you'll be there for her.* Rae had tried to squeeze my hand but she had no strength, no more fight in her. *She is your family. She has been for most of your life. Promise me you'll look after Cassie.*

The pleading tone in her barely there voice had tugged every which way at my heartstrings. I was haunted by this moment for a long time. This woman had brought me into her world, but now she acted like I was merely on the edge of it. There was no varnish on her feelings anymore; In death she knew who her true daughter was.

Rae was so weak then, her mind unable to focus for more than a few minutes. So I don't think she realized this: I didn't actually promise. I never uttered the words. Deep down I always knew I'd have to put Cassie behind me, somehow, someday.

I think that moment has come.

CHAPTER 20

Cassie

NOW

The bloodred liquid swooshes from side to side and my mind scrambles. The glass is on a shelf; the wine inside shouldn't be moving. What's left of it anyway. I'd like to finish it but that means reaching for the glass. I'm so very tired. Once again, my eyes close. I have to force them open.

I can't.

Maybe I drank too much. I try to turn my head to check the bottle, which is behind me on the floor, but my back slips against the cast-iron surface, making water splash everywhere. *Splash, splash, splash.* It's loud. So dramatic. Like I'm in a barge in the middle of the big great sea.

Where am I?

There's too much water in here.

Or not enough.

I reach over to the tap and turn on the hot water again. It feels nice as it flows over my stomach.

Today was weird. Did I make it up? No, something is wrong. Very, very, very wrong. I try to replay the events of the last few hours, but my mind can't latch onto anything for long. There was Olivier saying that he loves me and then leaving me alone all night. My wallet, *poof*, gone, when I needed it most. Some kind of weird-ass magic at the worst possible time.

Now I'm slipping, slipping, slipping, the back of my skull hitting rock bottom.

I have to push.

Get out.

Breathe.

I want to breathe.

My phone. Where is it.

This is all Darren's fault. If he hadn't dumped me, I would never have met Olivier. Would never have fallen for his sweet, devoted act. *I love you, Cassie.* Asshole! He was saying all the right things, did anything I wanted, made me believe I was special. And I let him because if I came back from the city with someone like him, I thought Darren would get it. I was a catch. If I could get a handsome, successful city guy, then I'd be good enough for him. I *had* been good enough for him before he started to get all serious on me, and I would be good enough again. I'd dangle Olivier in front of his face for a while, and he'd come crawling back.

But then…he didn't text me. Didn't really react when we "bumped" into each other around town or at a friend's place. It took me a while to under-stand what was going on: Darren didn't think things were serious between Olivier and me. The guy talked about the city all the goddamn time. The girls kept asking if I was going to go back to the city soon. Clearly Olivier was, wasn't he? Would I go with him? Was I going to abandon them all for the big city? I tried to look at him the way they saw him—with his accent and his pink shirts and his goatee. Not the kind of guy who was going to stick around our small town. To them all, Olivier was just a new fling. There was also the little problem of possibly going to jail if the government found out that our marriage was fake. For all these reasons, I had to go through with the "engagement." I had to show them all.

Shivers course through me. I reach over to turn off the hot water, but my arm doesn't go so far. My head lulls from side to side as water keeps streaming over me. I'll be asleep soon.

This is all my father's fault. When I learned he died, my first thought was, *good. Justice, at last.* It made no difference to me anyway. He didn't even bother coming to Mom's funeral, just sent a bunch of bland white flowers and called it a day. When I was younger, on the rare occasions he called, Mom hovered over me, and I didn't know what to say to him anyway. The most I got from him were birthday and Christmas cards. I'd rip up the envelope, hungry for the money. Would it be fifty dollars or seventy? Maybe a hundred? He switched it up all the time. Even though it pained me not to spend it right away, I'd leave it on the coffee table for a few days to make sure Taylor would see it. Would want it.

When Mom first told me I was getting a sister, I didn't hate the idea. Growing up in that house, everything felt stuffy. And I don't just mean the old furniture and the stale air. Mom didn't talk much. Didn't live much. I know she was depressed, but what about me? Then Taylor came and she was so fucking perfect. Clean and tidy and polite. *Yes, Rae. Of course, Rae. Anything you want.* She did her homework, put away her dolls—*my* dolls—set the table even before anyone asked her. *You're such a darling! Call me Mom.*

It's that wine Olivier ordered before he left. He opened it for me and even poured me a glass. Said it had to breathe, whatever that means. Such a gentleman. By the time I got into the bath, my lips were painted burgundy. With the fog in the mirror, it looked like I'd sliced my mouth open.

This is all Taylor's fault. When Mom got sick, Taylor acted like the responsible one, again. Came home from wherever she'd gone and took charge of everything. But making smoothies, bringing warm blankets, and calling people to invite them for the wake don't make you a daughter. You can cry all the tears in your basic little black dress. Still not your mother. And then, a few months later, *I'll come to the city with you,* she said. *You shouldn't be alone at your father's funeral.* I laughed. *I* wasn't alone. Not like her.

I read the story online a few years after she came to live with us. Until then, Mom had only told me the basics: Taylor's mom wasn't doing well and had done a bad thing. She'd forgotten about her daughter, just that one time, but because of that she had to go away to a bad place for a while. Taylor didn't have any other family, so she'd come to live with us. The real story was this: Taylor's mom was an addict. The news outlet didn't say it like that, but it's true. Booze or drugs or pills, I'm not sure.

It was the middle of summer, one of these hundred-degree days when you feel like you can't even think straight. An older couple was walking down the street and saw a little girl—she was five at the time—inside a car. It was parked, and there was no driver in sight. No parent. The windows were closed. It was so hot! The girl was pressing her sweaty palms against the window. She had red chubby cheeks, tears streaming down her face, and she was panting, sticking her tongue out like a dog. (I'm adding this last part, I can just picture her.) She wasn't even calling for help. She was so hopeless, used to being left behind. That's what people assumed later. Her mother said she'd only been gone forty-five minutes. No, twenty. Maybe it was an hour. Or two? She went upstairs to their apartment to drop off the groceries and then…she had no fucking clue. Anyway, she went to prison and left her burden behind for Mom and me to deal with. When she got out years later, she never even bothered to come back for her daughter.

At least that's what Taylor believes. She turned up at the house once— her mom, I mean. I was about eleven, home "sick" from school. Mom saw her through the window and bolted out the door, yelling at me to stay in my room. I didn't know who it was at the time—I only put two and two together later on—but of course I did my best to eavesdrop.

Not now, I heard that day. *She's doing well. We all are. Maybe when you're clean.*

But I am clean! the woman screamed. *Let me see her. I've waited so long to see her again.*

I'll think about it. Mom sounded terrified. Someone was coming after her favorite daughter! *But not now. Not now. Please, please, please.*

Eventually, the woman drove away.

My head won't stay up right. It's rolling against the edge of the tub. Left to right and right to left, and fuck I'm going to throw up.

I was supposed to go home. I have to go home.

The wine. It's the wine.

Once again I push on my arms to lift myself up, but I slip back further down.

Water swallows me whole.

My heart is pounding, my eyelids flicking on and off. It's like there's a loose wire behind the switch.

And I'm thirsty, so thirsty.

I should never have married Olivier.

She made me do it.

I need to leave.

Let me go.

Please.

I can't hold on anymore.

CHAPTER 21

Olivier

FIVE DAYS BEFORE THE HONEYMOON

lasted two weeks. Two weeks during which I didn't hold Reese in my arms, didn't feel her soft skin against mine. Two weeks during which I thought about her every minute of every day, picturing our future together. We'd be happy in the city. Reese had this fire inside her, and I knew she'd do great things with her life if she gave it a real shot.

Cassie, on the other end, was lazy and entitled. She'd also mostly given up on the pretense we were a couple. One time, a few weeks back, we'd been standing outside when a neighbor walked past with his dogs. Cassie had started introducing me, only to blank on my name. Her freaking boyfriend's name! *This is, um…Oliver,* she'd said. Everyone I'd met here called me that, the English version. Cassie never corrected them and I'd picked other battles. But I *hated* it. It wasn't that hard to call people by their names.

That day on the street, the man, Paul—see, not that hard!—had been full of questions. Where was I from in France? How long had I been in the States? Cassie had stared at me as I answered as calmly as possible. It was like she didn't know the answers, or didn't care enough to pretend she might be interested in this conversation. I'd given up on the idea we might announce an engagement and have that wedding she'd supposedly wanted.

I had never felt any kind of violent urge toward anyone, but that day, I'd wanted to slap Cassie. Because *I'd* done my homework after our meeting with the lawyer. I'd learned her birthday (May 7), her astrological sign (Gemini), her favorite food (burgers, how sophisticated) and what fragrance she wore (something chemically vanilla that made me feel nauseated, stupidly called Eau de Fantasy). I bought her flowers. I cooked meals—not great ones, but I did. I *tried.*

And every day, I woke up with the head-throbbing fear of ICE stomping on the door. Cassie *was* going to destroy my future. I was certain of it. My only remaining option: ruin hers first.

And so, after two weeks of going crazy with want, I went to see Reese.

"I just want to talk," I said as soon as I was certain no one could hear me. "Even if nothing I can say will change your mind. One more chance, and then I'll leave you alone. I promise."

She looked like me: tired, withdrawn, beaten. At least that's what I needed to believe, that she loved me as much as I did. Loved me more than anyone else. Because otherwise, after I'd uttered the idea I'd come to share with her, I wouldn't just be heartbroken. I wouldn't just be poor. I wouldn't just be deported. I'd be going to prison for a very long time.

"Not now," she said. "Tomorrow afternoon I'm going to Kingston to run some errands..." She trailed off, barely looked at me.

I filled in the dots in my mind. It was one of the bigger towns in the area, and we weren't likely to run into people there. We'd be safe.

The wait was excruciating, but it did give me time to do more research, to explore every potential scenario. There were so many ways what I had in mind could go horribly wrong, but if it worked, oh, if it worked...freedom would never taste so good.

The next afternoon, I'd barely sat down in Reese's car and closed the door before she was speeding ahead without even a glance at me.

"I love you," I said, the words tumbling out of my mouth. "You have to believe me. I love you. I want to be with you. If I'd met you first—"

"You married her," Reese said flatly.

"What if I wasn't married to her anymore?"

Her eyes remained focused ahead, but I took note of the twitch her face made.

She let a few seconds pass and cleared her throat. "You told me you had to stay with her for two years, that you couldn't get divorced before then. I'm not waiting for something that will *never* happen."

I'd expected that. Of course Cassie and I would get divorced. I knew that. But as long as I stayed with her, on paper anyway, Reese wouldn't trust me. She wouldn't believe I loved her more, wanted to be with her more. She'd been let down by guys too many times. It was one thing when she thought we were simply dating, that I was Cassie's guy du jour. But Reese wasn't going to be the longtime mistress in this scenario, and I couldn't blame her.

"Cassie and I won't stay married for the next two years," I said.

We were leaving town now and I felt a little better, noticing the fields on either side, the emptiness. I couldn't be too careful. Reese darted a glance at me. She was intrigued. She wouldn't have agreed to meet if she wasn't.

"We're going to fail our interview with immigration," I continued. "It'll never work. I'm sure of that now. So that leaves me with two options. I could wait until that happens, risk having the Department of Homeland Security investigate our case further before deciding that I'm a fraud and kick me out of the country…"

I paused and watched her hands grip the steering wheel, the way she held her breath.

"What's the other option?" she said, after I let the silence settle between us.

Our eyes met for a split second. Hers were full of rage, of confusion. Despair, also. Maybe. Hopefully.

It gave me enough courage to continue. "I researched all the immigration laws, the rules, the loopholes. I have to be married to an American citizen for at least two years to get a permanent green card so I can live and work here indefinitely. There's no way around it. If I divorce her now, I have to leave. Even if I married someone else, I'd have to start all over again. That would take time and a lot of money. It would also look suspicious as hell."

Again I waited, fear pooling at the bottom of my stomach.

"So there's no other option," Reese said.

"I'd marry you in a heartbeat," I said, suddenly realizing how presumptuous it was of me to assume she'd want that. Reese had been on her own one way or another for a long time. She didn't need anyone. Still, I chose to believe she wanted me.

"This is all about you wanting to stay here," she said. "In the States, I mean. You could go back to France…" She trailed off again but not before she glanced at me.

"I can't. I need to stay away. I don't even want to step foot in the country, not until I've sorted myself out."

There was another reason: I couldn't stop thinking about the money, which steadily seeped through Cassie's hands. I saw the shopping bags, the bottles of liquor, the receipts for expensive meals with her friends, the new iPhone. She was talking about buying a new car. She gave me cash every time I said I needed to get supplies for the inn, and never asked for the change. If we divorced, I'd get nothing.

I swallowed hard. I had *one* card to play and the time had come. "There *is* another option. Everything would be different if I were a widower."

Reese slammed her foot on the brake and the car shrieked to a stop, jerking both of us forward, then backward. I felt the wind knocked out of me. There was no one in front of us. No cars, no animals, no reason why she did that. We were just stopped in the middle of an empty road.

Reese turned to me, her eyes wild with shock. "*If* you were a widower?"

I couldn't breathe anymore but I had to get the words out. "If Cassie was…not alive, I could keep going with my application as I am now. With Cassie out of the way, I could make our 'love story' real. I read the fine print.

Immigration laws have a provision for foreign spouses of American citizens after they die. The government doesn't kick them out of the country just because their loved one passed away before the green card process is complete."

Reese's breathing grew ragged, but she said nothing.

So I finished my thought, nailed my own coffin shut. "I'd still be living here legally as her widower. I'd be in mourning. Devastated. I'd stay in the house. We…you and I, we could do everything we've been doing, just as quietly. And then—"

Reese wasn't throwing me out the car. She wasn't screaming that I was a psychopath who was proposing murder. In this bizarre and twisted world I now found myself in, there was hope. But also, she wasn't starting the car again. We were still stuck in the middle, both literally and figuratively.

"We could date openly, not right away, but in a few months. People grieve in strange ways. Things happen. It wouldn't be so hard to accept that you and I might fall in love."

A loud honk resonated behind us, and we both turned around to see a huge truck all the way back in the distance.

Reese put her hand on the ignition, but still didn't drive off. "I can't tell if you're being serious right now. You're talking about—" She gulped.

I spoke quickly. "I'm talking about being with you. After everything has blown over, we could get married. We'd be happy. Tell me you don't think you and I could be happy together."

The honks got louder but Reese was frozen in space.

"I love you, Reese. If you want to be with me, I could…"

She didn't blink. "You could…"

I spoke faster now, the words tumbling out. "The stairs in the house, they're uneven. Someone could easily trip and fall all the way to the bottom. I researched it; people die in the stupidest ways. Gas leaks. Cars break. Accidents happen."

Reese inhaled and exhaled deeply. The truck got even closer. For a moment I thought this might be it for us. *We* might die right here and now. "We could be together. You and me, no one else. I love you and you're not saying no. You're not telling me to stop."

Her breathing grew even heavier. "I love you, too. I freaking love you, too."

And then she started the car.

Hours later, when I got back to the inn, a strange sight awaited me: my wife, smiling at me from the porch. It was still steamy outside and my T-shirt stuck to my skin. I smelled of sweat and adrenaline, and felt the urgent need to take a shower.

"Here you are," Cassie quipped. She sounded like honey, the kind of tone I'd heard from her in the first few days in the city, but not since. "I've been waiting for you. Well, *we* have."

I'd left Reese a while ago, when she'd dropped me off after our little trip. Since then I'd been wandering the streets, making plans in my head. We hadn't discussed details. We'd talked very little, in fact. What else was there to say? I wasn't a murderer. It wouldn't *be* a murder. Reese loved me and she hadn't told me *not* to do it; that's all I needed to know.

Cassie grabbed my hand and led me inside, to the living room. My spine tingled as I checked myself in the stained mirror in the entrance. Something was off.

She perked up as she spoke, "I was just telling Taylor!"

There she was, sitting on the old sofa, with its saggy cushions and musty smell. I kept looking around, certain that someone else was there, too. I'd lived with the two women for almost three months and had barely heard them say two consecutive sentences to each other. On the rare occasions the three of us had dinner together, I made most of the conversation. I'd never felt more out of place than in those moments, watching the seconds tick by on the old wooden clock on the wall.

But no, there was no one else here. Cassie smiled at me some more before wrapping an arm around my waist. Then, she raised her cheek, waiting for a kiss. I obliged. I was still at her mercy. For a little while longer anyway.

Cassie grinned like a little girl. "You don't mind that I told Taylor before you got home, do you?"

"What did you tell her?" I said, keeping my tone cheerful. What the fuck was going on?

Cassie squealed and raised her left hand, her fingers spread wide. That's when I saw it, the blinding diamond on her ring finger. It was much larger and sparklier than the one I'd bought at the pawnshop in the city. "About our engagement last night!"

What? Cassie was unpredictable at the best of times but this was on another level. Although…this *had* been our original plan, if you can call it that: the City Hall wedding so I could get my green card application started, and then the bigger wedding with Cassie's friends. Meanwhile, her sister's face was impassive. She stared inside her glass of water, her feelings only betrayed by her white knuckles.

Cassie turned back to her. "I'm so excited. I know it's soon, but you're *such* a romantic!"

That last part was directed at me as she squeezed both my hands with excitement. She knew about the affair; that's what was happening here. She'd planned some kind of drawn-out punishment to make me pay for my mistakes. But no, that wasn't Cassie's style. She was impulsive, vengeful. If she knew, she'd lay it all out there and then. What else could it be?

She pulled me closer, practically pushing me down in one of the armchairs. I was barely settled in when she fell into my lap and wrapped one arm around my neck. And then it hit me. She was giving me exactly what I needed. We were "engaged" at last. We'd have the wedding she wanted. It was better this way. To carry out my plan, I needed us happy and in love, and she was handing that to me on a silver platter. Whatever she was doing, I could use it to my advantage.

I smiled openly. "I'm so happy you said yes!"

Cassie frowned, but just for a split second. I glanced at the diamond again. How much would that thing have cost? She had to be stopped.

I turned to her sister, avoiding Cassie's gaze. "And I'm excited we're doing it so soon. I know some people might think it's a little rushed, but this is exactly what we want. What we *need*." Then I looked back at Cassie. "I can't wait to marry you this Saturday." My tone was firm, my stance undeniable.

Her face fell. I somewhat expected that. Cassie wasn't that good an actress, especially when she hadn't written the script. But it wasn't just her. The air in the room had changed and both women stared at me with eyes narrowed. I'd said something wrong. Fuck, what had I said?

Cassie chuckled sweetly. "Um, no, we're going to Paris on Saturday," she said, her eyes fixed on me. "We booked tickets, remember?" Then she turned to her sister with a huge, knowing smile.

What. The. Fuck. But then again, why was I surprised? Cassie had gone and bought herself an engagement ring without even telling me. I had no idea what else she was capable of, but it felt like she was going to keep outdoing me until I put a stop to it.

"Of course, I remember," I said, buying some time.

My mind was spinning. I had to think fast. I had to stay away from France until I saved enough money to pay my debt back. But when Cassie said she'd booked tickets, I believed her. She'd never let me argue with her in front of her sister. If she had decided we were suddenly engaged and going to Paris to celebrate, then I didn't see how I could get out of it. I pictured myself landing at Charles de Gaulle, the finance brigade waiting for me, loudly proclaiming the level of my tax evasion. But how would they know? If I moved back to France, they'd find out eventually. But if I only went for a few days, the risk was minimal. Cassie had set things in motion, but that didn't mean I had to follow exactly on her terms.

"We're going for our honeymoon," I added, like *she* was the silly one for not remembering. Cassie tilted her head, confused, but I was on a roll, the plan forming in my head as the words came out. "We get married on Saturday and then I'm whisking you away to Paris. Nothing is too good for you."

I leaned forward and kissed her. I had to. Couldn't take the risk that she would contradict me. There was an awkward silence. I mean, another one. For a moment I thought Cassie would tear it all down again. She'd ruin everything. But, eventually, she shrugged and turned to her sister.

"You'll help with the food, right? And preparing the house? I need to focus on getting my dress."

Her sister's jaw was clenched. "I—Sure."

Cassie clapped her hands. "It's going to be amazing! Gosh, there isn't much time to organize everything. Is it tacky to send wedding invitations via text?"

Neither of us responded so she answered her own question. "I'm sure it's fine. It'll feel intimate. Spontaneous." Then she turned to me. "You're booking the hotel, right, babe? Paris is always a good idea."

Not that this was the most important thing right now, but *babe*?

I couldn't get another word out. She'd gotten engaged all by herself. Had booked tickets to Paris leaving this weekend without consulting me. What else was she planning? Did I really think I could get rid of her?

"Babe?"

Cassie looked back to me, her bony ass digging into my thighs. There was a threat in her tone, I could hear it loud and clear. "Yes, I'm taking care of everything."

By the time I'd finished my sentence, Cassie was staring as her sister got up and quietly left the room.

Then, Cassie jumped off me. "Better send those invites!"

So that left me sitting there alone, wondering what game Cassie was playing, and how much I was going to lose. Again.

Or maybe, just maybe…this trip was a stroke of luck. The perfect opportunity, if only I could seize it. It wasn't much time. But maybe, just maybe, I wasn't going to lose anything at all.

CHAPTER 22

Taylor

NOW

The walk from my hotel to theirs takes less than fifteen minutes. It was one of the reasons I chose it: on the Right Bank, far away enough that there was no chance of running into the happy couple, but still within reach for when I needed to see them. To watch them. To be sure.

After dropping them off at the airport, I couldn't go home. I couldn't walk away while Cassie went on *my* trip to Paris. Couldn't accept that she was happy and in love, despite all the evidence to the contrary. Of course I could have watched everything unfold on my screen, but it wasn't enough. I wanted to be in Paris. I wanted the honeymoon, too. And to be honest, I wanted to hurt Cassie long before I got on that plane.

All my life she taunted me, did everything in her power to make me feel sorry for being alive. For surviving and coming to ruin her life. After our— well, *her*—mother died, we managed to tolerate each other, just barely.

I was stuck. Broke. Rae's death had cleaned me out. When Cassie's father died, I felt sorry for her. Truly, deeply. I understood her pain, more than she could ever know. I had no concrete idea of why my father hadn't been in my life, but I felt abandoned all the same, clinging to the idea that one day we would meet again. One day all would be explained. I didn't have any hope that her father's death would bring Cassie and me closer—I'd given up on that a long time ago—but I had to be there for her. Couldn't turn my back on her at such a hard time. But, as always, Cassie slammed the door in my face and threw away the key.

I walk briskly southward, keeping my head down and my breath in check. The shortest way to go is through the Louvre, and the irony of it all might break me. I haven't been there yet—one of the most famous places in the city—because Cassie hasn't. And I only do what Cassie wants.

Not anymore. Stepping through the gate on rue de Rivoli, I have to fight the urge to stop and stare in awe. The glass pyramid greets me on the other side, standing majestically in the middle of the square. It's almost 9:00 p.m. and still light out, with many people taking selfies in front of the structure, even though the museum itself is closed.

I move along, quickening my pace even more. Cassie is waiting for me; she just doesn't know it yet. Leaving the Louvre behind, I go through the Tuileries Gardens and only glance at the Eiffel Tower in the distance as I cross over Pont Royal to the Left Bank. What a dream walk for a warm summer evening. I read that there are security cameras everywhere in the city, but I have my cap and feminine clothes on, so unlike Good Taylor.

Slipping into their hotel is easy, the lobby swarming with guests and staff. From the pictures online and Cassie's videos, I know exactly where the elevators are. I need to walk through with confidence. Tonight, there's no stopping me.

A few people are waiting at the end of the corridor and I slow down to make sure they enter the next elevator before I get there. No one can see me. No one can remember me.

On the sixth floor, my heart drums inside my chest as I walk down the corridor, looking for the right room. Every muffled step on the thick carpet takes me further away from the exit, all the way to the end, adrenaline dripping through my veins faster and faster.

Cassie was right about one thing. Two of us were too many. It didn't matter how big that house was, or how many times Rae told us we should be glad to have each other. Three made a family; that's what she liked to say. But not in our case.

Music filters through the door as I retrieve the key card from my back pocket, a pop song that's been playing nonstop in the shops over here. The singer croons about how we can have everything: the gorgeous boys and the great jobs and all of the power. Some of us would kill for that.

The music is so loud it drowns out the buzzing sound from the door. When the light on the key pad turns green, my heart drops. Even after all I've done, I can't help but feel like this is the moment I'm crossing a line. There's no way back from here.

I step inside.

The room feels familiar and foreign at the same time. The sheets look even whiter and crisper in real life, the balcony seems smaller, and the view is so much sharper. In an hour or so, it'll be dark enough for the Eiffel Tower to sparkle into the night for a few minutes, as it does hourly. Maybe I'll take the scenic route home to watch it up close. I don't have a balcony to watch it from, but I'll still have myself.

The door to the bathroom is halfway open, enough for me to see Cassie's head wobble from side to side and to notice the empty bottle of wine on the floor. She hasn't posted in the last ten minutes; I checked while I was going up the elevator. She must be really drunk. One might even say she brought this on herself.

I stand in the doorframe, the music drowning my thoughts. My brain is a pile of mush, my fingers tingling with fear. At the same time, I can almost feel the weight lifting off my shoulders at the idea of Cassie being gone. Out of my life forever.

It takes me a few more seconds to notice she has stopped moving. In fact, I'm not sure if she was moving before. If she drank all that wine... But that alone wouldn't do it. What is going on?

Another step further and I'm inside the bathroom, about to reach the edge of the tub. That's when I sense a presence behind me, the warmth of a body, a woodsy fragrance. Before I can process anything, a hand clasps around my mouth while another one grabs around my waist sharply, encasing my arms. I'm too stunned to even scream. I, too, drank a lot of wine, and I'm slow to react.

Next, I'm being dragged out of the bathroom, along the bottom of the bed. The upbeat music covers every sound as I try to free my arms, kicking at his sides. Just when I think I'm about to set myself free, I trip and fall backward.

And then the room goes black.

CHAPTER 23

Cassie

NOW

I t's not bad down here.

Cold, but quiet.

Peaceful.

Water surrounds me, submerges me.

I'm melting away. Letting go.

My mind wanders, my thoughts float around.

I'm okay.

This is okay.

Just when it feels like I'm so far gone that I won't be coming back, I'm yanked up, my lungs painfully filling with air as my face breaks through the surface.

I want to resist. I need to fight. But my body won't let me. My arms can't move. I'm powerless. *This* is when I die, isn't it?

Shivers, so strong.

Water droplets flick off me and onto the tiled floor as I'm being pulled out of the bath, out of the room. Onto a soft surface. The bed?

I'm scared but paralyzed.

My vision is blurry.

It's a man.

Darren!

No, Darren isn't here. But I'm too scared to think about who else it might be.

"You'll be fine." It's his voice. At least I think it is.

He sounds rattled, out of breath.

What is he going to do to me? What has he already done?

I have to go.

A towel is wrapped around me. A robe? It's thick and fluffy. I sink into it.

"I heard…" I start but can't form a full sentence.

I don't even know what I'm trying to say.

Some commotion? Someone here.

I was in the tub.

Tired.

So tired I couldn't keep my eyes open.

"Everything is fine, okay? *Nothing* happened."

Something happened.

I need to find my phone. Call Darren. The only one I can trust.

Help. Help. Help.

"You don't need help!" He's screaming.

Was I speaking out loud?

"Don't—" my voice is a whisper. "Let me—"

"You're dreaming. You're having a nightmare."

I'm stuck in a cotton ball. Muffled and comfortable, but unable to move.

"I'm awake."

This time I know I said it out loud.

One hand reaches behind my head, while another one slips inside my mouth. Two fingers press down the back of my tongue and then I'm rolling over, retching.

I throw up over the comforter, the disgusting smell only bringing up more, my hair caught in the slobbery mess.

I glance toward the door. It's so far away. He looms over me.

"Stop moving! You need to rest, Cassie." There's an edge to his voice. So sharp it might cut me.

"It's not a dream," I say, but I don't know if he hears me because I can't feel his presence anymore. His shadow is gone, along with that cologne he wears.

I must remain alert. I need to fight this.

I'm awake.

And then I'm not anymore.

CHAPTER 24

Taylor

NOW

Next thing I know, I'm lying on the carpet, alone, as a door slams shut. My heart stammers in my chest as I feel around my body. Nothing seems to be broken but my head feels like someone took a hatchet to it. I think maybe I hit it on…something. The bed frame? I'm so thirsty it feels like my tongue will remain stuck to my palate if I don't keep it moving.

My memory is fuzzy, but slowly it comes back to me. I was in Cassie's room, watching her in the bath. Trying to work up the courage to take a step forward, to do to her what…what I've often wanted to do, if I'm being honest. We didn't have to be friends. We didn't have to act like sisters. But she didn't have to be like this, either.

The light is bright and dizzying, and I struggle to focus on the brass number on the wall. Six. I'm right outside Cassie's room, where the music has been turned off. Patting down my pocket, I find the key card. Not that I intend to use it again.

My heartbeat doesn't slow down until the elevator door closes in front me. I check my phone: 9:39 p.m. It's been less than half an hour since I stepped foot in this hotel, since my plan went completely astray. At least my question has been answered. Olivier stopped me. I can still feel his hand on my mouth, his arm wrapped around my waist. Whatever I was about to do, he wouldn't let me. He loves her. He loves and will protect her always. Why am I so surprised?

Outside, the sweet summer breeze is at complete odds with how I'm feeling on the inside. I wanted her dead. But would I have gone through with it? I twist my brain over this all the way back to my hotel, but the truth is I'll never know the answer.

I'm still battling with these thoughts when I enter my own hotel lobby, my gaze fixed ahead on the much smaller and less swanky elevator. There must be some wine left in my room. Maybe I'll turn on the music and have a bath, too. A few more steps and I'll be alone. Again. Alone for good this time.

"Hey there!"

It takes me a moment to realize that the greeting is directed at me. It's coming from the front desk.

"Bonsoir!" Amir says, giving me a little wave.

His smile is so friendly that my instinct to make a beeline for the elevator is already vanishing. It would be rude to pretend I didn't hear him. I know that's Good Taylor talking, but still. I've been her more often than I've been myself.

"You look like you were in a different world," he says.

Taking a deep breath, I make my way to him. "I guess I was."

"How are you enjoying Paris?" He leans over the counter and rests his forearms on it, like we're two friends about to share a secret.

"It's not really going how I'd hoped." My smile is weak, but hopefully genuine. It's the truth, after all.

And now I know: despite everything, Cassie and Olivier belong together. Yes, they're liars and cheaters. Of course I know that. You'd think the big, fat engagement ring, the wedding, and skipping away on their Paris honeymoon would have been enough proof that Cassie and

Olivier were going to stick to each other no matter what. But I needed to be sure. So what if they have issues? What if she and Olivier don't have the perfect marriage or the dream honeymoon? They have each other. When it came down to it, he was there to save her. Maybe he's just after her money, when I thought it was the other way around. But it doesn't matter anymore. I know what I need to know: they deserve each other.

"We don't like to hear that your trip is not going so well," Amir says. "We want people to come to Paris to have a good time. You shouldn't go home and tell your friends you didn't enjoy it. That's bad advertising."

I attempt a smile. It leaves a bitter taste in my mouth. "Paris is not the problem." And there's no home for me to go to anymore. Cassie is selling the house. And Olivier will out me, won't he? He doesn't give a shit about what will happen to me. She'll make me pay for that, one way or another. A laugh escapes me now. It's dry and chalky. "I won't tell anyone I was here. Trust me."

His eyes drill into mine. "I have an idea."

I should run away before he shares it. There's something about this guy, with his overt friendliness and his dimpled cheeks, that screams trouble. Though maybe the trouble is me. It's followed me for so long, stuck to me like a bad smell. I can't get rid of it.

Amir looks around, double-checking that no one's here. "I get off work in twenty minutes. Come out with me. We'll go dancing, have a few drinks, and then who knows where the night will take us."

My head won't stop hurting. Rubbing against the back of it, I can feel a bump coming on. It makes me wince in pain, so of course I touch it again. The way this night started, there's no way it can end well.

But then Amir says something else. "You're only here for one more night, yes?"

He's right. When I got on that plane, I didn't have any real plans. Cassie and Olivier would be in Paris for a week, and I booked my own room for five nights. I wasn't thinking clearly, but I knew I should be home before they returned. Now I can't imagine going back.

"Do you have any painkillers, by any chance?"

He nods. Smiles as he hands me the packet. Then he watches me walk away; I can sense it. Because he knows what I will do. He knows it before I do.

Twenty minutes later, I'm freshly showered, made up and ready to go. When he sees me, Amir's jaw goes slack with awe, his gaze running over every part of my body, undressing me.

"Is that really you?" he says, aghast.

I'm wearing a black fitted dress, all cleavage—one I bought on my first day but haven't worn yet—thick eyeliner, and red lips. I dried my hair with my head down and now it's wild, like a mane. "It's a version of me."

For a moment we just stand there, gauging each other. The tension in the air is thick and hazy, making me feel like I haven't in a long time. Alive.

"You look different," he says, coming around from behind the desk and grabbing my hand. "I like it. A lot."

He pulls me tight alongside him, his hand warm but his skin a little rough, and then we're out into the Parisian night.

We go to Pigalle. The neighborhood is renowned for Le Moulin Rouge, the cabaret where feather-clad dancers perform the famous French cancan, but that's not where we're headed. Turning off bustling boulevard de Clichy, Amir and I pass by a few sex shops—with whips and vinyl lingerie in the windows—and stop in front of a black door. It's unmarked except for a purple neon sign above it in the shape of a key. Amir knocks three times, then two, then three again. A bouncer appears, to whom Amir whispers something I can't hear. A password, maybe. And then we're in.

Inside, the walls are painted a dark shade of violet and lined with matching velvet booths, barely big enough to fit two people. The lighting is so subdued I can barely make out where the bar is. The music is trancelike, with few lyrics. Still gripping my hand, Amir pulls me through the crowd of sweaty bodies to a booth in the back. He hangs on to me so tight that it sends electricity up and down my spine. He wants me here with him, won't let me go. The booth is even more private than the ones we've walked past, with black partitions going up halfway. We sit down.

"Taylor? Yoo-hoo, Taylor?"

Amir waves his hand in front of my face, the whiff of cooler air bringing me back. He must have been calling this name for a little while. I've always hated it. Taylor, it's so basic. For a long time I refused to answer to it. *It's just a name*, Rae would say with her kind, motherly smile. *You don't mind, sweetie?* I did. I still do. But that's what Cassie wanted to call me so, just like with everything else, I let her. Rae acted like it was Cassie's fault, but she left me no choice, either.

"Is this okay?" Amir says.

"This is perfect." Dark, anonymous, a million miles away from Cassie's swanky hotel room and her fucking husband. Truly fantastic. I'm so lost in my thoughts that I don't notice Amir has ordered drinks until they appear in front of us: clear liquid in no-frills glasses, with a couple of ice cubes that won't melt the liquor away.

"Santé!" I say lifting mine and clinking it against his.

Amir follows my lead with an amused smirk. "You speak French. You're here on a honeymoon, but with no husband. Are you married? Have you *ever* been married?"

I tip my head back, swallowing the drink in one fell swoop. It burns my insides as it travels downs my throat. Blurs my edges, too.

I slam the glass back on the table. "I thought we were going to dance."

Amir nods. "There's something dark about you. Something twisted."

He's a complete stranger and yet he sees me. Or maybe it's that I'm ready to be seen. To be myself. Free of Cassie, of...him. Of the crushing hope I felt for a few weeks. I glance at my empty glass. "What if there is?"

He leans out of our little black and purple cocoon to wave at a waiter, making the another-round gesture with his index finger.

Then he grabs my hand. "Did a man do that to you? Make you that way, I mean. Your ex?"

I shake my head. "It's the women who fucked me up."

All of them. My mother, who left me for dead and never came to get me back, even after she was released from prison. Rae, who looked the other way when her daughter tortured me every which way. *You girls! Stop fighting already!* But I never fought. I didn't have it in me and I knew I'd always lose. Cassie finished me. She thinks I'm the worst thing that ever happened to her, but she doesn't realize how mutual the feeling is.

Our next drinks arrive and are gone almost immediately. I want to dance. Amir follows as I pull him to me, my bare legs brushing against the soft velvet. On the dance floor, we melt into the crowd and the chemical, smoky air. My arms wrap around his shoulders, his around my waist, our bodies making one as we move to the mellow beat. Then he presses his lips against mine, working in his tongue softly, but eagerly, too.

It feels so good, better than I could have imagined. Why haven't I been living like this all along? Kissing this stranger in a Parisian nightclub tastes like an escape, like after all the disappointment and the heartache, there might still be something out there for me. We kiss for a long while, our arms traveling down each other's bodies, ignoring the elbows bumping into our rib cages and the drinks being sloshed down our shoes. I'm always so afraid of change, of messing with the course of things. Not anymore.

"Let's go back," Amir says, eyes burning with desire and pointing at our booth.

Next thing I know we're slipping down in our dark and quiet nook, and I'm straddling him while his hands search under my dress, unhooking my bra. Maybe I drank too much or maybe the partitions around the booth are as high as they look, but it feels like we're all alone.

I unclasp his belt and he lets out a hungry gasp. "I don't have a condom," he whispers in my ear.

"I do."

A spark lights up Amir's face as I retrieve the condom from my wallet and hand it to him.

"Here?" he says at last.

I don't miss a beat. "Here."

I need this. I need it fast so it can erase everything else. I need it hard so tonight is not the night Cassie won again. Amir reaches under the bottom of my dress, pulling my underwear to the side. I forgot how it feels to be wanted, to see that glow in his eyes, to feel the softness of his breath. To be one with somebody else, even for a few minutes. To be wanted for who I am.

Afterward, we both lean back, sweaty and panting, not looking at each other.

"This was…" Amir wraps his hand around my neck and pulls me closer for a kiss. "I was not expecting that."

I was not expecting the night to go this way, either. I smooth my dress back into place and reach for my bag as he pulls his pants back up. Then I check my phone. This is the longest I've gone without looking at Cassie's Instagram.

But I don't make it that far, because a text message has come through, from an unknown number, with the country code +33. A French number.

It's a link to Google Maps, with the red drop pin placed on a little square off Montmartre. The text is brief and to the point.

Please come

"Hey, listen," Amir says, his mouth on my neck. "The night isn't over yet and we could—"

I push him away, harsher than I intended. "I can't."

His forehead creases in surprise. "I thought we were having fun?"

It could be a trap. I stole her money, her wallet. I broke into their hotel room. But it doesn't matter, because there's only one thing I can do.

"Yeah, well, the fun's over," I say.

I shuffle across the seat and get up. Then, without looking back, I walk away.

CHAPTER 25

Olivier

I wait until Cassie is dead asleep to leave the room. Well, not dead, exactly. Not yet anyway. I was so close. The plan was working. The *pills* were working. Poor Cassie.

It was all going so perfectly until I'd walked into the room. I thought I was having the worst nightmare of my life and a heart attack all in one. I didn't mean to hit her. Technically, I *didn't* hit her. I grabbed her and pulled her back so she wouldn't take one more step into the bathroom. She'd been stunned—no shit, me too—and flailed her arms about, trying to get out of my headlock. That's when I tripped backward, and when she hit her head against the edge of the bed.

Now, over an hour later, I'm still shaking as I wander the streets of Paris. I should be back in the room with Cassie. That's what a husband would do.

What the fuck is she doing in Paris? For a while I just walk around, trying to wrap my head around it. And now, as I arrive at the edge of the little square in Montmartre, I'm so scared out of my mind that I can barely remember to breathe.

It could be a trap. There might be cops waiting for me. But what proof would they have? I was careful. The sleeping pills Cassie took, *she* bought them. Took them willingly. Not the ones I slipped in the bottle of wine, obviously, but no one saw me crush them and drop the powder in. Plus, I pulled Cassie out of the bath when she was about to drown. I made her vomit it all. I *saved* her. Though, of course, I'd rather not get into that with the police.

I check that the coast is clear, no one left or right, before jumping the short fence to the park. The tree leaves rustle loudly in the wind and my heart is racing, my palms sweaty. It feels like summer is over. I sit down on a bench far away enough from the street. The metal feels cold against my back. Cassie tried to fight me when I got her out, soaking my shirt through and through.

The sound of twigs being crushed on the ground startles me. Footsteps. The shape of a woman comes out of the night's shadow, haloed by a lamp-post on the edge of the park.

"Reese!" I say, jumping to my feet. "You came." My voice trembles.

Reese stands there, arms idly by her side. I can't quite make her face in the darkness, but her chest rises and falls in rapid movements.

"Are you okay?" I add. "I'm so sorry about what happened."

"What *did* happen?" Her tone is incredulous, her voice a whisper.

This conversation, us even being here, is beyond incomprehensible. We have so much to talk about, and so little time. "I protected you. That's what happened. Why are you here?"

"I hated you so much."

She sits on the other end of the bench, where I can see her better. There are tear streaks down her face. Her red lipstick is smudged all the way to her chin. Her hair is wild, like it used to be after we had sex.

"I know," I say. Of course she'd hate me.

"You lied." Her voice rises in the night. "You lied and you left me."

It kills me, not to touch her. "I didn't lie. I love you. I don't think you ever believed me, but I do."

I shuffle over to her. She flinches when I reach for her hand, but lets me take it anyway. It's soft and warm, just like I remember it. It was only over a week ago that I last touched her.

Her green eyes open wide as she stares into mine. Her shoulders start to shake, like she's convulsing. "You're right. I never believed you."

I want to wrap her in a hug but first, I have a lot of explaining to do.

So I start. "I fell for you that night we met at the bar, the first time we *really* met. By then I already knew Cassie and I were doomed. Our marriage was always fake, but it felt like it had all been for nothing. I thought my life was over. It was. And then I walked into that bar, and it's like you were there to rescue me."

I shuffle even closer to her until our thighs touch. I need to be against her. To feel her, like before. "I didn't buy the flashy engagement ring. The first time I saw it was on Cassie's finger that day when the three of us were in the living room. And I didn't plan the trip here."

I pause then, knowing Reese will want to protest. Because I tried to tell her already, after Cassie sprung that on me, on *us*. I can still picture it, the way Cassie looked at her sister, waiting for her pain to manifest. Then I thought Cassie had found out about us. We were careful though. Whenever we were at the house, Reese wouldn't even look at me, wouldn't allow me in the same room as her, even when Cassie wasn't home. *Especially* when she wasn't home. And Reese worked so hard—at a clothing store every weekend, at the bar most nights, at any other odd job she could pick up. But the moments we did have, we made them count. I had never felt so happy. Scared shitless, but happy.

Cassie must have guessed. She was fucking with us; hence the sudden "engagement." That night, after Cassie's bizarre announcement, I'd sent Reese a message. Soon after meeting, we'd each created new Instagram accounts (frenchguynewyork for me and thereseladouce for her) so we could communicate when we couldn't talk in the house. Reese wouldn't text using our phone numbers—too risky. But now the account was gone. I couldn't send her a message. I tried to talk to her, but she wouldn't let me utter a word. Reese thought I'd betrayed her, and she'd cut me out of her life in an instant.

Now she takes a deep breath, staring straight ahead at the trees. "You have to see why it's a little hard for me to believe you. You told me you loved me, that you couldn't stand being without me. That you might *kill* for me. A few hours later, Cassie announces that you two are engaged and going to Paris to celebrate. And then you come home and double down, talking about a surprise wedding, saying that the trip to Paris is actually your honeymoon. Sure, she could have been lying. Wouldn't be the first time. But you went along with all of it. You married her again, in front of everyone we know, and went off on your honeymoon as I watched you go. And that's not even all of it. I got into that suite and you stopped me. You saved *her*. You knocked *me* over and threw me out in the hallway."

"I *had* to do all of these things! That night, I saw an opportunity. After weeks of paying me little attention, Cassie was acting like she wanted to be with me again, with her blingy engagement ring and the tickets to Paris. It couldn't have turned out better, in fact. Suddenly, it all looked real between us again, the way it needed to be for my plan to work."

I take a deep breath and get up. I can't say what I have to say while looking at her.

I start pacing back and forth in front of the bench, aware of her gaze on me. "If you hadn't walked into our room tonight, Cassie would be gone." Reese lets out a gasp, barely audible, but it's there. I look at her. "Why are you even here, in Paris?"

She seems to ponder the question, hurt and confusion written all over her face. But she's not ready and I won't push her.

So I go on with the rest of the story. "That afternoon in the car, what I said about getting rid of Cassie… I was serious. And you didn't stop me. You didn't tell me I was out of my mind, or that you would call the police. You didn't throw me out of the car, and you didn't run away. That's all I needed to know. But then of course, Cassie had her own plans.

"You were mad. I got it. You didn't know I had nothing to do with them. And then I realized I couldn't involve you in any of it. I couldn't stand to be away from you, but it would all be worth it in the end. So I kept doing my research, and read an article about a woman who drowned in her bath. She was exhausted and drank too much. Most likely she dozed off, slipped to the bottom, and that was that. A friend found her body two days later.

"And then I read something else, about Americans dying abroad. That makes it hard for the government to get answers. They have to deal with the police in the other country, and the local law enforcement is going to care less about a foreigner, especially if her death appears accidental. So many people die every day. They can't investigate everything in too much depth."

Reese looks up at me, her eyes full of questions she doesn't want to spell out. I come to kneel in front of her and rest my hands on her thighs. "The hotel we're staying at... It's the one where I used to work."

"I noticed that, but I thought it was more proof that you *did* organize the honeymoon."

"Cassie had already made up that story about our engagement and booked the flights. There was no turning back. But then she left the rest up to me, a huge mistake on her part. I told her I had the perfect place in mind. When I worked at Bhotel, before I moved to New York, I was friends with some of the security guys. They often commented about the cameras on the sixth floor. They didn't work, so you couldn't see who was coming in out of the two suites at the end of the corridor, near the fire exit. The guys thought maybe it was because famous people sometimes stayed there and they wanted privacy. If you looked closely enough, you could see that they weren't even wired.

"That's the first thing I did when Cassie and I arrived. As soon as she got into the bathroom, I went to check the cameras. And then I found out that the security code to the service entrance at the back hadn't changed. I walked around a little, went to take a shower at the gym, and no one recognized me. Now, I couldn't hope that a little wine would be enough in this case. Cassie wouldn't die on her own. I wouldn't be so lucky."

Reese doesn't react. The sisters didn't just despise each other. The hatred ran deep. The name thing alone… Cassie and her mother wouldn't even call her by her real name? That was messed up. When Reese had introduced herself at the bar, I was so confused.

My name is not Taylor, she'd said as soon as it was just the two of us. *But Cassie couldn't pronounce my real name. At first she called me T. Then she settled on Taylor. Her mom thought it was cute and that it would help me fit in at school. A few years later, when she officially adopted me, she changed my full name to Taylor Quinn. My real name is Thérèse, with the accents. The French way. But Reese is easier.*

I sit down next to her and run a hand through her hair. I like the new color, the shorter length. It strikes me all over again, how beautiful she is. "Do you want to hear the rest of it?"

She nods, tilting her head so her cheek rubs against my arm. She always loved to be touched, could never get enough of being in my arms, pressed tight against my body.

I continue. "Before we left, I told Cassie that jet lag would be brutal, especially for someone who'd never experienced it before. She immediately called her dealer buddy, who got her a bottle of prescription sleeping pills. And then I had to wait for the right moment when it would make sense for me to go out for the night without her. Before I left, I ordered her room service, with a bottle of wine. When she wasn't looking, I crushed a handful of pills and poured them into the bottle. I just needed her unconscious enough; the amount couldn't look too suspicious.

"Then I went out with old colleagues from the hotel restaurant who no longer worked there. They'd been surprised to hear from me but I'd told them I was passing through on the way to visiting my parents. We hadn't been close but I knew they were big drinkers and even bigger partyers. They wouldn't notice if I slipped out for some of the night. I watched

Cassie's Instagram Stories, even texted her that I hoped she was having a good evening. Then I came back to the hotel and entered through the service entrance. I went up the staircase and into the hallway with the nonfunctioning cameras. All she needed was a little push under water, to be sure. Then I'd be gone again, seen at the bar with my ex-colleagues. I'd come back hours later to discover her body."

Reese swallows hard. "But I beat you to it."

"At first I thought you were an intruder. But when I realized it was you, I couldn't take the risk anymore. You would have shown up on the cameras. My alibi wasn't perfect but it existed. I couldn't let you take the fall for it."

She's silent for a while. When she speaks, her voice sounds hollow. "I couldn't let you go to Paris without me. And I couldn't let her get away with this. That's why I'm here. I did believe you that afternoon, when you told me you wanted to get rid of Cassie. I–I…"

She starts shaking as tears stream down her face. I wrap her in my arms, and to my surprise, she doesn't resist. There's so much more I want to say—that I *need* to say. Time is running out, but I can't take this moment away from her. So I wait until she's ready to continue.

"I wanted that, too," she whispers at last. "That afternoon, it hit me: there was a light at the end of the tunnel, a life without her. I didn't realize how much I wanted that until you said it out loud. I could move on from this. I could walk away from her. And then, maybe, there could be a life with you. It seemed too good to be true, but the way you said it, it felt possible, too."

She looks up and our eyes meet. I want to cry, too. We were so close. *So* close.

"Something clicked in me," she continues. "So yes, I did believe you that afternoon. I needed you to be telling the truth."

I take a deep breath. "I was!"

She shakes her head. "And then Cassie turned up with that engagement ring. It was almost comical. I sat there as she recounted how you'd gotten down on one knee the night before, how much money you'd spent on the diamond. I thought I was losing my mind. Reality came crashing down: I'd wanted my own sister dead and you had never really meant to do it."

"She's not your sister," I say meekly. I sound like Cassie, but I can't let Reese feel like she's done anything wrong.

She ignores me and continues with the rest of her story. "Maybe you loved Cassie, maybe you didn't. All I knew is that she had a ring on her finger, tickets to Paris, and that you were officially getting married in a few days. It was a wake-up call and a half. She had you, and I didn't. But then, after I dropped you two off at the airport, I opened the glove box to get a tissue, and there was my passport. I'd forgotten it was there."

"I remember you telling me about the trip to Paris you almost took, how Cassie ruined it."

She nods. "You must think I'm completely mad, turning up here."

It does complicate things. My plan required her to be at home. After I'd discover Cassie's body, I'd call her sister, obviously. She'd be able to testify how devastated I was. How much I'd loved Cassie. That it *had* to have been an accident.

"We're going to figure this out," I say, even though I have no idea how.

"I was so angry with you," Reese says, "or maybe with myself, for believing you. When Cassie turned up with a new phone and clothes, I figured she'd put it on one of her many credit cards. But then there was the engagement ring, the tickets to Paris, the wedding… I could only think of one explanation: you'd lied to me about being broke. The day before the wedding, I found money in a jar at the top of the kitchen cupboards. A *lot* of money. It didn't make sense that *you* would be using the jar to store it, but how would Cassie have that much cash? It *had* to be yours."

I let out a sigh. "I couldn't bring myself to tell you about the inheritance. First, because Cassie seemed dead set on having everyone believe that I was rich and spoiling her. I was afraid to mess with her plans. I was completely at her mercy. And then, when I realized how bad things were between you two, I couldn't be the one to tell you. I knew how much it would hurt you to know she suddenly had all this."

A car honks in the distance, startling us both.

"I had no idea who you were anymore," Reese continues. "One minute you're talking about killing her, and the next you're doing *this*." She gestures widely around her.

I shake my head. "Cassie and I were not doing *anything* together."

Reese snarls. It sounds cruel, coming from her. I've never seen her in this light. "You got married."

"For the papers! You know it was never anything more to me."

"And to her?"

I look away. "I guess I know now that it was about vengeance. She wanted to get back at her ex, and she saw an opportunity to make you suffer at the same time."

I've never put it so plainly before, but it's obvious. I remember the first time Cassie and I met. *You're French, from France?* I thought it was a dumb question. But no, Cassie was simply delighted she'd found the perfect mark. Her sister had always thought she had a French family and was dying to go to Paris. Cassie was going to rub me in her face whether I knew it or not.

"Well, she succeeded," Reese says, untangling herself from my arms.

"If things had gone my way tonight, Cassie would be gone. But you still don't believe me, even now that I've told you everything." Though, of course, I haven't told her about the money *yet*.

She doesn't answer. We sit in silence for a long while. Eventually I wrap an arm around her shoulder again and she places her head in the crook of my neck. We fit so perfectly together.

"Do you like Paris?" I whisper in her ear. "Is it what you expected?"

Reese lets out a sad laugh. "It's a great place for a honeymoon. So romantic."

"We'll come back here. Together. We could try to find your dad's family. I haven't forgotten about that." The certainty in my voice surprises me.

She shakes her head, then sits up straight to look into my eyes. "I thought you never wanted to come back here."

"I don't want to live here again, no. But with you, I'd visit Paris any day. For you, I could do anything."

"If I hadn't walked into your room tonight—"

I cut in. "I'll find another way." Everything feels possible when I'm with her. "If that's what you want."

"I never get what I want."

Now was not the time to tell her that she was going to get all of Cassie's money. It was better if she didn't know, so she could act genuinely surprised when it happened. She had to be one hundred percent innocent; that was the key to all of this. She'd have an ironclad alibi—being an ocean away—and I'd have no motive. But what if she screws it up again? I haven't come so far, gotten so close, to give up now.

"I think you could, this time. Thérèse, please look at me." Back home, when it was just the two of us, I'd sometimes call her Thérèse, reveling in how her eyes lit up every time I did. It felt so intimate to call her by her name when no one else did. Now there's a softness to her face, like she really wants this to be true. "Give me another day, okay? I'm going to get you everything you want, and so much more."

CHAPTER 26

Cassie

NOW

My throat feels like it's on fire.

"Are you there?"

I wait for a sound, my heart pounding. That's when the smell hits me: vomit, all over the sheets. It's still wet to the touch. I'm guessing it's mine, though I don't remember it happening. On my nightstand, the lamp casts strange shadows around the room as I turn it on. It's enough to see the proof I didn't dream this: the empty bottle of wine and the puddles of water on the floor between the bathroom and the bed. My hair is still damp and I'm naked under the sheets.

"Olivier?"

Please let him be gone forever. I need this nightmare to be over. I lift myself up in bed, trying to think. My mind is fuzzy, my limbs weak. I have to get out of here. But first, I check my phone and discover that I sent Darren a message. Judging by the time, I was in the bath then.

Don't believe anything. He's dangerous.

Darren has texted me back a few times.

What do u mean?

Cassie? Please, ur scaring me.

R u coming home?

Lifting myself up against the headboard, I flick through my recent calls and tap on his name.

Please pick up. Please please please.

He does. "Cassie! What's going on?"

I try to take a deep breath, but the air tears through my lungs, and stars dance in front of my eyes. "I think I was drugged."

"What? Where are you?"

My mouth is dry. "In the room. In bed."

I flick off the sheets and slowly set my feet on the floor.

"And where is he?"

"Gone. I think. He dragged me out of the bath and then I vomited everything and—"

"I don't understand. I thought you'd left him. You told me he was okay with it."

Did I say that? I can't think. My head hurts so much.

"My wallet was stolen. I couldn't book a new ticket."

I pluck my underwear off the floor and slip it on. Then, I put Darren on speakerphone. I need to get moving.

"Why didn't you call me?"

"I'm calling you now!" I clasp my hand on my mouth, regretting how loudly I just screamed.

Olivier could be outside the door. He could be lurking around, waiting to hurt me for good.

"Cassie, please. You're not making sense. Do you need money to get home, is that it?"

I sigh, hearing the judgment in his question. My days of asking him for money are far behind me, but I can't explain everything to him now.

In the closet, I quickly flick things off the hangers. A few of them dangle before falling with a clatter. I run back into the room and start stuffing clothes into my suitcase. I bought all this with my own money—the trendy dresses, the designer shoes, the Chanel! They all think I'm worthless. Good for nothing. But look at this! It's all mine and I'm not leaving without it.

"Darren," I say, buttoning up my jeans. "If something happens to me—"

"You're going to be fine."

"He drugged me!" I jam the last pile of dirty clothes in before zipping my bag closed. "He's out to get me."

Darren lets out a sigh. "Look, I never liked the guy, his smirky face and that goatee. But why would he do that?"

"I'm telling you he wants to kill me. Please believe me."

"You're scaring me," Darren says softly.

"Oh *you're* scared? I need you to know, in case something happens to me. In case I don't make it home."

I put on my sneakers, lacing them so tight I can feel the blood flow cut off on top of my feet.

"You told me he was fine with you two splitting up," he says, lowering his voice even further.

I sit back on the bed, pressing the palms of my hands against my temples, trying to calm myself. "It's not true, okay? He's not fine with us splitting up. He won't let me go. I can't explain everything right now but—"

I can't explain for many reasons, including the fact that it doesn't quite make sense to me. Not long after we arrived home, Olivier started to disappear for hours on end. Back in the city, he'd told me how special I was, how deeply he'd fallen for me. Now he seemed to only care about putting on a good face when we'd meet with the immigration officer. Darren didn't seem to be taking the bait and I was trying hard to forget I'd married a total stranger, all for nothing. I started to think about calling the whole thing off, but before that, I had one more idea: the sudden proposal, the ring, the trip to Paris.

That changed everything. With Olivier, at least. The morning after, it was like we were back in New York. He was happy. It was all about me again. Olivier made me coffee and toast with peanut butter. He'd set up a little tray and carried it to my room before I was even up.

I really appreciate everything you've done for me, Olivier said, sitting close to me on the bed, *and I want you to know I don't take it for granted.* He had dark circles under his eyes, like he'd been pondering this all night. *You have all this money and this house, and I think you should protect yourself. I shouldn't have any right to it. It's not mine.*

It's not *yours,* I'd agreed, before taking a sip of my coffee.

*That's my point, Cassie. We're already legally married. If something happened to you—*He'd trailed off, looked away.

The idea made me feel queasy, but the guy had a point.

You don't have a living parent anymore, Olivier said sadly, like he felt sorry for me, *but there's your sister.*

I'd frowned. *Where is this coming from? Did she say something to you?*

I don't talk to her, Olivier said, like he was offended by the thought of her. *You know I don't. And I only care about you. You saved me, Cassie. I don't ever want you to think I'm taking advantage of you.*

He was right. There was no way he should get everything. The next day, when I called my father's lawyer, I'd resented having to put Taylor's name down. But I told myself it was a security thing, a grown-up thing. I was proud of myself. When I told Olivier I'd done it, he looked so relieved. Like he'd accomplished his job of keeping me safe. Of doing right by me. At least that's what I thought was happening.

"But what, Cassie?" Darren says impatiently. "Why are you so sure your own husband wants to hurt you?"

That's when I see it again, the bottle of sleeping pills, partially hidden by the alarm clock. I unscrew the cap—and it's almost empty. I didn't take that many. Not by choice anyway.

My throat feels like it's closing up. "He tried to kill me. Can you please trust me, this one time?"

A few seconds pass before he responds. "Fine. Let's get you out of there. Call me as soon as you're in the taxi."

But I still hear it in his voice: he won't fight for me. Like he didn't when I came back from the city, or when I dangled my engagement ring in his face, or when he came to the wedding. I'm all alone, aren't I? This is the hard truth. I'm an orphan. No one understands me or what I've gone through. No one even knows why Olivier and I got married. I don't even really know myself. I didn't have to do this. I brought this all on myself and now I can't get out of it. A wave of nausea hits me and I have to rush to the bathroom.

I may be all packed up and ready to leave, but somehow I'm not sure I'll make it out of this hotel alive.

CHAPTER 27

Thérèse

NOW

Three months ago, I wasn't all that surprised when Cassie came home with Olivier in tow. She'd always been impulsive. If trouble was hiding somewhere, she'd be sure to drag it out so she could play, like a cat hunting down a mouse.

I studied Olivier as he pulled their bags out of the Uber's trunk. He was handsome and polished—wearing a neat polo shirt and fitted dark jeans. He also looked a little shocked as he took in our decrepit house. The poor guy seemed to have no idea what he was getting into, and it was obvious that he didn't fit in. All of that faded away when my darling sister told me his name, and then when Olivier opened his mouth. She'd found a French guy this time, and she knew exactly how that would make me feel.

After we canceled our trip to Paris, my desire to go hung in the air. Cassie would catch me using my Duolingo app and laugh mercilessly at my bad accent. She used my Netflix account and railed against the French movies in my recently watched list—*Subtitles? No, thank you!* I didn't need to tell her that I'd signed up to all these DNA websites, that I continued to research my and Mom's names—Thérèse and Jacqueline Ronald—and that I'd contacted everyone involved in Mom's case, to no avail. Cassie knew I'd never stopped hoping that one day, the pieces of my life would come together.

Now we were both orphans and that didn't sit right with her. She and I could never be the same. The French boyfriend made sense in that way. Me, on the other end, I was done playing games. I buried myself in work, asking for more shifts at the bar and at the store, taking everything I could get. I got up earlier for breakfast. When I wasn't working, I'd lock myself in my room, watching the last two episodes of *Sex and the City*—the ones when Carrie goes to Paris—on repeat.

Ignoring my sister and her new boyfriend worked pretty well for a couple of weeks. I must have exchanged all of two sentences with him after the day he arrived. Then there was the night he walked into the bar. His eyes were empty, his shoulders slumped. He looked beaten. There was no way this was his kind of drinking establishment—I pictured him sipping fancy cocktails in tufted leather booths instead—and as he slouched over the sticky linoleum surface on the counter, I almost felt sorry for him.

When he saw me, his jaw went slack. The bar was ten miles away, in the next town over, and it felt like it was mine, one of the only places where I was comfortable leaving Good Taylor at the door. I'd wear the fitted tops I'd found at thrift stores or in Cassie's wardrobe. I put on bright-red lipstick and thick eyeliner, trying a different version of me, the one I might become if I ever got out. Of this town. Of this life. Of under Cassie's thumb.

It wasn't my intention to talk smack about Cassie, so when Olivier asked why my colleague called me Reese, I told him the official version. Poor little Cassie couldn't say my weird name, so she changed it to Taylor. That's what most people in town called me, but this was my workplace, my turf. Cassie never came here—there were other bars with better music and nicer-looking guys.

I'd expected this would be the extent of our conversation, but Olivier had shaken his head. *That was your name! She shouldn't have taken that from you. Does she always play with people like that?*

It was a slow Tuesday and I poured us both a drink. We moved on to the topic of the inn, and Olivier mentioned Cassie's idea to renovate it. I almost spit out my drink all over the counter. His face fell even further as the pieces clinked into place. *It wasn't her idea, was it?* I shook my head sadly. Olivier seemed like a smart guy, but Cassie was a pro at make-believe.

Now he looked even more dejected, but I felt a little better. Olivier got me. He didn't know it yet, but that's what was happening: someone in this world understood what I'd been up against for so long. Someone felt the same way. I could have an ally. Maybe this was the turning point I'd been holding out for all along, why I'd stuck around in spite of everything.

As the evening wore on, filled with talks about our pasts, our hopes, and his dreams—I didn't have any at the time—I stopped thinking of him as Cassie's boyfriend. This wasn't the first time I'd flirted with a guy at the bar, though it was the first time the guy looked like Olivier. And the first time a guy looked at me the way he did.

The thing is, I'm not innocent. Good Taylor doesn't really exist; she was all about survival, a little girl who had been left for dead and was scared of what terrible thing might come next. So I'll admit this: when I walked to the restrooms at the end of the night, I was testing something. Just this once, I wanted to see if I could prove Cassie right and *actually* take something from her. When Olivier came over and kissed me, I only thought about how much I wanted to hurt her. This new guy would be gone from her life soon enough anyway, and it would never go any further between us. Olivier was too good to be true. It was a moment of weakness on his part.

But here I am in Paris, sitting on a bench in the middle of the night, shaking from top to bottom because I can't stand being so close to him and not nestling myself in his arms.

"I love you," Olivier says again. "I meant every word that afternoon in the car."

Every time it cuts deeper into me, past the shell I've had to build to protect myself. He loves me. He wants to be with me. Just like he said that afternoon, when he talked about getting rid of Cassie. I thought he was playing a sick joke on me. Who would do that to be with me?

I wanted to believe him so badly. Despite what I said, and despite what happened the last time I followed a guy to his hometown, I would have come to live here with Olivier, if he'd wanted to. We could have started over in Paris, together. But he didn't want that, so instead I pictured the two of us in New York. We'd be together every night, sharing tidbits about our day over delicious meals at dimly lit restaurants. Walking through Central Park hand in hand, surrounded by strangers. A fresh start, with him. It filled my heart to the brim and more. It all felt very possible.

A few hours later, Cassie announced Olivier had proposed to her. *Look at this ring!* They were going away to celebrate. Where to? Paris, *obviously*. Did I forget Olivier was French? It'd be the trip of a lifetime. How wonderful! Didn't I think it was wonderful? Of course I did. Good Taylor always thought everything Cassie did was absolutely fucking wonderful.

I get up from the bench, trying to clear my head. When Olivier looks at me like that, I feel exposed. Naked.

"You went along with all of it," I say. "And then, not only were you going to Paris; you also were going there on your honeymoon."

"Because I realized it was easier that way. The happier Cassie and I appeared, the better it would look after her terrible accident happened. And then, of course, I wanted to protect you. You could never be suspected of anything, even though you'd get all the money."

My blood turns to ice. "What are you talking about?"

Olivier looks right and left, checking that we're completely alone. Somewhere in the distance, a man lets out a drunken yowl. "That was always going be the tricky part. If something happened to Cassie, all eyes would be on me. It's always the husband. And when the police found out Cassie had inherited a packet of money, I'd look doubly guilty. It wouldn't matter how tight my alibi would be; they'd never let me go. So I had to make sure I *wouldn't* get her money."

"But if you're not—" I say, pretty certain I'm misunderstanding him.

"*You* are," he says, looking deep into my eyes. "All of the two million dollars. Or at least what she hasn't wasted away already. And the house."

"No, that's not possible." My voice sounds squeaky. Olivier nods. "She hates me."

"She does," he agrees, "but she has no one else. You're her family, whether she likes it or not. I'm just a stranger she married on a whim without thinking it through. And she must have realized that because it wasn't hard to convince her. She called the lawyer herself and everything. You're her next of kin."

"I don't want her money," I say, sitting back down. In spite of me, my foot starts tapping on the gravel, making little crushing sounds. I think about the stash of bills I took, how dirty I feel to be using them. I want what's mine. Nothing else.

"That's why I had to stop you in the room," Olivier says. "Well, one of the reasons." I bring my hand to the back of my head, where the bump has only grown bigger. "I'm really sorry about that, but I couldn't let you do anything. You can't be near Cassie."

"You threw me out into the hallway."

The pain on his face looks real, too. "I'm so sorry, mon amour. I had to think fast. I wasn't even sure it was you until you were lying on the floor unconscious. And then I had to get you out as quickly as possible. I did it all to protect you."

"Come here," he says now, opening up his arms. "Please, I've missed you so much."

I can't resist anymore and bury myself in him. The warmth of his body sends a rush of pure relief through mine. It was only over a week ago that we were last together, but every second since then felt like someone was pricking at my skin, letting me bleed out. All my life I told myself I was fine being on my own. I'd gone without real love for so long; I could keep going, and going again. But then I met Olivier and all of my beliefs blew right out of the window. I wanted him. I needed him. Couldn't imagine living without him.

Tears fall down my cheeks and onto his shoulders. "I screwed everything up. I–I'm sorry."

"I'll find another way," he says, rubbing my hair. "I have no motive and dozens of social media posts showing Cassie and me madly in love. We still have three days in Paris."

He sounds like he's trying to convince himself more than me, but this time I want to trust him. We're together now. I didn't make this up. He would have gone all the way, if I'd let him. He told me he loved me and I chose to believe Cassie instead. More thoughts bubble up in my head. *Don't go back to her. Stay with me. She's not worth the risk.* I picture the look on her face when she finds out he chose me. But then I remember how I felt in the car that afternoon when I imagined her dead. The anger, the relief. I know why I walked to their hotel, why I slipped into the room. I was so close to doing what Olivier had promised. But I'll never know what would have happened if he hadn't stopped me.

I don't say any of this, only what matters. "I love you."

And then I bring my lips to his. Our kiss is like a soothing balm on my wounds, but it doesn't last long enough. When I start to relax into it, Olivier pulls away.

"I have to go. I should get back to Cassie before she wakes up."

"And what do I do?" For once I want someone to tell me, to take care of me.

Olivier wraps his hands around my face. "You go home. Right now."

I force myself to nod, even though I hate the idea of leaving him here. With her.

"I mean it, Thérèse. Go back to your hotel, erase any trace you were in Paris, and get on the next flight." He checks his watch. It's 3:00 a.m. "Get to the airport as soon as you can. You could be home by the afternoon."

I nod more forcefully now. "Okay."

"Then, when you get there, do whatever it takes to look like you never left." He bobs his head up and down like he's trying to psyche himself up. "Does anybody know you're here?"

"No, I never planned to come. I didn't even pack a bag. The bar cut some of my shifts, as you know. And now the store won't need me again until the holidays."

"Good. Great. And here in Paris, you don't know anyone, right?"

He's asking, but not really. There's only one possible answer to this question.

"Right," I say, my throat tight.

"Do you think anyone might recognize you?"

"What do you mean?"

"If it ever came to it, could anybody testify that they've seen you here?"

I picture Amir's hands all over my body, his eyes trained on mine. The guy knows my name. He has a copy of my passport. He saw the cash. He heard the story of my fake honeymoon. But I can't tell Olivier any of that. I can't be the one to ruin this, again. He convinced Cassie to give me all that money. He's doing this for me. For *me*.

"Reese? Did you meet anyone in Paris?"

I take a deep breath and shake my head. "I'm very forgettable," I say with a laugh.

"You're not."

I can tell he's waiting for more. He wants to be sure. I've never lied to him before.

"There's no one else," I say.

Olivier exhales slowly. We believe what we want to believe. "Okay. Go home. Act like you never left. And whatever you do, don't call me."

"What if—" I start. There's so much I want to ask. So many ways this could go wrong.

"No," he says, his hand wrapping tighter around mine. "You can*not* call me. As far as anybody knows, you're my wife's sister. We barely know each other, all right?"

I nod. I'll be rich and we'll be together. He's doing this for me. "I love you. I trust you."

He kisses me one more time and gets up. "I'll see you soon, okay?"

Without looking back, he walks out into the night, jumps over the small fence, and disappears.

CHAPTER 28

Olivier

NOW

B y the time I'm walking through Bhotel's service entrance and up the stairs, my confidence has fizzled. I'm not a violent person. Except for that one time my brother and I got into a fight—he started it—I've never hit anyone in my life, never even got into those war video games. I'm a good guy, I just made a mistake—several mistakes. Fine, too many mistakes. But I can still make them right. Thérèse and I could technically move here. Though of course, the tax office would find out soon enough. They'd come at me. Them and everyone else. It'd take a lifetime to pay it all back. Meanwhile, Cassie is sitting on a fortune. Shouldn't Reese have a right to *something*? The house, at the very least.

The moment I open the door to the suite, I know something is off. First, the light is on. A suitcase, Cassie's, is stashed by the entrance. I lift it up. It's full. It was on the floor by the bed when I left, so Cassie must have packed it. Cassie is awake. And then I notice something else: the pill bottle is no longer on the nightstand, but on the dresser. In full view.

Before I can wonder where she is, the toilet flushes and then the faucet is turned on. A moment later, out comes Cassie, fully dressed. A little too alive. She looks pale and her hair is in disarray as she wipes her mouth with the back of her hand, as if she threw up again.

When she notices me, the gasp that escapes her lips sounds like the howl of a dying animal.

I don't have much time to think.

"How was your night?" I say.

I'm all smiles as I step further into the room.

"I want to go home," Cassie says quietly. "Please let me go home."

She has nothing on me. She can't prove it. I didn't do *anything*. "What are you talking about, sweetie? We're going home in three days."

Not taking her eyes off me, she walks across the room and grabs her denim jacket from the back of the chair. "I'm going now."

But I can't let her. Moving quickly, I close the distance between us and reach for her hand. She flicks it off, which makes her jacket fall to the floor. Letting out a yelp, she bends down to pick it up.

"Let's take a minute, okay?" I say. "Whatever is going on, I'm here for you, Cassie." I need more time to think, to plan. I'm not giving up yet. Not the money, not Reese.

Cassie is shaking as she stands back up, but my focus soon shifts from her to the floor, where the jacket just was. Pieces of paper have spread all over the carpet.

My throat ties in a knot as I look closer. She takes the opportunity to make for the door and grab her suitcase.

I recognize the gold lettering now, the bits of my photograph. That bitch tore my passport to shreds.

"What did you do?" I ask, as the answer washes over me.

She's leaving me. After everything I did, all the shit I put up with, she thinks she can get rid of me? Not so fast, *babe*. I don't wait for her response and instead lunge toward the door, pressing against it. Cassie jerks back so hard her suitcase drops to the floor with a loud thump. This only makes her jump more.

"I called the lawyer," she says, trying to sound calm, but not doing a great job of it. "She knows our marriage is fake and that I want out."

"Hold on a minute," I say, going for my most soothing tone. "I feel like there's been a misunderstanding. I want to be married to you, Cassie. I love you."

I put on a smile and slowly go to sit on the edge of the bed, the one closest to the door.

"You tried to kill me," she says, eyeing the exit. I let out a deranged laugh. "You drugged me. I was in the bath… I felt myself…go."

I point at the empty bottle of wine on the floor, which I must have kicked out of the bathroom when I was dragging Cassie. "Hey, I don't judge you for treating yourself on your honeymoon. But I wasn't here. You drank that all by yourself."

Making sure to stay as far away from me as possible, Cassie walks over to the dresser and grabs the pill bottle, which she shakes in front of her. "I counted them. The bottle is almost empty. I only took a couple every night."

She's not sure. I can read it on her face. Cassie might throw accusations around, but she has nothing concrete.

"You're not the only one who felt jet-lagged," I say with a shrug. "I took some as well."

I get up and walk over to her. If she really believed I wanted to kill her, she would have tried harder to get away from me.

"Don't come near me!" she screams.

"Come on, sweetie. Let's take a deep breath."

She shakes her head, her eyes practically bulging out. "I told Darren about what you did. I'm serious. He *knows*. If something happens to me, they'll…arrest you."

Oh. Oh! I'm done, aren't I? Cassie is going to walk out of here freely and I'll never step foot in the U.S. again. I think she sees the realization on my face even before I open my mouth. She's gone too far, said too much.

"You little bitch!" I snap. "So used to getting your way. You *wanted* to marry me. All you cared about was messing with your ex and destroying your sister."

Cassie steps back until she's against the wall, but there's a hint of relief in her eyes. She didn't make this all up. "And I won. Darren and I are getting back together. I'll divorce you and then I'll be with a real man. One who can take care of me." Her voice is shaking, but her eyes are full of hatred.

"Is that right? You think he's going to stick by you now, when he dumped you before because you were never going to be good enough for him? He wants a nice little wife, the house, the snotty kids. They'll hate you and you'll end up like your mother."

She takes a shaky breath as she tries to push past me, but I wrap my hand around her wrist, squeezing it tight.

"It's over," she says, her face contorted in pain. "You can't get back to the States without a passport, and you can't live there without me. I almost feel sorry for you. Your big dream has gone—" She presses the fingers of her other hand together, then spreads them out wide in front of her face. "Poof! And here's the difference between us: you still need me but I don't need you anymore." She's trying to sound tough but there's regret in her eyes. Fear.

"Geez," I say, releasing my grip just a touch. "It's no surprise no one loves you. You think Darren does? Then why isn't he here with you? Why did he let you marry me?"

"You—" Her jaw quivers. "You don't know anything."

I need to buy time until I can figure out my next move, and it's working. To show good faith, I release her wrist.

"Your sister definitely can't stand you."

A spark goes off in her, angst turning into anger. "What does Taylor have to do with this?"

"Her name's not Taylor." If Cassie is determined to ruin my life, I'm not going to go away so easily. "And she's a much better person than you'll ever be."

Cassie scoffs. "She's a loner and a weirdo. Her mother almost killed her. Wait, is something going on with you two?"

A thought flashes in my mind, so simple and yet unfathomable. What if I explained the truth? I married the wrong sister for the wrong reason. I could be with Reese, and Cassie could be with whoever the fuck she wanted to. Cassie and I could still pretend to be happily married. I could work harder at convincing her to invest more money into the inn, to let me handle it. It could work. In theory, at least.

"We're in love," I say, feeling like a teenage boy declaring my feelings for the first time. Jittery and full of crushing hope.

When Cassie opens her mouth, it's to let out the highest-pitched shriek I've ever heard. Then, she whips around. I grab her by the waist so forcefully she stumbles back onto the bed. Before she can move again, I straddle her, pinning her down on the sheets. I'm about to take hold of both her wrists when she turns her head to the left, looking for something off to the side. I do the same to see what's so interesting to her, and our eyes land on the iron at the same time. It's on the board, in the middle of the room. The distraction lasts only for a split second, but it's enough for Cassie to push me off her. Then she reaches for the iron, just as I do, too.

Like I said, I'm not a violent person. But in that moment, all I can think of is how good it will feel to smash the cool metal piece into her ugly little face.

CHAPTER 29

Thérèse

NOW

Any place would feel dull after Paris, but the house seems dreadful as I park my car out the front. Before going in, I spin the flowerpot and grab the spare set of keys, the one the Realtor used to get in. I'm not interested in receiving visitors.

Everything is quiet inside, just as I—we—left it. The smell of rotten leaves and pollen from all the flowers Cassie spread around the house for the wedding fills the air, making me want to retch. I haven't slept a peep since I left Olivier, and only picked at the meal I was served on the plane.

For the next hour, I focus squarely on settling back into my life. Good Taylor's life. I take off my clothes—the jeans, T-shirt, and leather jacket I wore when I left—and have a shower. The rest is still in Paris. Before leaving the hotel, I folded all my new clothes and wrote a note to the cleaning staff that they should enjoy them. It killed me, but I couldn't take anything back. Olivier was clear about that: there should be no trace of me, no signs that I was ever there. I only kept the cap, which I wore until I got into my car at JFK airport. I dumped it in a trash can when I stopped for gas on the way home. Of course, if it ever came to that, the police could check my travel records. But they'll only do that if I give them a reason to.

I can't help checking my phone every few minutes. He can't call me. We won't speak until it's done. Where is he now? Has he alerted the police yet? Did he get that far? Yes, he did. I have to stop doubting him. My job is to act like everything is normal, like I didn't disappear off to the other side of the world to follow my sister on her honeymoon. Like I haven't always, to some degree, wanted her dead.

My eyes heavy with sleep, I make a batch of brownies and don't even wait for the dish to cool down. Instead, I grab my keys and head over to Ms. Richardson's house. It's a little late, almost dinnertime, but hopefully she won't mind. Madeline is one of the town's notorious gossips, so visiting her is the quickest way to spread the word.

She must have seen me through the window because she opens the door before I even knock. She's been expecting me, I guess. I never called her back.

"Taylor, you changed your hair!" she says as she envelops me in her frail arms. Her fragrance is strong, something floral and too much of it.

"Oh, um, yes." I'd forgotten about that. "I felt like trying something different."

What if she asks where I got it done? There are only two hair salons in town, and Madeline maintains her red mane religiously.

"I brought you something," I add, meaning the brownies. She waves me inside, and I follow her toward the kitchen. "I'm so sorry I didn't call you back. It's been a busy few days."

"Of course!" she says, looking over her shoulder. "With the wedding and everything. If you can call it that. All that beer…at a wedding? Pizza slices? Phew, Cassie's friends are a loud bunch. Anyway I'm sure you had a lot to do with the planning. I bet it was you who made the finger food and arranged the flowers."

"Maybe." This is Good Taylor speaking, with a heartfelt smile. It doesn't matter how hard she works, she always deflects. I can't say I missed her in Paris.

Madeline's kitchen is cozy and bright, with cupboards painted canary yellow, a green tiled backsplash, and an assortment of tea towels featuring illustrated cats.

"You know I always appreciate a visit," Madeline says, retrieving two tall glasses. "I get lonely in here. The children don't come anywhere near as often as I would like."

I'm grateful for the change of topic. "How old is little James now?"

"Two and a half. Such a sweetheart. I'm hoping for more grandchildren, but I try to be good and wait patiently." She mimics zipping up her lips, as if she hasn't badgered her son to have babies since the day he got engaged.

I lean back against the counter while she pulls a jug of iced tea from the fridge. She cuts up two slices of brownie and we mosey over to the porch at the back of the house. It must have been hot all day here because the air is stuffy, almost suffocating.

She waits until I take my first sip to launch into the matter at hand. "I was worried about you. First, I didn't see your car and then—"

I smile brightly. "I really should have called you back. The thing is—" I scrunch up my nose, like I'm so excited I can barely contain it. "I didn't want to say anything before I knew it was serious, but I met someone."

Madeline chokes on a piece of brownie, unable to contain her surprise.

"That's where I was the last few days. Amir—that's my boyfriend— lives in Albany. Since I was off work for a few days, I figured I'd stay with him."

"Your boyfriend?" She says, avoiding a repeat of her near spit-take.

I came up with the boyfriend idea on the flight home. Olivier and I didn't have much time to work out the details, but he's going to stay at the house when he comes back. Of course he'd live in his wife's home. But, after a while, people might get suspicious. If they think I have a serious boyfriend, it'll be easier to keep Olivier around.

"Yes, my boyfriend. Amir wasn't at the wedding because I didn't want to take any attention away from Cassie."

Madeline nods. Everyone would expect Good Taylor to put Cassie's needs first.

"We met at the bar almost three months ago," I continue. "I know this might sound corny, but it was love at first sight."

"Ooh!" Madeline says excitedly. "Just like Cassie and Olivier! By the way, have you heard from your sister? How's the honeymoon going? I've always wanted to go to Paris."

My throat tightens. Suddenly I'm so angry for us, my fake boyfriend and me. We can't even get one minute in the spotlight. It's always Cassie, Cassie, Cassie. But once the rage clears, I see the opportunity. And I take it. "It's going great, from what I can tell. And yes, we've been in touch. They seem really happy."

"Um," Madeline says, taking another bite. A few crumbs fall on her lap. "That's good. I keep thinking of what Rae would have made of this. They did get married awfully fast. Sending invitations via text message? With three days' notice? I know people don't send mail anymore, but still. Does Cassie even know that much about Oliver?"

"It's *Olivier*, actually." I can't help with whatever he's doing right now, but at least I can do that for him. "And yes, she does. The two of them are such a great match. It's wonderful that they found each other. When you know, you know, right?"

I feel sick thinking about what is happening—has already happened?—in Paris. In fact, I still haven't touched my slice of brownie. But I have to do this. When he comes back, Olivier will be scrutinized. They already talked so much behind his back these last few months. The more people believe he and Cassie were the real deal, the easier it will be.

"It's really noble of you to say that." Madeline reaches over and pats my thigh like I'm an obedient dog.

I smile, resisting the urge to punch her in the face. Olivier is right. There's nothing keeping me in this town. As soon as the dust settles, we'll be in the city, where nobody knows us, and no one can come and stomp all over our happiness.

"I mean it," I say. "I've seen them every day these last few months. Cassie and Olivier really love each other."

"Soon there'll be wedding bells for you, dear. Everyone gets their turn eventually. Just you wait."

Sometimes I think the worst people in my life have been the ones who pretended to wish me well. The ones who felt, without knowing, that they could decide what was best for me. Like the passersby who called the police when they saw me in the car. If only they'd minded their own business. Mom was going to come back for me. These assholes told themselves they were saving me, but all they did was ruin my life.

"I hope so," I say, smiling so much my cheeks cramp.

"So what does Amir do?"

"He works at a bank. He's very smart. I'm so lucky." If I'm going to have a fake boyfriend, then I want a good one. "He makes a pretty decent living, too." I look down, like I'm blushing.

"I'm happy for you, sweetheart." Madeline glances sideways as if to check that no one is eavesdropping. Over the fence, her neighbors are tending to their garden. "When Cassie came back with Olivier, I couldn't help but think... I mean, he is certainly handsome. And he's helpful, too. He carried my groceries a few times, put them away and everything. Good manners are important; I don't want to discount that. But he seems so out of place here. For a while I thought he'd run back to the big city as soon as the novelty of country life wore off."

I try to keep my face still, chasing away the image of Olivier finding country life novel. "He's very invested in the inn," I say. "It'll look amazing when he's done."

"Hmm," Madeline says absentmindedly. That doesn't fit with her narrative. "Well, I hope you'll have a real wedding. That party these two put on..." She grimaces. "Maybe I'm just old-fashioned, but in my time, people who got married so fast only did it for one reason." She raises an eyebrow as if to check that I'm getting her gist. "Cassie's pregnant, isn't she?"

My heart drops, my mind going to the question I've been avoiding all along. Did they sleep together in Paris? And then it hits me all over again. *I* slept with someone else. I betrayed Olivier and almost ruined everything.

"You'll have to ask her," I say at last. "All I know is that she might not have gotten the big wedding, but the honeymoon is more than making up for it."

Madeline takes another sip of her iced tea, then stares at me for a while. "So, this Miles—"

"Amir," I correct. "It's an Arabic name. His mother is from Morocco." I don't know if it was a trap, but I was prepared for it nonetheless. I wonder what the real Amir thought when he noticed I'd checked out early. He probably just moved on to the next lonely, screwed-up woman who came through the door.

Madeline puts a hand in front of her mouth. "Oops! Do we get to meet him soon?"

"Of course! I think you'll like him."

I haven't decided what will happen to Amir yet. Will he have met someone else? That's the obvious choice. But for once, *just once*, I'd like to be in charge, to set the rules of my own relationships.

I say my goodbyes to Madeline soon after, promising to return with a man who doesn't exist or, at least, not on this continent. But I don't head home yet. Instead, I take a detour via Main Street. I need to make sure people see me, if it ever comes to that. I stop by the drugstore, the only one open late, exchanging a few words with Marco, the cashier. When I exit, clutching a bag full of cleaning supplies I don't need, I spot a familiar face on the other side of the street: Cassie's ex-boyfriend Darren.

These two were an odd match: she the wild child who wanted to try everything, the drugs and the parties and the boys, and he the serious student who always said please and thank you, and mowed his grandma's lawn after church every Sunday. Their endless cycle of breaking up and getting back together went on for so long I often lost track.

I wave at him quickly, only briefly making eye contact. I need to get some sleep before the police come.

"Taylor!" He's crossing the street now, he and his determined gait catching up to me in no time. "Have you heard from Cassie?"

His face is one big frown. This isn't a casual question.

"Of course," I say with what I hope is a warm smile. "She's having the best time in Paris." I fight the urge to keep walking; I don't want to arouse his suspicion.

"Right, but, um, have you spoken to her today? In the last few hours, maybe?"

I try my hardest to keep my face blank, even though of course I know Cassie hasn't posted anything since she was in the bath. I have so little to go on, but that has to mean the plan is working.

"Cassie's on her honeymoon. She has better things to do."

He opens his mouth, but nothing comes out. Then he smiles weakly. "I've been calling her, but she's not picking up."

I give him a pained smile. "Cassie's married now. And they're so happy together."

"That's not true." Darren says. He sounds sure of himself, but at the time, I can tell he's searching my eyes for validation.

Could it be that... Has something been going on between them since she came back home with Olivier? No, no, no, that will mess everything up.

"Haven't you seen her pictures from Paris?" I say. "It almost makes me wish I was there."

"I'm worried about her. Something's not right."

Crap. He needs to let this go. "I'm sorry this is painful for you, Darren. You're a great guy."

I wave at him again and get walking before he can say anything back. I don't really breathe until I'm home, dropping the shopping bag on the floor in the foyer and staring at myself in the antique mirror. What was that all about? What does he know? Like me, I'm sure he's seen all of Cassie's fun on his phone. He might be jealous but there's no reason he should be worried. These thoughts play in my mind over and over as I make myself an egg on toast. I sit at the dining table and stare into the distance, letting the food go cold. Was it fear I read in his eyes? But why?

His face keeps haunting me as I pace the room, replaying our brief conversation. If anyone suspects Olivier and Cassie had a less-than-perfect marriage, this could create a real problem. But what did Darren say, really? Maybe all the pretty pictures of the newlyweds got to his head. I can't blame him.

And then, when I think my nerves can't take it anymore, that I've twisted my brain into too many knots, something truly bizarre happens. I hear a key inserted in the lock, the latch releasing. I rush to the entrance as the front door opens, the hinges squeaking angrily.

Someone's home.

CHAPTER 30

Cassie

NOW

Taylor stares back at me, her mouth hanging open. The honeymoon was supposed to last two more days, so of course she wasn't expecting me so soon. It'll seem odd, but as long as I stick to my story, I'll be okay. God, I *have* to be okay.

"Surprise!" I say, my voice all croaky.

If she notices it, I'll blame it on the air-conditioning on the plane. It was so damn cold in there. Or maybe I felt frozen inside because of everything that happened.

"You're here."

It could be the bad lighting, but Taylor looks like the color has been drained from her, like life has left her body. She still doesn't move, blocking my way.

I push my suitcase against the wall. "I came back early."

Captain Obvious over here, but I need to distract her from the fact that my legs are still shaking. They have been since I walked out of that room.

Taylor's eyes dart behind me, to the front door. "Alone?"

I can't help but look back, even though I know the answer. I mean, I closed the door behind me, so use your brain, Taylor. But I don't say that because I need her on my side. She *has* to believe me.

"Yes, alone. Can we sit down? I've had a long trip, but I need to talk to you."

I walk into the living room, not turning back to check if she's following me. It's Taylor—of course she's following me. She does what I tell her to do. That's always been our thing.

I take off my sneakers and cross my legs in front of me on the couch, but Taylor remains standing, staring down at me.

"Sit, please." I can't keep the irritation out of my voice.

"Where's your husband?" she says, once again looking toward the entrance.

As if Olivier might be about to walk in.

"I said I needed to talk to you."

She studies me coolly, and for a moment, I think she's going to make it harder than it needs to be. But good old Taylor can't afford to hurt my feelings, especially now she knows I own the house outright.

"So tell me."

She sits down on the armchair as far away from me as possible, her butt only half on, as if she wants to be ready to escape.

"Yes, well, I was about to. Here's the thing… Olivier and I broke up. Or what do you call it when you're married?"

"I wouldn't know."

"I guess we're going to get a divorce now. I'm not sure how these things work."

Taylor looks down at her fists, which are clenched tight. "And he's okay with that?"

"What does that even mean?" It wasn't my intention to snap, but the last twenty-four hours have been a lot, to say the least. It's not every day that someone tries to kill me. "Of course he's okay with that."

"I thought he was so love with you he couldn't wait any longer to propose." She's sitting so still that if she wasn't talking, I'd wonder if she'd turned into wax, like a lifeless doll.

"He was." I catch myself. "He *is*."

Olivier's words from last night come back to me. *We're in love.* But that was a sick joke, right? Something he said to hurt me. There's no way. No way...

Suddenly, Taylor gets up. She pats the pocket of her pants and pulls out her phone. "I need to..." she says, already halfway to the other side of the room.

"Not now, please. There's more..."

She looks from her phone to me, takes a moment to think it through, then comes back to sit down. Taylor has always liked to feel needed. She loves it when it seems like we will all fall apart without her.

"I know I don't always show it," I continue, "but I appreciate how you've always been there for me in the hard times. When Mom died—" I trail off, pressing my lips tight. I want to cry and scream and throw things around. What happened to me? When I dare a glance at Taylor again, she looks stoic, expressionless. I move on. "As soon as we got to Paris, Olivier was acting a bit funny." That's the nicest way I can put it. The asshole was planning on murdering me. I know it. *I know it.* "He started talking about how much he missed it. He used to live there, you know?"

"How would I know?"

Her tone is sweet and cutting at the same time.

A few days away from her, and it takes me five minutes to remember why I hate her so fucking much. "So, as I was saying, Olivier started asking if I'd ever see myself living in Paris. Like, maybe not forever, but for a few years." A spark of anger flashes in Taylor's eyes. Shit. Wrong thing to say after she never got to go on that trip. "And, um, I'm not you. Paris is nice. I mean, it's beautiful and everything, but living there? Not for me. People don't even speak English that much. Plus they have stairs and dog poop everywhere." My face twists in disgust.

I expect Taylor to argue on that point, to grumble about how I married a French guy and now I don't appreciate what I have. And why do I always want more? Because that's what people do, Taylor. We. Want. More. Not everyone can be content with scraps. And most of us don't have to. Instead she just nods, her head bobbing up and down. She glances at her phone again, then presses it against her thigh, facedown. What is up with that? Taylor doesn't have any friends. She doesn't have a life. Does she?

My mouth feels so dry, but I can't stop now. "It was a big surprise at first, but then I remembered that when we met, he was talking about moving back to France. So I told him if he really wanted to be there, I shouldn't be the one to stop him. I could have seen that coming, but we fell in love and—" I stop there, because there's only so much bullshit one person can make up, even when that person is me.

"Oh right," Taylor says like something has clicked in her mind. "So, after you met, he stayed in the States for you. He never wanted to be here."

I shouldn't have talked to her as soon as I got home. I waited for hours in the airport; there were no seats available for most of the day. And then I still had the whole flight to think about it, but I haven't ironed out my story enough yet. Ironed. Bad choice of word.

"Anyway," I say, ignoring her comment. "Last night, he told me he was unhappy."

A sick smile forms on Taylor's lips. "With you?"

Bitch. But point taken. I shouldn't say that Olivier was unhappy with me. That won't work. "Not with *me*, with his life in general. We talked for hours."

"I thought he was out with his friends. Didn't you have a night to yourself in your honeymoon suite? That bath looked amazing. At least that's what you posted on Instagram."

A burst of satisfaction courses through me, but it doesn't last. Taylor was watching, and carefully so. Maybe too carefully. "We didn't literally talk for hours. It was more like snippets of conversation we had since we landed in Paris. But in the end, it was very amicable. A super healthy breakup, in fact. And then I figured I should go home."

"Why?" Her tone is cool but I can see how tightly her hand is gripping her phone. "You were having *soooo* much fun."

Can't she let anything slide? I shouldn't have to justify myself to her. "Excuse me if I care too much about doing the right thing, but if we're getting a divorce, then it felt weird to stay on my honeymoon. Even if Olivier wanted the breakup, too. I mean, 'wants' the breakup. It was mutual, is what I'm saying."

I try to shake the image away, but it pops into my mind anyway: Olivier lunging at me, grabbing the iron from the board just as I was trying to. The raw scream that escaped my mouth. How I managed to wrangle it out of his hands, and then...

"So where's your husband now?"

Who does she think she is, interrogating me like this? Leave it to the police, Taylor. Wait, no. Not the police.

"Why do you care?" The question slips out of my lips, and Taylor recoils. I force a smile. Fuck I'm so tired. "We still had the room booked for two nights and I didn't want to leave him in the lurch. I told him he should stay there, and then he'll find somewhere else. He has friends in Paris, obviously. I'm sure he'll be fine."

We're silent for a long while. The old wooden clock Mom liked so much ticks on, making a more excruciating sound with every passing second. Taylor stares off into the distance.

When she still doesn't say anything, I get up and head to my room. There, I take a long, hot shower—I won't be getting in a bath anytime soon—and change into pajamas. Of course I don't sleep that night. Olivier's face haunts me as soon as I try to close my eyes, and then he stays while I stare at the ceiling, studying every crack and bit of chipped paint, hoping he will leave me alone. Olivier was going to ruin my life, but I think I ended up doing that all on my own.

Daylight peaks through the curtains, the sun rising into the sky and pushing its way into the room from behind the velvet fabric. Seconds, minutes, hours pass, and I still haven't looked at my phone. I just want to lie there, away from everything, where the outside world can't get to me. My mind is in shambles as I turn over to face the wall, my back to the window. I'm aching all over, my eyes are paper dry, and I can't bring myself to move. Suddenly, the doorbell rings. And rings, and rings. There's no ignoring it.

"Taylor!" I cry out. "You going to get that?"

But I hear no footsteps, only the shrieking tone, which won't stop. I drag myself out of bed and have to push off the mattress with both hands to stand.

"Cassie? Cassie!"

Darren's voice filters through the door before I've even opened it. When I do, the first thing I notice is his face contorted in worry, his crinkling eyebrows.

He bursts into the foyer. "Cassie, oh my god! I thought something had happened to you. What the hell?" There's no harshness to it. Only fear deep inside his eyes.

And then he's hugging me, wrapping his arms so tight around my body it hurts. I drop my phone onto the console in the entrance so I can hold on to him better.

But then he pulls back. "What happened? I was worried sick!"

I take a deep breath. Wordlessly, I start leading him to my bedroom, but catch myself. If anyone sees us together in there, it won't look good. We go in the living room instead, where I sit down. I feel restless and unable to carry myself at the same time.

"I must have texted you a hundred times!" he says, towering over me.

"I'm sorry I didn't respond. I was…embarrassed." The words barely come out of my mouth. "Can you sit? You're making me nervous."

He does but his knee bounces up and down so much I feel seasick. "You said he was violent—"

Shit.

"No, I said… I didn't… It wasn't like that." The iron. Olivier grabbed it first. I would never have done it. "I was annoyed with him. That's all."

Darren comes to kneel beside me and hangs on to both of my elbows, making sure I'm paying attention. "Cassie, you don't have to lie to me. If he did anything, I'm here to protect you. And if he ever shows his face here again… I mean, he better not show his face here again."

I want to laugh, it's so pathetic. I really thought Darren and I were going to work out this time. We'd learned our lessons; all the mistakes had been made. I couldn't imagine that the worst ones were yet to come.

Darren leans over, close enough that I can feel the warmth of his leg through his slacks. "I went to work this morning but I couldn't focus. You weren't responding to me! So I gave my boss an excuse and rushed over here. I thought… You said he was trying to kill you, Cassie. That's more than a little joke. Even for you."

Fuck. He's not going to let this go. When I needed him that night, he wouldn't take me seriously and now… Darren has always been so straight and narrow. I don't fit in his world.

"You know me. I get a bit dramatic sometimes. Olivier and I broke up. He decided he wanted to stay in Paris because he doesn't like it here." I make a sweeping motion around us, my hand grazing his cheek in the process. That part of the story won't be hard to believe, because it's true. "So we're over. I didn't react so well at first."

It was all going to work out perfectly, but then Olivier had to come back into the room before I had time to leave. He had to see his passport ripped to shreds. He should have known it was all over for him, but he had to try again. The poor guy was so desperate. He couldn't let me go. So I had to make him.

I can't explain any of that to Darren. Maybe it's the lack of sleep, or the adrenaline I've run on since I left the hotel, but there's no happy ending here.

"This doesn't make sense, Cassie. You told me your husband was out to murder you."

"It was a horrible joke, okay? You of all people should get me."

Darren exhales slowly as he stares at a dent in the walnut coffee table. "Everything's a joke to you, isn't it? You came back with this stranger and then went and married him three months later, and then you tell me—"

I cut him off. "I think we misunderstood each other."

"So what happens now? You're here, you're safe. Without him." He crosses his arms against his chest as he lets out another sigh.

"What happens now is that you leave," I say at last, looking at the doorway. "I'm sorry about what I said. I can't do this right now. I need to get through my divorce first." I swallow hard, needing to catch my breath. "I want to be alone for a while."

The words feel itchy against the insides of my throat. Because of course it's a lie. What I want is to erase the last few months of my life. I want to go back to when Darren and I were together, and I want to fight for him. For us. Because that means I would have never met Olivier. I would never have gotten myself into this fucked-up mess. And, maybe for the first time in my life, no one can help me out of it.

I have to do this alone.

I *can't* do this alone.

What I did… There's no coming back from it.

CHAPTER 31

Thérèse

NOW

Something terribly wrong happened in Paris. That's the only logical explanation. Cassie's story didn't make sense, and I think she knew that. I saw the way she wrung her hands as she talked, how she jumped every time the tree rustled in the wind outside the window. I could have asked questions. There were so many holes in her twisted tale. But if I did, I wouldn't be closer to the truth. There's only one person I trust and he's not here. Where is he?

All night long, I stare at my phone, placing bets with the devil. Would it really be so bad if I called him? I could do it from the landline or from Cassie's phone. That way it couldn't be traced back to me. But what if I screw up everything again? Olivier was clear about that. We can't take any risks. If I had listened to him in the first place, it would all be over by now. We'd be together. I'd be free.

Hours keep on ticking by, and still no Olivier. No sign of life.

But maybe that's part of the plan. Maybe Olivier has it all figured out, and I just need to wait.

By early morning I'm like a lion in a cage, bouncing against the bars with too much energy to spare. I need to do *something*. I've spent way too much of my life feeling like other people were in charge, that I had to go along with whatever they wanted to put me through. For now there's only one thing to do: I must get out of the house, away from Cassie.

I end up at the grocery store, mindlessly wandering the aisles as the wheels of my empty cart stick to the dirty tiles. If this were a normal day, I'd be planning what to make for dinner. That's what Cassie would expect, especially after coming back from her big trip. Just because she's acting like a lunatic doesn't mean I can afford to do the same. Today, I'm a doting sister welcoming her beloved sibling home. This is still my life. For now.

"Ma'am."

I look up to see a tall man in a uniform frowning at me.

"You're blocking the way," he adds, pointing up and down the aisle. He's right. I'm standing in the middle, making it impossible for the mom behind me to push past with her stroller. "Ma'am? You shouldn't be standing here."

That's true; I should be in Paris with Olivier. I didn't get a chance to talk to him about this, but I want to go back there on *our* honeymoon.

"I'm sorry," I say, finally stepping to the side. "Your little one is so cute," I add, turning back to the mother, without even looking inside the stroller. It's what Good Taylor would have done—defuse any possible tension with a compliment. She's still in there somewhere. I can't wait for her to die a quick and painless death.

Mac and cheese. That's what I'll make tonight. Some good old American comfort food to help Cassie deal with the breakup. Does she seriously think I believed her? That *anyone* would? She always underestimated Good Taylor. And I've waited long enough for the day it would come back to bite her in the ass.

I get home loaded up with two bags of food, even though I hardly remember buying anything. Cassie's money—the stash I took before going to Paris—is dwindling fast. Based on the life she was living over there, I'm not sure hers is going to last very long.

I hear Cassie before I see her. She's in the living room, talking to someone.

"I'm sorry," she says. I stand in the foyer, so still and quiet I almost forget to breathe. "I was being dramatic. It all went so fast. I–I shouldn't have said that to you. Can we please pretend it didn't happen?"

Oh god. Olivier is here. He's fine. He's alive! Only now do I let myself accept how scared I was for him. Every muscle in my body loosens up at once. I'm like jelly. I can't even feel my legs anymore, but I don't care. He's safe. Everything will be okay.

My first instinct is to walk in there. I have to see him, but I'm afraid of what will happen when I do. Cassie will read the look on my face, the love and the pure joy. These last few weeks, it's been hard to fathom why she couldn't see what was happening right in front of her. But every day Olivier and I got away with it, we became a little more reckless. Soon it almost felt like a game. If Cassie couldn't see I was sleeping with her boyfriend—I didn't know they were married then—that only made me want to move closer toward the fire, afraid of getting burned, but pulled in by the flames nonetheless.

"Please," Cassie says now. "Can we forget everything?"

I grip tight onto the shopping bags, the blood draining from my fingers. My temples pulse against my skull. Soon this will all be over. Olivier and I will be together. I'll do whatever it takes. Or else I'll lose my mind.

But then another voice filters through the doorway. "This doesn't make sense, Cassie. You told me your husband was out to murder you."

It's not Olivier.

Cassie *knows*.

Cassie *knows* and Olivier didn't come back.

I manage to stop the scream that wants to come out just in time. Instead it feels like I'm choking, like there is no air around me. Breathless, I turn around, which is when I see Cassie's phone on the console. Moving one shopping bag to my right hand and wincing at the weight, I grab it. Then,

I slowly open the door, clenching my jaw as if that will mitigate the noise. Outside, I shove the groceries back into the trunk of my car, holding on to the hood so it doesn't slam shut. I can't be too careful.

After that, I'm walking down the street, my pace quickening with every passing second. I need to talk to Olivier. Now. Cassie has her own birthday as her password, which she clearly hasn't changed since we were teens.

I flick through her contacts until I find Olivier's number, and press Call. *Pick up pick up pick up.* The ringtone goes on endlessly, or at least that's how it feels, until his voicemail message begins.

Hi, you've reached Olivier Laurent. I'm sorry I'm unavailable right now, but please leave a message and I'll get back to you as soon as I can.

Paul, our elderly neighbor three houses down, waves at me from his lawn as Olivier's voice fills my ear. The old man's two German shepherds bark, drowning the sound of my beloved promising he'll get back to me.

I wave back, my smile tight, and hang up. Another try, same result. *Please, Olivier. I'm sorry I stormed off that day you told me you were married. I'm sorry I couldn't bring myself to believe you, but I do now. Give me another chance. I need you back. Please.*

Any moment now, Cassie is going to notice her missing phone. I should stop. Give up. I can't stop. At first, I don't plan to say anything. I just want to hear his voice—soft and sweet, not to mention his melodic accent—one more time. When the beep resonates after his voicemail message, I can't help but stay on the line.

"Olivier, it's me. I miss you. Please, I want to know if you're okay. Give me a sign. Anything. I love you. I always will. I'm sorry about what happened, all of it. Forget everything else, I just want to be with you."

My voice sounds shaky, but he'll know who it is. He'll find his way back to me. *Does anyone know you're in Paris?* I lied to my love. And now I'm doing the one thing he told me not to. If I've blown this again, I won't be able to live with myself.

I turn around, rushing back toward the house as quickly as I left it. I've only been gone a few minutes, but the car that was parked on the other side of the street earlier is no longer there. It must have been Darren's.

Before going in, I wipe her phone against my thighs, though my palms are so sweaty that it won't make a difference anyway. But Cassie is not looking for her phone. In fact, I find her sitting on the couch. She's looking down at her lap. Tears drop onto her new satin robe, leaving a watermark on the shiny pink fabric.

"Oh, it's you," she says, looking up and rubbing her eyes.

"What's wrong?"

I put the phone back on the console on the way in, but I'm still holding the memory of Oliver's voice.

"I'm fine," she says getting up and noticing the grocery bags in my hands.

She heads to the kitchen. I follow her.

"I need to eat something," she says, rummaging around the cupboards.

For once she doesn't ask what cereals we have left, if I can grab her the milk from the fridge, and how about I start a fresh pot of coffee because I know how to make it better. Today, she makes her own breakfast and sits down at the round Formica table while I put the groceries away.

When she speaks again, she sounds lighter. Almost chipper. "I should have let you come with me to my father's funeral. I wasn't in my right mind then. That whole thing with Olivier—I should never have married him."

I turn around, clutching the carton of eggs. "Then why did you?"

She scoffs. "You always think people are so black and white. Good or bad. We all know which one you are. Don't tell me you didn't love it, being the perfect daughter."

"It wasn't hard, being better than you."

Her phone chimes from the entrance and we both jump a little. She tries to rest her spoon on the side of the bowl, but it clatters on the table, splattering milk-soaked cereal around her. Ignoring the mess she made, she starts to get up, but then changes her mind and sits back down, shaking her head.

"Anyway, it's you and me again now," Cassie says. "And we have to be there for each other."

A desire burns inside of me as I look down at the eggs in my hand. I want to throw every single one at her and watch their shells smash against her pretty little skull. We have *never* been there for each other. *I* have been there for her time and time again. Cassie would break Rae's favorite vase and immediately point the finger toward me. She'd steal a twenty from her mother's wallet and swear she saw me take it. I never said anything because I couldn't.

"Cassie—" My voice is so small, so shattered, that I'm not even sure I'm speaking out loud. "Are you going to tell me what happened in Paris?"

She picks up her spoon again, wiping the table with the sleeve of her robe. "Don't try to make it more complicated than it needs to be, Taylor. Everything will be fine. We're good. We're sisters, right?"

But here's what Cassie doesn't understand: I'm done being good. "Aren't you selling the house and kicking me out on the street?"

I turn back to the fridge, depriving myself of her reaction. Or maybe I don't want her to see my flushed cheeks, my tight chest. I've so rarely stood up to her.

"I'm sorry I said that." I freeze. This. Is. Not. Normal. "And I have more to tell you."

I turn around slowly, staring at the groceries that have now spilled out of the bag, the jug of orange juice, a bunch of asparagus, and a jar of peanut butter rolling against the toe kick underneath the cupboard. I bend down to pick it up.

"Leave it!" Cassie says, louder.

I do what she orders and drag a chair back. It scrapes against the floor, making us both wince. "What is it, Cassie?"

She puts on a smile and looks me deep in the eyes. "I still want to renovate the inn. You know, the way Olivier planned."

"You mean the way I suggested and you told me at the time it was a dumb idea?"

She exhales loudly. "Yes, fine. You were right. That's what you want to hear? You. Were. Right. But just because he decided to stay in Paris doesn't mean we can't do it ourselves. He got the paint cans already, and did you know he ordered tile samples for the bathrooms before we left? They should arrive soon. We could choose together."

"You can't be serious." This is the last thing I thought we'd be discussing right now.

"Of course I am. And there's something else. My dad left me some—" The doorbell rings, interrupting her. Cassie's eyes bulge out. "Are you waiting for someone?"

I shake my head. "Nope."

She swallows hard.

I start to get up, but she puts her hand on my forearm. "Maybe we're not home," she says quietly. Pleadingly.

I get up anyway. "Why wouldn't we be?"

"We're not always home!" she scream-whispers.

My spine tingles as I head out of the kitchen. "Our cars are out front. We're definitely home."

"Taylor, no! Don't!"

I quicken my pace toward the front door, Cassie on my heels. Fearing she'll try to stop me, I swing it open with a little too much force. It slams against the stopper, which makes a popping sound. Two people stand on the porch: a fortysomething Black woman, tall and slender, and a white guy with red hair and a beard. Both are dressed in street clothes, but the woman is already pulling out a thin wallet, flicking it halfway open to reveal a gold insignia.

My heart crushes inside my chest. "Yes?"

"Ms. Quinn?"

I feel Cassie react behind me, but I'm faster. "Yes."

"Ms. Cassie Quinn?"

The next few seconds go by in a flash, like I'm not really here. Somebody else is experiencing them.

I step aside.

Cassie nods slowly, not glancing at me.

The woman presents her badge. She's a detective, she explains. They both are.

They ask to come inside, their faces solemn.

And then they utter the words I feared the most for the past day, the ones I sensed deep down were coming, the ones I prayed I'd never hear.

"Ms. Quinn, we're so sorry to inform you that your husband, Mr. Olivier Laurent, was found dead in his hotel room in Paris."

I don't know what Cassie does, or what she says. I'm unable to process anything. The only thing I hear is the scream, screeching and feral, that permeates the air around us like thick smoke. It's been going on for a few seconds when I realize it's coming out of me.

And still I can't stop it. In that moment I already know I can keep screaming and screaming and screaming, the pain will never go away.

CHAPTER 32

Cassie

NOW

S ome coffee would be nice. For our guests?" I give Taylor a stern look, then wait for her to take the hint.

Annoyingly, she doesn't move, but I still feel like I should give her a pass: that earsplitting scream she let out diverted the attention from my reaction. Or lack thereof. Still, we don't want to be rude or give a bad first impression.

"Taylor, please?"

"We really don't mean to be a bother," the woman says. She introduced herself as Detective Jackson and she's all smiles now, but I bet that won't last long. "Maybe we could sit down?"

"Of course," I say, leading them toward the couch, my mind spinning.

I expected this. I prepared myself for it. Everything will be fine.

As soon as the four of us are seated, I launch into it. "I was just with him. I can't imagine… That's… I can even think of the words. Oh god, tell me. What happened?"

Detective Jackson and her colleague, Detective Collins, look at each other with a mix of pain and confusion. Am I not doing this right? Fuck. There should be a how-to guide for the perfectly distressed widow.

Detective Collins clears his throat. "The cleaning staff at the hotel found him. The 'Do Not Disturb' sign was on, but they have a policy of checking in with guests if they haven't cleaned the room in more than forty-eight hours. Fancy hotel, and all that."

"Hmm," I say, nodding repeatedly as I press my lips together.

"But of course you'd know that. You were there," Detective Jackson says.

I force a smile. "Can you tell me what happened? Olivier was fine when I left Paris. We had a really good, peaceful conversation, and we haven't spoken since. What... How did he—"

I shouldn't finish that sentence. A distraught wife would react like that. She would be confused. Hurt. Freaking out.

"We're still waiting for more information, but the cause of death was most likely an overdose of sleeping pills," Detective Jackson says.

Taylor gasps before I can.

"Your husband also seems to have suffered a concussion on his head," Detective Jackson adds. "So that's giving the detectives pause."

"Aren't *you* the detectives?"

Detective Jackson sighs. "The *French* detectives. Since it happened over there, they're in charge of finding out exactly what went down. Our job is to assist them in any way we can."

"That's so kind of you."

I glance at Taylor, who's nodding almost imperceptibly, her fingers twisted together on her lap.

"Really the reason we're involved is you. A French man dies in France; it's their case. But a French man who lives in the States with his American wife, who was with him hours before he died... That's where we come in. Do you know anything about that concussion, Ms. Quinn?"

"Please call me Cassie. Ms. Quinn was my mother. And I'm Ms. Laurent, actually." I pause, but she's clearly waiting for me to continue. "Yes, Olivier hit his head. A day or two before I left, maybe? I can't remember. Between the time difference and the jet lag, I'm not sure. So, um, he got up in the middle of the night and tripped on the ironing board. We'd left it out from the night before. Olivier fell and the iron landed on his head. I slept right through it; I don't really remember the details."

Before I can take in the detectives' reactions, Taylor turns to me with eyes wide open, her mouth slightly agape. What's her problem?

"None of that woke you up?" It's Detective Jackson. Her smile is kind, but that doesn't mean anything.

Shit, I'm not thinking clearly enough. "I was still jet-lagged. Olivier bought these sleeping pills for the trip, and I guess they worked a little too well."

"Didn't *you* buy the sleeping pills?" Taylor says.

"What does it matter?" I say, too sharply.

"It does matter," Detective Jackson cuts in, with a half smile. "So *you* purchased the sleeping pills?"

I look down, stopping myself from shooting daggers at Taylor. I wish we'd get off this topic already. I didn't exactly get these pills legally, and I'm in enough trouble as it is, but it looks like I have to answer so I face the detectives again. "Olivier, my *husband*, suggested the sleeping pills. He came with me to get them. I paid for them so I guess, *technically*, I bought them. I never thought Olivier would…" I pause, like I'm about to cry, my chin quivering.

I'm good at this. I used to fool Mom all the time as a teen. I could do the worst things and get away with them. But of course, no dead bodies were involved then.

Detective Collins takes a deep breath. "Ms. Laurent, we're very sorry for your loss, and we know this must be a lot to take in, but it's important we help our colleagues in France with their investigation."

"Investigation?" I say, bringing my hand to my chest.

"That's generally what happens when someone dies like this."

I swallow hard. *Come on, Cassie. You can do this. You'll be fine. They can't prove anything.* "I mean, could Olivier have maybe committed suicide?"

I say it like it just occurred to me, like it wasn't my plan all along. To be fair, I didn't mean to hit him with the iron. He grabbed it first; it was self-defense. But then he held it over my head and froze, his eyes pooling with anguish. I took advantage of a split second of hesitation on his part. It was him or me. When it smashed against his head, it startled me, like I wasn't the one doing it. I thought he might be dead for a moment. I could picture the police rushing into the room and clasping handcuffs around my wrists. And then I realized: I *wanted* him gone. That way there would only be one side to the story: mine. No messy divorce, no risk that he'd come after my money, that he would try to kill me again. He wouldn't let me go, so he'd get what he deserved.

He was starting to come to and I was enraged, determined to keep him away forever. That's when I saw the bottle of pills. Two could play at this game. So I gave him a glass of water, but he wouldn't take it. He tried to fight me, but he was too dizzy to resist when I straddled him, my knees digging into the crook of his elbows, and poured the liquid down his throat. Just some water. Some cloudy water. Three sips for the marriage he tricked me into, and three more for getting in my way. Like I said, it was self-defense. Then the glass was empty, and as I walked out the door, I tried to forget exactly how many pills I'd crushed into it.

"You're correct that suicide is the most reasonable explanation. But there are a few outstanding elements we need to clear up."

Detective Jackson glances at her colleague, who takes over. "Ms. Laurent, why did you leave your honeymoon early? And without your husband?"

I let out a deep sigh, then turn to Taylor. She has to be a part of this, whether she likes it or not. "I was just telling Tay about this. It all happened so fast."

Slowly she turns to me, like I awoke her from a spell. I never call her *Tay*. It's something I just made up, but sisters have little nicknames for each other, don't they?

I continue. "My father died recently. We were estranged and I had no idea he was living this glamorous life in the city. I met Olivier at his funeral, about three months ago."

The detectives nod encouragingly, and I explain the rest of the story, the one I thought through all the way home. The official version I feed them is this: I was distraught—dead dad, so hard!—and met a handsome French man. It was intense and passionate right away, and before I knew it, we were on our way to City Hall. Yes, it was fast and, well, really spontaneous, but we were having so much fun. I thought I was in love. Olivier is, *was*, a great guy. I had gotten out of a long relationship only days before and got swept off my feet. Shit happens when you want to be happy.

"But your wedding was only recently?" Detective Jackson says. Her right eyebrow rises so high it might touch her hairline.

"Yes, I was getting to that. After we got married, we realized it had gone a *little* too fast. I don't have family anymore and Olivier's is in France—"

The two detectives glance at Taylor in unison. What did I say?

Detective Jackson addresses her now. "We're deeply sorry for your loss, too. Do you need to take a moment? You look very shocked."

Shit, so they noticed, too. What the fuck is wrong with her? Once again, I remember what Olivier said. I'd pushed the thought to the back of my mind, certain he was only trying to rile me up, but now it's staring back at me. Taylor does seem distraught. More than me? She can never let me have anything, not even this.

"They were close," I say quickly, reaching for Taylor's hand. She stares at mine. "When Olivier and I came back here, the three of us started hanging out. I mean, Taylor works hard so she's not around much. But it was important to me that they get along."

"And you did?" Detective Collins says to Taylor.

She starts to open her mouth, but I can't let her talk. "May I have some water? I'm feeling a bit faint. This is all too much."

Taylor takes a deep breath, and for a few seconds, nobody moves. "Yes, we were close," she says.

Then, she gets up and walks off to the kitchen. The three of us sit in horrifying silence, the sound of the tap running our only soundtrack. Taylor comes back out carrying four glasses of water on our old wooden tray, but her hands shake so much that it spills all over.

Detective Jackson waits until she's sitting back down. "I don't think we've been properly introduced."

I gulp down my water, noisy gargles drowning everything else for a moment.

"I'm the sister," she says. "Cassie's sister. Taylor Quinn."

"My mother adopted her when she was a teen," I say. "We're not, like… *blood*. Her mom was a distant cousin of my mom."

"Legally, we're sisters," Taylor says plainly.

Detective Collins frowns in my direction. "You said you had no family left. It's a bit confusing, is all."

"My husband died."

"The husband you left during your honeymoon," Detective Jackson says. "Why'd you leave, Ms. Laurent?"

"Olivier and I *both* realized we'd rushed into it. It was fun while it lasted, but we weren't *really* ready to commit to each other for life. After a few days in Paris, he told me he missed France too much. He wanted to stay there, and we both knew that meant without me."

"And you were okay with that?"

I nod. "We made a mistake."

"Hmm…except Mr. Laurent is no longer here to make mistakes."

Finally, *finally*, the tears come. Not many, and I have to force them a little, but here I am, the broken wife, the widow. At last. When I start sobbing, they leave me alone for a couple of minutes. The three of them sit there, watching me cry. Then, Detective Jackson asks me to relate my last hours in Paris, step by step.

I tell them about my night of self-care, how relaxing that bath was. And that wine, *yummy*. Olivier came home a little drunk—understandable!— and woke me up. We had a long, calm, and loving discussion. No harsh words were exchanged. And no, Olivier was never violent with me. Such a kind, honest man. You know aside from the fact that he drugged me and tried to murder me. Twice. How good it felt to smash the iron into his head. To watch him be completely at my mercy as I poured the water down his throat. I didn't know what I was doing. I wasn't thinking clearly but it felt so right in the moment. Of course I don't share that last part.

"After we were done talking, I couldn't go back to sleep. So I got up and packed my suitcase. I thought about booking another room but I checked online, and the hotel was full. It felt like a sign that I should go home. I took a taxi to the airport and waited there most of the day to get a seat on a flight home."

I didn't actually check if the hotel was full, so I have to hope it was, in the middle of summer. For the rest, I can only assume they have video footage of me leaving the suite, then the hotel, then getting into a taxi. I was calm then. So relieved. When I'm done talking, the detectives remain still, their faces blank.

"Mind if we ask you a few questions now?" Detective Jackson says to Taylor.

For the first time since they arrived, I really look at her. She's even paler now, if that's even possible. Her eyes are red-rimmed and tears threaten to stream down her face. It's *my* husband who died (bless his soul) and she's out here stealing my thunder. Again.

I have to stop her. "I'm sorry, but this is all such a shock. I think I need to go lie down. We both do."

"Okay," Jackson says. "We don't want to keep you too long for now, and we'll be in touch as soon as we have more information."

I smile painfully, then we all get up and I lead them toward the door, where they give me their condolences one more time. I don't exhale until they're back in their car, driving away from me.

In the meantime, Taylor has disappeared off into the kitchen. I find her leaning over the sink, her palms pressing on either side of the counter. At first it looks like she's throwing up, but in fact she's sobbing hard, so much that it sounds like she's choking.

"What?" she barks after a minute without looking up.

It hits me for real this time. Olivier wasn't lying. Something *was* going on between them.

"What indeed," I say coolly. "What was that all about in there? What aren't you telling me?"

She straightens up and takes a deep breath before turning to me. "You killed him. You two had a fight and—"

"We didn't fight," I cut in, crossing my arms against my chest. "We had the best time in Paris. You know that. Everybody knows that." Twice she opens her mouth to respond. Both times she closes it again without saying a word. "What reason could I have to kill my husband? Please, find one. I'll be waiting."

"You—" She lets out a strangled breath and doesn't finish her sentence.

"I didn't do anything. And you should be very careful what you tell anyone. You wouldn't want to accuse your darling sister without proof."

We stand there for a while, staring at each other. Taylor has always been my downfall. The one who stole love, space, time. I'm not going to let her take my freedom, too.

CHAPTER 33

Thérèse

NOW

She killed him. She's lying. *Of course* she's lying.

A dozen times, I grab my phone to call the detectives and tell them. Cassie's story doesn't hold up one bit. Olivier didn't want to die. He didn't, he didn't, he didn't. He loved me. What he wanted was to be with me. I even look up the number to the police station online, then immediately close the tab. I can't prove anything. As far as the world knows, Olivier and Cassie were happy. That's what the photos show. Cassie has the receipts. And what do I have? Nothing.

Worse. I'd have to explain that I was having an affair with my sister's husband. They would press me with endless questions and I would for sure crack under the pressure. I'm not like Cassie, a cold-blooded murderer, almost smiling as she was told her husband had died. Even if I could keep my face straight, I'd be forced to admit that I followed them to Paris, that I stalked them under my cap and behind my sunglasses like a damn sociopath. And if that didn't make me sound unhinged enough, I'd have to explain that Olivier had a plan. That he drugged her that night. That *he* was going to kill her.

I know my sister killed her husband because he was out to kill her. And he was out to kill her to be with me.

I play the conversation in my mind over and over again, and it never sounds like anything less that the fantasies of a deluded, lonely, pathetic woman. Which is who I am. Who I've always been.

And then there's the doubt. It seeps under my skin, crawls all over my body. What if Olivier lied to me? What if he never intended to kill her at all? What if he was so unhappy with the way things had panned out that he took his own life? Cassie is not telling the truth, but there's still the possibility that *some* of it is true. And that's enough to keep me away from the police.

Which means I have nothing else to do but stir in my despair. Cassie and I have barely been alone since the officers left us two days ago. People, neighbors and friends, have been dropping by to pay their respects. They come armed with casseroles and condolences, sharing platitudes about a man they didn't even know.

Every time someone rings the bell, Cassie uses the occasion to show off one of her new black dresses—straight from Paris—in which she looks a little too good. She stares at my red puffy eyes. I take in her perfectly applied makeup. We say nothing.

And no one speaks to me. *She's* the bereaved widow and she loves it. Parades around, pretending to blow into a tissue every now on then. Marvels at the flowers they brought, swearing they didn't need to, while displaying the arrangement front and center with a smirk on her fucking face. The attention makes her glow like a neon light; it's Rae's funeral all over again.

Madeline comes by and though *she* asks how I'm doing, Cassie overhears it and quickly brings the conversation back to her. Her grief, her husband, her utter and total shock. I picture my own two hands around her neck, pressing hard, watching her choke. Slowly. Then I walk away.

It's another two days before the police come for me. Not literally, but the detectives call and ask me to come by the station. Alone, they insist. As soon as possible. I'm grateful for the escape, though it feels a little like I'm sending myself off to my own slaughter.

The station is a twenty-minute drive and I blast the radio all the way, drowning my thoughts.

He loved me. Did he love me?

I read the few articles I could find online, hoping my French was good enough to make sense of what they said. A man died in the suite of a luxury hotel, where, strangely, he used to work. Was it suicide or overdose? His wife—they called her Carrie, she would have hated that—had left him hours before. She knows exactly what happened in that room. The rest of us will probably never find out.

Inside the police station, the air-conditioning makes me shiver and I almost go back to the car to retrieve my leather jacket from the trunk, but I want to get this over with as quickly as possible. Unbelievably, it's still only August, the height of summer. The red dress I bought in Paris pops in my mind; I didn't need to get rid of it after all. Didn't need to worry about Amir telling anyone I was there. Didn't even need the fake boyfriend.

Detective Jackson comes to greet me, then leads me to an interrogation room, where she offers me coffee. I decline. I can't take anything from them because whatever they want from me, I won't give it away.

We sit on opposite sides of the table. There's a camera in the top-left corner of the room, and I bet this one works.

After a few words of introduction and more condolences, the detective gets right into it. "So your sister goes off to New York City for her father's funeral, and she comes back with a husband."

I wait for a question, but it doesn't come. So I nod. "I didn't know they were married. They kept it secret."

"Even from you, the sister? You lived with them."

"They kept it a secret." My voice sounds robotic. I've cried all of the tears over the last few days. I have none left.

"Okay. So Cassie comes back from a few days away with a brand-new boyfriend. Did you find that strange at all?"

"My sister has always been impulsive. Though I think she'd call it spontaneous."

"Can I get a yes or no?"

"No, I didn't find it that strange. Cassie has had many boyfriends. I was a little surprised, but I got over it quickly."

"And they seemed happy?"

Did they? Did I ever believe, from the moment they arrived, that they loved each other? The truth is that I don't remember. I tried so hard to block them off, to not see anything.

"Cassie and I aren't very close. I can't say I paid too much attention."

"But you welcomed Mr. Laurent into your home and you two became friendly. At least that's what your sister said."

Except it's not my home. It never was. I nod. "Olivier was a great guy."

That's when I allow myself to think what has been burning inside me all along. He died because of me. He'd still be alive if he hadn't met me. Or if I hadn't gone to Paris. Or if I hadn't walked into their hotel room that night. Or if I hadn't let him go back to her. I could have stopped this so many times, in so many ways. I did this. I lied to him about the fact that no one knew I was in Paris. I let him believe he could still get away with it, and then I sent him off to die.

"Allegedly, they agreed to separate that night. It might have been tense, heated. Do you have any reason to believe that Cassie and Olivier may have been fighting? I mean, beyond a few harsh words, maybe physically?"

"No."

"That was a fast response. Did you ever witness them fight?"

"No."

"Do you have any reason to believe that, up until that night, they were anything other than a married couple enjoying their honeymoon?"

"No."

"Do you have any reason to believe that any foul play was involved in the death of Olivier Laurent?"

I say it louder this time. "No."

"So he was a great guy you became friendly with, and when his wife left, he suddenly was heartbroken over it and took his own life, even though it was supposedly his idea to stay in Paris without her. Is that what you think happened?"

"I have no idea what happened."

"Because you weren't there?"

My throat feels like it's closing up. Do they already know I was in Paris? They could have spoken to Amir. But it would have come up by now. I have to hang on to that.

The detective lets out a pained sigh. "You were very distraught when we came to your house."

This time I stare into her eyes. "People keep dying around me. It's not a great feeling."

"I can only imagine. Is there anything you would like to add at this time? A man was found dead in his honeymoon suite after his new wife walked away from their marriage. We don't want to draw conclusions too quickly unless we're certain."

But I think she knows the answer before I open my mouth. In fact, she's eyeing the door. I *have* to let them draw these conclusions, because the truth is so much worse. I have nothing else to say to her. So she lets me go.

And now I have to live without him. As I drive home, tears blurring my vision, fingers gripped tight around the steering wheel, all I can think about is that I have to end this. I can't go on like this, knowing what happened.

But I'm still alive when I get back to the house. Because as much as I want to beat myself up for what happened to my love, I want to hurt Cassie a whole lot more.

CHAPTER 34

Cassie

NOW

The wake felt like having another wedding, only over a few days and with less dancing. Somebody else was bringing the food—I have enough to eat for a week—but even the flowers looked the same. All along, I couldn't shake the feeling that I was being tested. People had so many questions. Were we fighting? Did I ever see the dark side to him? Why didn't I stay? I was having so much fun! And why didn't I want to live in Paris with him? It sure looked like I was loving it.

The detectives call again, several times. Once, it's to confirm that Olivier did die of an overdose of sleeping pills. Hearing it knocks the wind out of me. I'm not a monster. None of this would have happened if he hadn't tried to kill me first.

The second time, it's to ask about his visa status and green card application. For one spine-tingling moment, I wonder if the immigration lawyer told them about our phone call. I asked about a divorce two days before Olivier supposedly suggested we call it quits. But I stuck to my story. We fell in love. We got married. And if I could help Olivier get a green card, then why not? I wanted him to stay here. It made sense. I don't know much about how it all works; Olivier handled that part. Yes, I think his application was in progress. Though of course, he wouldn't need it any-more since he changed his mind and wanted to stay in Paris.

The detectives don't mention talking to the immigration lawyer, so I have to assume what I said to her really is confidential information. I'm too scared to call her—what if the police are tracking my phone?—so I look it up online. She might have to divulge the content of our conversations if I was suspected of murder. Which, well...but that's not going to happen. If the police suspected me, then why aren't they here already? Why wait? They have nothing on me. It was self-defense. They can't prove anything.

Finally, the moment comes when I have the house to myself. Even Taylor is gone, who knows where. She's been acting weird all this time. I mean, even weirder than usual. At night I lie in bed listening to the sounds around the house. The ticking clock, the creaky stairs. Taylor's bedroom is down the hall from mine. There should be no creaking. I can't squash the feeling that something is coming. This can't be the end of it. I killed someone. I could have walked out of that room after I hit him. But no one will ever know. It was self-defense. I have to keep repeating it in my head. If it comes to that, I'll be ready.

In the kitchen, the smell of the beef stew Madeline brought over per-meates from under the pot cover. It makes me want to throw up. Trying to shake the feeling away, I drag a chair against the counter and get up to check the striped cookie jar.

The money is gone. I can tell even before I lift the lid. When my inheri-tance came through, I couldn't help but stare at the number on my account. It felt unreal. Ridiculous, even. Olivier kept rambling on about everything he needed to buy to work on the inn—tools and supplies and whatnot—but I wasn't comfortable giving him my credit card details. I never trusted him, not even as he watched all these YouTube videos, painfully trying to learn how to patch holes in the wall or how to fix a squeaky door.

I checked my bank balance several times a day, feeling paranoid. What if it suddenly disappeared? So I took a bunch of cash out over time, gave some to Olivier, and stuffed bills around the house. If something ever happened, I'd have that, at least.

Now I wouldn't put it past my dear husband (RIP) to have stolen from me, especially since he was the only one who knew about the money, aside from that day I was hungover and blabbered to that sleazy Realtor. I should never have told Olivier but I was so stunned when that cow agreed to give me so much. All that money was about to flow right into my pocket! It wouldn't feel real until I told *someone*.

What if Olivier didn't steal the money? It could have been Taylor. She knows this hiding spot better than anyone else. Maybe Olivier told her about it? I never really saw them talk, but then again, I didn't pay that much attention after we came back. I was too busy dangling Olivier in everyone's faces. But Taylor doesn't get to steal anything else from me.

Her room has always given me the saddest vibes. Everything is organized and tidy—not one bra littering the floor, no snack wrappers on the small desk by the window. It smells like the green tea candle she likes to burn and freshly vacuumed carpet. Like a life not lived. The nightstand drawer only confirms this feeling. It's full of half-used ChapSticks, a box of tissues, and a notepad with a grocery list. Poor Taylor.

In her tiny closet, the T-shirts are stored by color (black or gray), the underwear is stacked in a neat pile, and two belts are wrapped in a tight circle. When we were younger and Mom complained about the state of my room, I'd make Taylor clean it up for me. The first time I asked, it was almost a joke. No, a dare. But she did it, so I kept asking. Maybe she *should* stay living with me. The house is too big for me to maintain on my own. Just kidding. I can't wait to never see her again.

There's no money anywhere. Definitely not twenty-thousand-dollars' worth of it. As I keep searching, Olivier's words come back to me once again. He wasn't just saying that to hurt me. Something was going on. And maybe it doesn't matter, or maybe it will make all the difference. I'm not out the woods yet. But if I go down, it won't be on my own.

I pull some of the clothes out of the closet. There's got to be a clue somewhere. Or maybe I just need to keep busy. For the first few days after someone dies, people are all over you, pretending that your feelings are the most important thing in the world. And then they go away. Grief has an expiration date, apparently.

Taylor owns all of three pairs of jeans, which she wears in constant rotation, even in summer. She doesn't like her pasty white legs, feels too girlie in a skirt. At least that's how I'd feel if I were her. I yank the jeans out a little too hard, and one pair drops onto the floor.

When I pick it up, something falls from the pocket. It's a black paper sleeve wrapped with a plastic card inside. I recognize the logo even before I kneel down to retrieve it. The cursive B I saw all the time when I was in Paris, and the room number. 609. This is the key card to my hotel suite, the one I kept in my wallet, the very one that was stolen at Café de Flore.

It has to be—there's a red stain from the day my lipstick opened in my bag and smudged onto the paper—and yet, it makes no sense at all. I sit down on the bed, struggling to catch my breath. Taylor was here and that card was lost—stolen—while I was in Paris. The only way Taylor could have this is if she was in Paris herself. But of course that can't be. She was here. Home. The whole time. Or was she?

My phone rings, startling me. The name on the screen sends my body into panic mode, but I answer it anyway. I don't think I have a choice.

"Detective Jackson," I say.

I need to tell her. Taylor was in Paris. She followed me around. She stole my wallet, she… What? What did she do? But that's for the police to figure out.

"Ms. Laurent. I'm glad to catch you. I have some important news."

"Me too," I say without thinking.

"Oh?"

"Yes. I have…something." I don't know how to put it. Taylor was in Paris. How?

"Okay, well, if you don't mind me jumping in. We had a call with the detectives in France this morning."

My heart stammers in my chest. Clutching the key card in my other hand, I walk out.

"Ms. Laurent?"

"I'm here."

"The investigation is complete. The French police have ruled your husband's death an accident. An accidental overdose, most likely. The relatively small amount of sleeping pills found in his system makes it hard to conclude it was death by suicide. Though of course that's still a possibility. I'm sorry to say we'll never know for sure."

I exhale quietly. "No, I guess we won't."

"To be honest, there are still aspects of this case that don't sit right with me."

"Yes!" I say without thinking.

This is when I tell her about Taylor, right? But the detective speaks again before I can cut in.

"So, I want to ask: why didn't you tell us about the voicemail?"

"The voicemail?" I can't contain the surprise in my voice. Did Darren speak to the police? But I never left him a voicemail.

"The one you left on your husband's phone."

"Excuse me?"

"The day after you returned from your honeymoon, you called your husband multiple times from your cell phone. Didn't you?" the detective adds when I don't respond.

My mouth goes dry. It must be a trap. I *should* have called him to check in, shouldn't I? If the breakup was so amicable, I should have called to say I'd made it home and see how he was doing, the poor husband I left behind in Paris.

"I think I'm still in shock," I say tentatively. "It's all been very upsetting."

"That's understandable."

I swallow hard. "I don't even remember what I said. My memory is fuzzy."

"Well, I know what you said. I read the transcript."

Wait, did I *actually* call Olivier and I don't remember? "Will you read it to me?" I say.

"I'm not supposed to."

"Please! I–I want to hold onto every possible memory of him."

She sighs. "I guess there's no harm in it, now that the investigation is over." She clears her throat and then I hear the shuffling of paper. "This is what the transcript says: 'Olivier, it's me. I miss you. Please, I want to know if you're okay. Give me a sign. Anything. I love you. I always will. I'm sorry about what happened, all of it. Forget everything else. I just want to be with you.'"

This wasn't me. I didn't say any of this. And if it was from my phone…

Detective Jackson lets out a sigh. "Let me reiterate, once again, how truly sorry I am for your loss."

"Um, okay, thank you. So, this is it? You won't be… I mean, it's over?"

"Not quite. You said you had some news?"

"What?"

"Before, you wanted to bring up something?"

The edges of the hotel key card feel rough against my palm. I make a split decision. "No, I–I guess I'm just tired. I have nothing to say."

"Are you sure?"

I'm not. But I need to think about that. Because if the investigation is over, why would I risk them reopening it and coming to a different conclusion? "Yes, I'm sure." At least for now.

"All right. I wish you a good day, Ms. Laurent. Take care of yourself. Oh, and you might want to know the French authorities are releasing your husband's body to his family today, if you wanted to be in touch with them."

"Right, yes, his family." I pause, still in shock. "I guess I should call them?"

"That's entirely up to you, Ms. Laurent."

So I won't. I'm not even sure what they know about me, if anything.

Minutes after we hang up, my shoes are on and I'm out the door. I texted Darren to ask him to come get me, and his car rolls around the corner before I've reached the end of the street.

I slide into the passenger seat, a grin plastered on my face in spite of me.

"What's going on?" Darren says, starting the car again. "You're freaking me out."

I squeeze my lips together; I can't let him see my true feelings. "The police called. It was an accident. Accidental overdose, they said."

Darren shoots me a glance out of the corner of his eye. "Okay."

"I'm so relieved, you know. It was… I mean…"

"You're *relieved*?" I don't respond. "Cassie, where are we going? What is happening right now?"

"Just drive," I say, waving at the air in front of me.

He does.

We sit there in silence as I gather my thoughts. "I'm sorry about everything that happened. What I said on my last night in Paris. I know it must have sounded weird—"

"Weird? You told me you were afraid for your life. That your husband wanted to kill you and that you had to run away. And then *he* turns up dead."

"It's not what you think."

"Then what am I supposed to think, Cassie? You weren't answering my calls and texts. When the police came to me—"

"They came to you?"

We're stopped at a red light and Darren turns to me. "Of course they came to me. Your husband died during your honeymoon right after you left him. Do you realize how suspicious that made you look?"

"What did you tell them?"

A car honks behind us. The light has turned green. Darren keeps driving. "Cassie, what happened in that hotel room?"

"What did you tell them?" I say, more forcefully this time.

Darren takes a deep breath. "I *didn't* tell them what you said. Our conversation on the phone that night. I–I can't be involved in anything like that."

"Like what?"

He jams his fist against the steering wheel. "Man, I don't know, Cassie. Something happened. It doesn't matter what you say. Something messed up went on between you two, and I want no part of it."

I can't believe this. I went through hell to get Darren back. Now we can finally be together, and all he cares about is preserving his flawless reputation. "I was leaving him to be with you, Darren. We're good now. Everything is fine."

"Nothing is fine. Your husband is dead. And you don't—"

I put my hand on his thigh. "And I don't love him. I love *you*. It was always you. And now—"

"And now, nothing."

"We can be together," I say, hating the pleading tone in my voice. He shakes his head. "Darren?"

A moment passes. What is wrong with him to only want me when he can't have me? He has no idea what I did for him. For *us*.

"I'm taking you home," he says.

"We'll wait a few weeks. Or a few months, if you want to. It'll all blow over soon."

But it's like he's not listening. He does a U-turn at the next intersection and we drive all the way back in silence. The blue sky is so bright it makes my eyes sting. And then Darren doesn't actually take me home. He parks two blocks before, down a quiet street.

"What are you doing?" I say, turning to face him. I try to grab his hand, but he won't let me.

"We can't be seen together."

"Darren, everything is fine. We *can* be together. We will be."

"No, we won't. I can't." He's breathing heavily now. "Are you even sad?"

It takes me a moment to understand what he's asking. "Of course I'm sad. I never wanted any of this to happen."

"*What* happened, Cassie? Please tell me." His tone is urgent.

For a moment I almost do. Because what's the alternative? Am I going to keep this secret for the rest of our lives? The investigation is over. I'm safe. But I know he can't hear the truth, not even a fraction of it, so instead I lean over. I did all of this to be with him. I did it *for* him. But he'll never understand.

When I kiss him, he doesn't pull back. Not at first anyway. It's gentle, the way Darren has always kissed.

"I'm sorry, no." He says, pushing me away.

"Darren…" I lean forward again, but this time he jerks back.

"I can't. Please, get out of the car." I don't. "Cassie, I need you to get out of the car. Forget what I said. I don't want to know what happened. Get out the car, please. Get out of my life. I don't care what you did to him. You and I are over. Forever."

Maybe for the first time, I believe him.

And as I start walking home, I know only one thing for certain: my life started going off its rails the moment Taylor walked into my house. Mom and I would have been fine together, if she'd let us. But Taylor doesn't get to win. She doesn't get to walk away in one piece. In fact, I'm going to make sure she doesn't get in my way ever again.

CHAPTER 35

Thérèse

NOW

Her husband's body is not in the ground yet, but Cassie is out here kissing her ex-boyfriend like nothing happened. When I saw them in the car two streets back, I couldn't believe my eyes. Was Cassie really driving around town with him for anyone to see? I tried to tell myself that it didn't mean anything. To my knowledge, Darren hasn't come by the house since news of Olivier's death spread around town, but it's possible I missed him. All of this could be explained away. Until the kiss. The kiss tells me everything I need to know. It answers all of my questions.

The kiss is the end.

I drive home slowly, staying back from Cassie, who's walking along the sidewalk, her head down. Every now and then, she wipes her eyes with the back of her hand, like she's drying tears. But she won't fool me anymore. I wait until she's inside the house to pull into the driveway.

A sense of calm overwhelms me as I go up to the door. It's over. She killed him. I know it and there's nothing she can do to stop me. No tricks she can pull on me.

"Cassie?" I say when I walk in.

Her strangled voice comes from the living room. "Here."

For a few seconds we stare at each other. Her eyes are puffy, her lips swollen.

"He loved me," I say. The evenness of my voice startles us both. I keep going. "He fell in love with me. I know it's completely unfathomable to you, but he did."

"Not now, Taylor," she says, starting to turn away.

"Yes, now, Cassie. You don't get to boss me around anymore. You don't have anything. You're going to jail."

She chuckles dryly. "No, I'm not. Nice voicemail you left my husband, by the way. It almost moved me to tears." She must see the shock in my eyes, because she adds. "Oh yes, I know about that. Actually, I think it helped my case a lot. Because the police think *I* said that. I left my husband and then I regretted it. I couldn't have done anything to him if I called him the next day to say I was in love with him and wanted to get back together."

I can't breathe. "I'll call them now. I'll tell them everything."

"Sure you will," Cassie says, walking closer to me. I flinch. The look in her eyes, it's deadly. "And you'll tell them you were in Paris, too." She pulls something out of the pocket of her dress, a black plastic rectangle. "You'll explain to them why I found the key card to my hotel suite in *your* jeans. That's right, Taylor, I know you were there."

"I—You—" No other words come to me.

She shakes the key card in front of my face. "Oh yes, sure. Maybe I can't prove it myself. But what if I called the detectives and told them to check your passport? Or maybe they could look up if there was a passenger with the name of Taylor Quinn on a flight to Paris recently?"

She grabs her phone, pretends to go through her contacts. Or maybe she really does. "Shall I call them?"

"You killed him."

"See, Taylor. I kind of think that you did. You slept with my husband. You followed us to Paris in secret. I knew your voice sounded weird on the phone, but I couldn't put my finger on why. Now I know. Maybe you planned this all along. Somebody stole my wallet, the wallet in which I kept the key card to my suite. And, that same night, I was drugged and left for dead in a bathtub."

"I didn't drug you," is all I can say back.

Her eyes go wide with shock, and for a moment neither of us speaks. She wasn't sure until now, but I confirmed it all.

"Even if you didn't," she says at last. Her voice is a whisper. "Do you really want the police to know all that?"

I start pulling my own phone out of my pocket. "I want them to know you killed him."

She lunges at me, flicking the phone out of my hand. It lands on the floor with a thump, at equal distance from each of us.

"I have money now," she says. "More money than you can ever dream off. But of course you already know that. You stole that from me, too."

I let out a laugh. "Didn't you use to say that Mom should never store money in the cookie jar? That it was the first place anyone would look?"

Cassie's jaw clenches. "She wasn't your mother."

I crouch down to get my phone, but she's faster than me. She kicks it and it slides under the sideboard.

"You think you're so fucking smart, Taylor."

"My name's not Taylor."

"You're so much better than me. Sure, call the cops. And why don't you tell them you're going to inherit my millions if something happens to me?" I wince. "But you already know that. You two had a plan, didn't you? You were going to kill me and run away with my money. And you, specifically, were going to be the biggest winner of all if Olivier had gone through with it. Do you want to tell the police that, or should I?"

"You killed him," I say. She still hasn't denied it. Only one person died, and she's responsible for that. It's not a crime for me to have been in Paris. It's not even a crime for me to have been sleeping with Olivier.

Cassie sighs. "Nothing's going to bring him back now."

Tears pool at the corner of my eyes and start streaming down my cheeks.

Cassie's face softens as she speaks again. "I'll share my money with you, fifty-fifty. We'll do up the inn, make it all nice and pretty. I'll handle the paperwork so it belongs to us both. Wouldn't you like that, to have your own home, at last?"

I don't respond.

"It's more money than you'll ever see in your life. And Olivier was right, this house has so much potential. If we do it well—" I cough, and she corrects herself. "I'll help. But, fine, if *you* do it well, and I know you will, because you do everything so fucking perfectly, it could be a huge hit. We'll make so much more. You won't have to work these shitty jobs anymore. You'll be free."

"I'll never be free as long as I'm with you."

She takes a deep breath, waits a moment. Then: "You were right about your dad. He's French. Or he was at least."

I shake my head. I'm numb. She's a born liar. "I don't believe a word you say."

"Denis, his name is. Mom told me when she was dying. I think she was having regrets. Maybe she felt like she should have helped you find out more about your family. She said he might still be in Paris. That's all I know. I swear."

"If your mom knew about my dad, she would have told me. She was loving and kind."

Cassie rolls her eyes. "That's what you tell yourself. If she was so kind, why didn't she tell you your mother came by to see you after she was released from prison? She wanted to be in your life again but Mom shooed her away. She was terrified of losing you and being stuck with me. So she told your mother to leave. You could have seen her again before she died. Honestly, I'm pretty sure that's why Mom adopted you. She felt guilty that she kept you away from your family for her own benefit."

To say that this new information stuns me is an understatement. My mom came for me. My dad might still be out there somewhere. And yes, Cassie could be lying. She's so desperate right now, she'd say anything. But somehow she sounds more genuine than she ever has before.

"Why are you telling me all this?"

"I'm trying to get you to see that we're stuck together now. We are sisters, after all."

She crosses her arms against her chest, daring me to contradict her. But I can't. As much as it kills me to admit it, she's right. I can't prove that she killed Olivier. I could share everything I know and it might still not be enough. Cassie could spin this. She could spin anything. And what would happen to Olivier? I don't want his memory to go down as the man who tried to kill his wife. That wouldn't solve anything.

As for me...well, I could lose everything, again. If I give away Cassie and the police don't convict her, I'll have nothing. No house, no money, no Olivier. And, like always, she'll have won.

"Do we have an agreement?" Cassie says, staring me down. "I hope you understand that I can't let you walk out of this room until we do. And I'm going to keep a close eye on you from now on. I can't take the risk of you running off to the police with your crazy little theory. So what's it going to be, Taylor? Do you want to be poor and miserable for the rest of your life, or do you want to be like me?"

B	ubbles simmer quietly on the water's soapy surface. Underneath, her pale skin is creamy, her hair undulating like tentacles. Daylight seeps through the bathroom's window, making the brand-new tiles shine.

It was her choice, the minimalistic style, white with a few touches of black. It reminded her of this beautiful hotel suite in Paris, so chic. The guests have been raving about it; it's all over the reviews.

Recently renovated and simply beautiful. We loved staying at the Qu'inn while visiting the Hudson Valley. The two sisters who own it did a wonderful job. Definitely recommend!

After a moment, her bluish lips rise, regaining some of their original color as her face breaks through. She takes in a lazy breath, as if she hadn't just been deprived of air.

It's the middle of the afternoon, when everyone is out, and she turned on the music loud on her phone's speakers, something pop and upbeat. She bobs her head sideways, miming the lyrics, even though she doesn't know them.

The last few months have been stressful, to say the least. She never imagined it would be this much work, that it would take all of her strength and energy. At last she can relax, feel at peace with herself. Her dance moves are a little too abrupt in this confined space, and suddenly she slides down, her head once again dipping below the water. Her pruned hands grip the tub's sharp rim and she pulls, but something holds her back.

Someone.

An arm wraps around her neck, pressing her down. Another one grabs her wrist, flipping her onto her stomach. Now both of her hands are held tight behind her. Her shoulders hurt, but it's the least of her problems. She tries to throw her head back, as hard as she can, to get some air. But as she rises to the surface of the water, she is pressed back down more forcefully.

She tries to kick her legs around, fully aware that time is running out. She must do something, tell someone.

I know what you did.

You'll never get away with it.

Nothing happens for a while. She just floats away, her forehead bumping against the hard bottom of the brand-new tub.

The surface fizzes for a few angry seconds.

And then the bubbles vanish.

Author's Note

The following note contains major spoilers for *The French Honeymoon*. Continue reading at your own peril. You have been warned!

One night, as I was pondering what kind of novel I wanted to write next, I found myself thinking about Émile Zola's deeply dark and twisted novel, *Thérèse Raquin*. Published in 1868, it tells the story of Thérèse, a motherless young girl who is taken in by her aunt, Madame Raquin. The older woman has a sickly son she dotes on, Camille. When the children are of age, she decides that they should marry, for convenience.

Soon after, Thérèse meets Camille's work colleague and friend, Laurent, and the two begin a passionate affair. They dream of being together for real so, mad with love, they plot to murder Camille. Once he was gone, they'd wait a few months until Madame Raquin and her friends realized what a good match Laurent would be for Thérèse, and then they would not only be together, but would eventually inherit Madame Raquin's meager savings.

Thérèse, Laurent, and Camille go on a boat tour on the Seine outside Paris and Laurent kicks Camille overboard, maintaining him underwater until the deed is done, while Thérèse watches in horror.

But after killing Camille, Thérèse and Laurent can barely stand the sight of each other. Crippled by guilt, they live in fear of being found out, and in full view of Madame Raquin's insurmountable grief. Thérèse and Laurent descend further into madness and eventually reveal themselves as murderers. There is no happy ending for them, or anyone.

I've always been drawn to stories about forbidden loves, love stories that simply can't be. Of course, in modern times, Thérèse could have simply run away with Laurent and divorced Camille. Though, maybe not. This got me thinking about my group of foreign friends here in New York City. Many got married before they wanted to. Why? Usually because one person in the relationship was offered a job in the Big Apple and the only way their partner could legally join them was if they were married. What ensued were rushed trips to city halls, sometimes kept secret from friends and families, but with tons of photographic evidence to present the immigration officers (with big smiles, so they wouldn't pay too much attention to the extremely recent wedding bells). That also meant that the couple couldn't divorce for as long as they wanted to stay in the United States, or else one of them would lose their visa or green card and would have to leave the country.

It gave me what I needed for this story: a reason for Olivier Laurent to rush into marriage with the first person who would have him, Cassie Quinn, and an even better reason to stick to the marriage despite the unhappiness.

Another aspect I wanted to explore was a honeymoon gone wrong, like the case of the newlywed killed by her husband while scuba diving in Australia (another water-based death). How wrong can things be in a relationship—a brand-new marriage, at that—for one of the spouses to murder the other? Isn't a honeymoon supposed to be one of the happiest times in one's life? Then again, ask many recently married couples, and you'll often hear plenty of horrifying wedding planning stories. The happiest times in our lives can often coincide with the worse ones, something I find endlessly fascinating.

By morning—I didn't sleep much that night—I had the broad strokes of a new story, themes to explore, and even a title, *The French Honeymoon*. All of which eventually became this novel.

While I personally didn't obtain my green card, and eventual naturalization, through marriage to a U.S. citizen, I did my best to accurately portray the lengthy and complex process of green-card marriages. However, I took a few liberties and simplified some details for the benefit of the story. For example, applicants are allowed to travel outside the United States while their green card is in progress, but they need to apply for advance parole, so Olivier could only have gone to Paris if he had submitted that form earlier on.

The details shared in this book around marriage fraud are also genuine, as best as I could research them, including just how widespread the practice is and how wise immigration officers are to it. For what it's worth, I believe Olivier was right: he and Cassie would never have gotten away with it. He needed that plan B, though if you're reading this, you know how that turned out for him!

READING GROUP GUIDE

Please note that the following reading group guide contains spoilers for the novel. If you have not finished reading *The French Honeymoon*, we kindly suggest you do so first.

1. When we first meet Taylor, she's alone, sans suitcase but with wads of cash, and claims to be on a honeymoon. In these early pages, what did you think happened to her? What did you guess right or wrong?

2. In her mind, Taylor has a fantasy version of what a perfect Paris honeymoon looks like. Have you ever fantasized about a place you wanted to visit? And if/when you visited it, did it meet your expectations?

3. Cassie turns up to her father's funeral heartbroken, and she leaves with a hot new boyfriend/husband and a hefty inheritance. How do you feel about her actions during her few days in New York City, especially when it comes to her father's widow? What would you have done differently?

4. Olivier first moves to New York City as a way to escape his debts and responsibilities. What do you think about his choice? Is it always better to stay and face your problems?

5. Cassie is determined to portray her life as perfect on social media to make the people around her jealous. But this makes her vulnerable too. What do you think her social media presence says about her? And what would yours say about you?

6. Olivier and Cassie marry within days of meeting each other. Theirs is obviously not your typical love-at-first-sight romance. Do you know anyone who got engaged and/or married very quickly? What was the story there?

7. "Sometimes, Paris is a terrible idea." Which character do you think this line applies to the most? Who *really* shouldn't have come to Paris?

8. What was the most shocking moment for you in this novel?

9. Cassie and Taylor have a conflicted relationship from the moment Taylor comes to live with them. Do you think Rae could have done anything differently, or was their sisterhood always doomed?

10. All three main characters in the novel do terrible things at different times: stalking, cheating, plotting murder, actually murdering... Pick one character and discuss the justifications for their behavior.

11. Reese wasn't sure if Olivier loved her and really wanted to be with her. Discuss her thought process and the reasons why she was or wasn't justified in her thinking. Do you think Olivier really wanted to be with her?

12. At the end of the novel, Cassie makes a proposal to her sister. They could do up the inn and run the business together. What do you think really happens in the few months afterward, before the final scene in the novel?

A CONVERSATION
WITH THE AUTHOR

The following conversation contains spoilers for *The French Honeymoon*. We kindly suggest reading it once you've finished the novel.

What was your inspiration for the novel?

Two story ideas came to me at the same time. One was inspired by the nineteenth-century novel *Thérèse Raquin* by Émile Zola. In it, two lovers, Thérèse and Laurent—you might recognize the names—plan the murder of Thérèse's husband, Camille, so they can be together. It's a very dark novel that got me thinking about the timing of life. What if you met the love of your life but couldn't be with them? What would you do to change that? The other idea was about a honeymoon gone wrong, specifically a brand-new husband murdering his wife. What could compel a man to kill his wife during what should be one of the happiest times in their lives? It took many drafts, but eventually I combined these two pieces of inspiration into *The French Honeymoon*.

How much has the novel changed since you started writing it?

A lot! The final novel is so different from the first draft it's almost unrecognizable. The title and the love affair were there from the start. So were the honeymoon in Paris and the motive for the (attempted) murder. But the first few drafts centered around Taylor/Thérèse and Olivier *after* he returns from the honeymoon alone. Rae (Cassie and Taylor/Thérèse's mother) was alive; Cassie was not. In fact, the chapters from Cassie's point of view were a later addition.

Is there a character you relate to more than the others?

I did not feel this way when I set out to write this novel, but now, I believe that they are all broken in their own ways. No one's innocent, and no one's a total villain either. My heart breaks for all the pain Taylor/ Thérèse has endured in her life. But I see Cassie's side too, and I have empathy for her desire to shape her life into something it's not, to make these decisions (however bad!) as she tries to escape her reality. This may sound surprising, but I feel the same way about Olivier and respect his desperate attempts at turning his life around over and over again. He just wanted the girl and the money and to be happy, you know? Sometimes you gotta do what you gotta do.

What was your greatest surprise in writing this story?

I'm a romantic at heart, and I was really rooting for Taylor/Thérèse and Olivier to walk off happily into the sunset at the end. Yes, I was writing a thriller, and yes, I always intended for murder to happen, but for me, this novel was originally about their twisted romance, the injustice of meeting the love of your life at the worst possible time. I wanted them to get away with their plan so badly! But as I got to the middle, I found myself with these three characters in and out of the hotel suite on that fateful night, and I realized what *needed* to happen to Olivier. I know it sounds cliché, but in that particular moment, I felt like the scene with the iron wrote itself. My fingers on the keyboard dictated how it was going to be, regardless of what *I* wanted. I like to say that, in this book, no one leaves Paris unscathed, but I was pretty sad when Olivier met the fate he did. Once it happened though, there was no going back. I knew it was the right turn for the story.

Is there a scene that was particularly difficult to write?

The bar scene when Reese and Olivier "meet" for the first time was incredibly tricky, but I was determined to make it work. I wanted to be as true as possible to the reader, and it was a delicate balance to portray this interaction in a genuine way while still serving the plot I had in mind. Olivier has this awful day. He's exhausted, depressed, and thinks he's doomed. And then he walks into that bar, and *Wait! Is that who he thinks it is?* They're in a completely different context, and she looks so unlike herself. It couldn't possibly be. Even as he's talking to her, he has these moments of doubting himself. He's so attracted to her, which is the worst thing that could happen to him since he *has* to make things work with Cassie.

And one that was easy?

Some of the easier scenes were the ones in the middle when Cassie is getting ready for her night of self-care, as she calls it, and then, when she's in the bath, feeling like something is off. As a writer, there are few moments when I feel like I'm pulling the strings. More frequently I feel like the novel is beating *me* around. But while writing these scenes, I was gloating. I kept thinking, *Go on, keep drinking that wine, Cassie! Get in the tub! Think your petty thoughts!* The other scene that came really naturally was the one where Reese and Olivier are in the car, admitting their love to each other and discussing what they could do to be together. I'm a visual person, and I could so clearly see that road, the truck honking behind them, the panic and the passion all mixed up within that small space. It might be the scene I'm most looking forward to watching if *The French Honeymoon* is ever adapted for the screen.

Let's talk about that ambiguous ending. Seriously, who dies?

What could you possibly mean by "ambiguous ending"? Joke aside, in my mind, the ending is crystal clear. The clues are peppered throughout the book, and they all lead to the grand bubble-bath finale. I love a novel that delivers twists until the very last page and one that keeps me thinking after I finish reading, so that's what I wanted to attempt here. I know that, as a reader, I would analyze every line of that last page and try to decipher the who's who of what's going on. I also know who I would be rooting for. We'll say it was an accident, of course. *Someone* should enjoy all that money.

ACKNOWLEDGMENTS

TK

ABOUT THE AUTHOR

Anne-Sophie Jouhanneau is a bilingual French author based in the U.S. She has previously published novels and nonfiction books for teens, which have been translated into more than twelve languages. *The French Honeymoon* is her debut adult novel. After graduating university in France, she moved to Amsterdam to begin a career in advertising. She then spent a few years in Melbourne before settling in New York City, where she lives with her French Australian American family, two gorgeous cats, and a whole lot of passports. Find her on social media @asjouhanneau.

Printed in the USA
CPSIA information can be obtained
at www.ICGtesting.com
JSHW021347110924
69344JS00012B/12